THE VENICE CODE

A James Acton Thriller

By
J. Robert Kennedy

James Acton Thrillers
The Protocol
Brass Monkey
Broken Dove
The Templar's Relic
Flags of Sin
The Arab Fall
The Circle of Eight
The Venice Code

Detective Shakespeare Mysteries
Depraved Difference
Tick Tock
The Redeemer

Special Agent Dylan Kane Thrillers
Rogue Operator
Containment Failure
Cold Warriors

Zander Varga, Vampire Detective
The Turned

THE VENICE CODE

A James Acton Thriller

J. ROBERT KENNEDY

Copyright © 2014 J. Robert Kennedy

CreateSpace

All rights reserved. No part of this publication may be reproduced, stored in or introduced into a retrieval system, or transmitted in any form, or by any means (electronic, mechanical, photocopying, recording or otherwise) without the prior written permission of the publisher.

This is a work of fiction. Names, characters, places, and incidents are products of the author's imagination. Any resemblance to actual persons, living or dead, is entirely coincidental.

ISBN-10: 1497403251

ISBN-13: 978-1497403253

First Edition

10 9 8 7 6 5 4 3 2 1

For Tom Clancy, an inspiration and a pioneer.

THE VENICE CODE

A James Acton Thriller

"I believe it was God's will that we should come back, so that men might know the things that are in the world, since, as we have said in the first chapter of this book, no other man, Christian or Saracen, Mongol or pagan, has explored so much of the world as Messer Marco, son of Messer Niccolo Polo, great and noble citizen of the city of Venice."

Marco Polo, The Travels of Marco Polo, 1299 AD

"Let all who are under a yoke as slaves regard their own masters as worthy of all honor, so that the name of God and the teaching may not be reviled. Those who have believing masters must not be disrespectful on the ground that they are brothers; rather they must serve all the better since those who benefit by their good service are believers and beloved. Teach and urge these things."

1 Timothy 6:1-2, The English Standard Version Bible

PREFACE

Marco Polo was only seventeen when he left on his now famous journey to the Orient. Led by his father and uncle—the brothers having already spent many years in what is now China—their journey was long and hard, but they knew the rewards at the end would be tremendous, the leader of the Mongol Empire, Kublai Khan, already having befriended the brothers on their first trip.

Their journey was eventful but predictable, a near straight route east to what is now known as Beijing, except for one strange detour that had them suddenly head north. Bearing gifts and messages from the Pope for the Khan, this deviation delayed their delivery significantly, something that would be unimaginable unless the Polo's had good reason to stray from their planned route.

And only one reason would be found acceptable.

If the Khan himself asked them.

Approaching Karakorum, Mongol Empire
March 23rd, 1275 AD

Most would have screamed, but it wasn't in Giuseppe's nature to do so, even if a knife was stuck against his throat, the blood already dripping from where the tip of the blade had penetrated. Instead he glared at his attacker—at *their* attackers, his eyes flicking over to his master who seemed to be taking their current predicament in stride, his face barely registering any surprise at these turn of events, their guides having betrayed them.

Why did my master ever agree to this side trip?

It had made no sense at the time—at least not to him—why they would change such well-laid plans on such short notice, but he was a slave, a mere servant to his master and not always privy to such things. Though he had to admit his master was kind, never beating him, never depriving him, never raising his voice, he was still a slave. But after serving his master for over a decade, since a boy, he had come to think of the man as a brother, the two nearly the same age. He knew his master was twenty-one, but wasn't quite sure what his own age was. He was certain it was something similar, but when he had been sold into slavery, he had known little of himself beyond his name—Joseph, which his new masters had changed to Giuseppe, the Italian version of the name.

He was just fortunate to have been sold into the family he had, their kindness and generosity known throughout their home of Venice.

Which was why he eyed his master with concern, he now being held at knifepoint by three of their attackers, two holding his arms behind his back, the other searching him for valuables as a heavy snowfall began to engulf them all.

A triumphant shout from the searcher as he held up a long, narrow gold tablet engraved with words Giuseppe could not read, but knew by heart. It had been presented to the master's father, Niccolo and uncle, Matteo, when they had stayed with the leader of the Mongol Empire, Kublai Khan, in Khanbalig years before. It guaranteed them safe passage through the Mongol Empire, including access to any provisions as needed—with no need to pay.

Though it had been granted to his elders, his master's father had decided to give it to his son on this side journey just in case the need of its protection should arise. Giuseppe knew his master would never use it to purchase goods, as that would be an abuse of the trust placed in his elders by Kublai Khan so many years ago, but the inscription and the symbol engraved might just buy them out of situations such as the one they now found themselves.

"What is this?" demanded the man now holding the tablet.

"It is a 'gerege', given to my father and uncle by Kublai Khan himself."

A hush settled over the narrow canyon they now occupied, it in retrospect an ideal location for an ambush. Giuseppe wondered how many travelers had fallen prey to these scoundrels, and hoped their modus operandi was to merely steal rather than steal and kill.

The warm blood trickling down his neck and beneath his fur trimmed jacket had him thinking the latter.

"What does it say?" asked the man, his voice subdued, the fear the man now felt palpable, even the tip of the blade in Giuseppe's throat retreating slightly.

"It says, 'By the strength of the eternal Heaven, holy be the Khan's name. Let him that pays him not reverence be killed'."

"What does that mean?"

"It means that Kublai Khan himself is a friend of the person who possesses this gerege, and Khan himself guarantees their safe passage and any provisions they should need."

"I don't understand," whispered the man, backing away slightly, suggesting he did have at least an inkling of what was meant by the words his master had spoken.

"It means that should you harm us any further, should you disrupt our passage in any way, you will have made an enemy of Kublai Khan himself, and you will die."

The man stepped back, waving over several of his men—Giuseppe guessed his lieutenants—and an animated discussion was soon underway. They were speaking Mongol, a language Giuseppe had learned for the journey, and had become quite proficient at, and the tidbits he could hear were terrifying to say the least.

It appeared the decision was leaning toward the option of killing everyone so there would be no witnesses.

Giuseppe eyed his master who remained calm during all of this, his eyes never still, taking in everything around them as if searching for hope, yet no hint of desperation could be seen. Then again Giuseppe couldn't remember ever seeing his master perturbed in the least on any occasion, though he had to admit this was the most difficult position he recalled them being in, despite over four years on the road. At times he forgot what Venice looked like, the lagoons of the city state the only home he remembered, his youth a memory purged, its horrors only revisiting him in his dreams now, those thankfully forgotten quickly.

His only clear memory was his mother, her beautiful face and her long black hair framing her smile as she gazed down at him, tucking him into bed.

And the horror on her face as she had been hauled out of their humble home, her arm outstretched, trying to hold on to him, never to be seen again.

Where that was he didn't know, what had happened to her he dared not imagine, and how old the memories of her he could merely guess—he only knew they weren't old enough to fade away with the rest of his childhood.

The small group of renegades broke from their meeting, the leader approaching Giuseppe's master, a grin on his face.

"We will kill you all," he announced, the tip of the blade almost forgotten now pushed tightly against Giuseppe's throat once more.

Giuseppe's heart slammed against his chest as he realized they were all about to die. He wished the master's father and uncle had accompanied them. At least then their party might have been large enough for these marauders to have let them by unscathed, or at least a better fight might have been made of it. Instead they had been surrounded within moments, and not even a blade clashed with another before they had been subdued.

But not if the brothers had been here!

The brothers and the master together were a force to be reckoned with, and with them rallying the troops, the servants and guides would have fought at their side, to the death if necessary.

At least that's how he felt about it.

Yes, he would die for his master. He wasn't sure how the others felt about that; it wasn't a topic that came up often while preparing the meals or performing his other duties that involved interactions with the other servants. He only knew how he felt. He loved his master like a brother and would happily give his life to the family that had given him a home and treated him with respect all these years.

"That is one option," replied his master, his voice still calm. "It's not the path I would have chosen, but then I have the benefit of education and foresight."

The man looked confused, apparently not used to hearing one of his victims speak so calmly and with such eloquence. A surge of pride filled Giuseppe's chest and swelled through his body as he watched his master bravely face down these fiends.

"You annoy me!" screamed the man, raising his sword in the air, the fatal blow only moments away. "Kill them all!"

Suddenly the man gasped in pain, his shoulders jerking back, his neck hyperextended, his gaping mouth and wide eyes revealing the shock he now felt as he slowly turned away from Giuseppe's master. He heard a thud then the knife at his own throat jerked. He refused to shout out the horror he felt, instead keeping his eyes focused on his master who stood less than ten feet away, a slight smile on his face.

That was when Giuseppe's captor collapsed to the ground, finally forcing his eyes from his master. The man was now at his feet, an arrow protruding from his chest. Giuseppe looked at his master, then the leader of the ruffians, and saw another arrow protruding from the man's back.

It had all happened in seconds, and now several more thuds were heard, more of their attackers collapsing, including the two holding his master, who immediately dropped to the ground, grabbing a blade and rushing toward one of the few remaining targets. Giuseppe grabbed the blade from his own attacker's scabbard and rushed forward to join his master as the surviving ruffians looked about in confusion.

A confusion that only lasted seconds, decisions quickly made.

They fled into the dusk, the ever thickening snowfall obscuring their escape.

Giuseppe rushed to his master's side, warily eying the lengthening shadows and wondering who had come to their rescue. A shape moved and Giuseppe instinctively placed himself between it and his master. He felt a gentle hand on his shoulder then heard his master's voice.

"Do you not think that those shadows might be friends?"

The thought had occurred to Giuseppe, but he was unwilling to put his master's life at risk again.

"They might very well be friends, Master, but they may also be the same scoundrels who just fled, returning in greater numbers."

The hand patted Giuseppe on the shoulder, then he saw his master step forward, his sword drawn, even with Giuseppe as the number of shadows approaching increased.

"Then we shall fight them side by side as brothers."

Giuseppe's eyes almost glistened at the words, and he couldn't honestly say that a tear hadn't escaped, the snow melting against his flushed cheeks perhaps mixing with a salty bead. He was just happy his master hadn't seen his moment of emotional weakness. But the pride he felt at that moment was unrivaled in his lifetime of service. To be called a brother of his master? He could imagine no greater honor. He knew any words he said at that moment would trivialize what had just been said, so instead he merely nodded, squaring himself for any possible attack.

"Are you okay?" came a voice from the darkness that Giuseppe immediately recognized as his master's father.

Giuseppe's shoulders sagged as the tension of the past ten minutes was wiped away with those three simple words. He turned to look at his master who grinned at him as he tossed his commandeered weapon and retrieved his own, Giuseppe doing the same.

"We're fine, Father," replied his master as the shadows cleared with the approach of the rest of the travelling party he had thought left behind. The master's father and uncle emerged from the darkness along with their servants, all armed, all still on their guard.

Hugs were exchanged amongst the family, Giuseppe standing respectfully aside, instead turning his attention to the leader of the ruffians who lay on his side, moaning nearby. He kicked him onto his back, the arrow pushing farther into his body with a gasp.

The three kinsmen circled the man, gazing down at his agonized form.

"Wh-who are you?" he gasped, looking from man to man.

The master's father took a knee, prying the gold tablet from the man's hand.

"I am the rightful owner of this, not you," he said, rising and handing it back to his son.

"I think it's perhaps best if you held on to this, Father."

He shook his head. "No, I think you have earned it. Your suspicions were correct and you were indeed ambushed. If it were not for your foresight, we would have all been captured and murdered. Instead, your idea of having us follow you proved genius. When you meet the Khan, I have no doubt he will honor you with one of your own."

Giuseppe's master smiled, taking the tablet and returning it once again to the security of an inner pocket.

"Who—?"

"Who am I?" interrupted his master, taking a knee beside the dying man. "Who am I, the architect of your destruction?" He leaned forward, his mouth almost at the man's ear. "I am Marco Polo, and you are no more."

And with those words, Giuseppe's master slid a knife between the man's ribs, ending his suffering.

River Road, Potomac, Maryland
Present day

Grant Jackson's head vibrated against the glass of the large Cadillac, his legs stretched out in the backseat, his eyes closed as his left hand cradled a glass of eighteen year old Macallan, the ice clinking against the edges of the crystal. His throat was a bit sore and a glass of water would probably do him better, but until they invented water that helped numb the entire body while quenching your thirst, he'd stick to the scotch.

He took a sip blindly, the smooth liquid setting fire to his mouth as he rolled it around, enjoying the flavor. Finally he swallowed the smoky brew and sighed in satisfaction, returning the glass to its perch on his knee. He had never had a drop of scotch until his dad had died, and in a fit of anger and sorrow, he had grabbed a bottle of his father's favorite and drank it until he learned to like it.

It was definitely an acquired taste with him.

He had thrown up that night, and he thanked the malt masters that had created the golden liquid for their skill in brewing excuses, for he wasn't certain it was the alcohol that had made him vomit. The fact that his father, the President of the United States, was dead was shock enough, but to find out he had been murdered, in the White House, by a man Grant had known since he was a baby was even more shocking.

His mother had nearly become a recluse, retreating from society and refusing to speak of it, and whenever he asked questions about what had happened, he was stonewalled at every turn. He considered himself an intelligent man, and he knew something wasn't right. There was no way Lesley Darbinger, his father's closest friend and most trusted advisor, would just kill his father for no reason. There had to be a reason. The marines had killed him moments after they heard the shots, but they had been too late to save his father, and too effective in their response to gain any intelligence from the shooter.

The investigation after the fact indicated that Darbinger had a brain tumor and most likely wasn't in control of his actions, which would explain his ordering US Special Forces troops to assassinate a group of students in Peru under the guise they were a terrorist cell, and to pursue the survivors to London, England to eliminate them, all under the supposed orders of his father.

To Grant it sounded like bullshit, but what was the alternative? If Darbinger wasn't guilty, then did that mean his father was? He wanted to know the answers, he was desperate to know, and he knew there was only one way he was going to find out, and that was from the inside.

Which was why he was now running for Congress. He'd ride his father's coattails into the inner sanctum and try from within to get answers, and if he couldn't get them, he'd run for President if he had to. He had the looks, the education and the pedigree to win, and he was determined to do so.

The car jerked to a halt sending Grant flying forward, his glass slipping from his hand. His head smacked the B pillar, stunning him momentarily as he heard shouts from the front of the car, then another slam, this one sending him backward as they were hit from behind. He pushed himself back into the seat, rubbing his head with his hand as the sounds of the front doors opening seemed far too distant.

"This is Sierra One, we've got a situation, send backup immediately, over!"

It was Mike, one of the Secret Service agents assigned to him whose voice brought Grant back to reality.

What the hell is going on?

Several shots rang out and Grant's heart leapt into his throat as his pulse began to race. His shaking hands reached for the door but it was suddenly torn open, Mike's free hand reaching in and grabbing him by the shirt. He was hauled out onto the pavement and into a puddle, the light rain from earlier in the evening still making its presence known.

Several shots were fired over his head and he looked at where the gun was aimed. A large black SUV was jammed against their bumper, a man using the passenger side door as cover. He looked behind them to see another SUV blocking the street, perpendicular to the Caddy. He was about to open his mouth to warn Mike when one of their attackers raised a weapon and shot. Mike's shoulder blades jerked together, his chest bursting forward in pain and confusion as he dropped to his knees. His eyes met Grant's as he collapsed.

"Run!" he gasped before his face hit the pavement. Grant jumped to his feet and sprinted toward a nearby alley. As he reached the entrance he felt something slam into his back and he flew forward, smacking the pavement hard. The sound of footfalls rushing toward him was all he could make out as a sudden warmth spread through his body, his muscles relaxing as he slowly blacked out.

And as his eyes flickered shut, he saw a man's hand reach down to grab him, his watchband slipping slightly, revealing a small tattoo made of three parallel lines, the third slightly thicker and rounded up toward the other two.

Approaching Karakorum, Mongol Empire
March 24th, 1275 AD

About the only good thing that Giuseppe could say about the past day was that their attackers hadn't returned. And that was all. What had started as light snow flurries had turned into a squall that had lasted all night. It was unlike anything Giuseppe had experienced before, Venice not known for its snowstorms. His master, Marco, seemed thrilled with it, volunteering to take the first watch and letting his father sleep through his turn.

Giuseppe merely shivered in his furs, sitting at Marco's side through four hours of the storm, huddled at the entrance to a cave they had discovered, a substantial fire continually fed by Giuseppe merely taking the edge off the icy wind.

"I've never seen such snow!"

It was at least the third time Marco had uttered these words, the excitement suggesting he was unable to contain himself, each outburst a release that would slowly build again over time, to be relieved temporarily by the next outburst.

"Neither have I, Master."

It was the third identical reply, then nothing else would be said until the next utterance from his master.

"I guess you're wondering why we left our planned route."

Giuseppe's eyebrows shot up in surprise at the unexpected statement. "It is not my place to wonder why."

"Come now, Giuseppe, we have known each other long enough to be honest with one another," said Marco with a smile and a wink.

"I have always been honest with you, Master!"

As if sensing his shock at the accusation, Marco leaned forward and grabbed Giuseppe's shoulder, giving it a squeeze.

"Relax, Giuseppe, I'm only joking with you!" he said, laughing then letting him go. "We have known each other since we were children. We have played together, drank together and fought together. There can be no greater bond between men!"

"I serve at the master's pleasure."

"Hmm," was the reply, Giuseppe's heart immediately racing as he could detect the displeasure in Marco's tone.

"I'm sorry if I offended you, Master."

Marco shook his head. "No, you didn't offend me. I sometimes forget your station, that is all. It is not my choice, you understand. If it were up to me, you would be a freeman, and we would be equals on this journey. But my father says that cannot be. Only family and servants will be permitted at the palace in Khanbalig, all others will be denied entry." Marco grinned at him, a gleam in his eye. "And you know I wouldn't survive without my trusted Giuseppe by my side in the great city!"

"Your words honor and humble me, Master."

"I wish you would call me 'Marco'."

"I could never."

Marco batted the words away with his hand. "I know, I know." He looked at the entrance and the wind howling to gain entry. "I will tell you why we are here."

Giuseppe said nothing, instead leaning forward.

"Kublai Khan has asked us to undertake a mission for him of the utmost importance."

Giuseppe's jaw dropped. There was no hiding his shock at the news, or the renewed awe he felt for his master. If the Khan himself had asked the

Polo family for this favor, it surely indicated the esteem in which the great leader held them.

And yet he still remained silent, daring not ask the questions that filled his head.

"As you know, my father and uncle returned from their journey with a message from the Khan for the Pope. We currently carry the reply to that message along with many gifts from the new Pope Tedaldo for the Khan. This makes our journey important as we have an opportunity to spread Christianity throughout the Khan's territory." Marco lowered his voice. "You remember the envoy? The one that met us before we changed our route?"

"Of course, Master."

"He had a message from the Khan. Apparently there is a problem in the former capital of Karakorum which is where we are heading now. What you might not know is that Karakorum was built by Genghis Khan to be his capital after he defeated the Khwarezm Empire. His successors built it into a great walled city with a large palace that made it a center for politics that spanned the entire Mongol Empire.

"But something went wrong, and when Kublai Khan claimed the throne he abandoned the city, relocating the capital several times, finally settling on Dadu which we now know as Khanbalig. What wasn't known before was why he abandoned the former capital. The messenger provided the answer, an answer I can hardly believe."

Giuseppe had been given the benefit of an education thanks to his masters, but only in the basics. He could read and write in several languages, he understood mathematics but not to any great degree—he could handle himself in a market—and knew the Bible and the history of the Church. But world geography, that beyond Europe, and history outside of his own continent? He had almost no knowledge. He had made every attempt to overhear the stories told by his master's father and uncle upon their return, and when he had been informed he would be accompanying them on their second journey along the Silk Road, he had been thrilled.

And this little tidbit into history and world politics had him enthralled.

"What is it, Master? What was the reason?"

"It appears that the locals, pagans and Saracens alike, had turned to idol worship."

Giuseppe's head jerked back, the very thought of it abhorrent, the worship of an idol heresy, a sin and violation of one of the Ten Commandments.

"What kind of idol?"

"Some crystal carving. The Khan isn't certain what it is, except that it was brought in by a trader who claimed it had great powers. The city administrator purchased it and later claimed it spoke to him. At first it was his inner circle that began to worship the idol, then word spread through the servants of its power, and soon much of the great city had devoted themselves to this false idol. When Kublai Khan returned from an expedition to the north, he found the mosques and temples abandoned, the famous Silver Tree missing from the city square, and instead a temple in its place with a crystal form at its center. Troops once loyal to him held him back and he was forced to retreat from the city."

"The Khan was defeated?"

Giuseppe's heart slammed in his chest. If the Khan was defeated by the followers of this pagan idol, what hope did this tiny expedition have?

"No, but he was forced to retreat. He returned in force, sacking the leadership, but not before the skull was hidden away somewhere. It wasn't until recently that the Khan learned where it has been hidden, but everyone he sends to retrieve it is met with suspicion, and the idol is never found."

"What can we, I mean you, with all respect, Master, hope to do that the Khan couldn't?"

"As Europeans, we will be met as scholars. It is hoped that we will be able to gain access to it through the local priest. Apparently he knows where it is located from time-to-time, it moved regularly to keep ahead of the Khan's soldiers."

"What does he want with it?"

"He wants it removed then transported to the Holy See in Rome. Apparently the city's economy is now failing, worshippers looking for answers from the idol rather than from themselves, leaving their duties and businesses to decline in favor of seeking blessings from this crystal figure in the hopes of instant gratification."

"Does it work?"

Marco recoiled at the question. "Of course not! What kind of Christian are you?"

Giuseppe's chest tightened, his face slackening at the thought of insulting his master. He opened his mouth to apologize when a grin spread across Marco's face.

"You should see your face, my brother." Marco reached forward and slapped Giuseppe's shoulder. "I asked the same question of the messenger. All he would say is that enough rumors of it working have spread that the truth no longer matters."

"You said he wants it sent to the Holy See. Why?"

"I personally think he's too superstitious to destroy it himself. If I had to guess, he hopes the Church will deal with it for him."

"Will they?"

"I'm certain they will. I can't see the Pope being scared of some crystal carving. I could see him saying some prayers over it though, just in case!"

Marco made the sign of the cross, silently apologizing for the subtle insult to the Holy Roman Church's leader. Giuseppe did the same, rewarded with a smile from Marco.

"In all seriousness, this is a dangerous journey as we've already seen, and that had nothing to do with our ultimate purpose. First we must reach the city, infiltrate it, meet with the priest, find the idol, overwhelm its guards, exit the city with the idol, and escape its worshipers' pursuit."

"It sounds impossible."

"Nothing is impossible, my brother, as my father and uncle proved with their first journey. Nearly impossible? Absolutely. I suspect we may not survive the attempt."

"Then why do it? Why not let the Khan take care of his own problems?"

Marco smiled, shaking his head. "Giuseppe, we must. A great trust has been placed in our family by a greater man. For us to deny his request would be to dishonor our family name forever. If we fail, we die with honor, and that I can live with. But if we succeed, we shall go down in history. And in time, no one will forget the name Polo."

A strong gust of winter wind howled through the cave opening, the fire almost forced out, only small blue flames able to resist the wind battling it. Giuseppe covered his mouth with his hand so he could breathe, then suddenly the wind stilled inside, the fire springing back to life, and he found himself sitting alone, his master having risen.

"Let us sleep, brother, for tomorrow we have a difficult journey."

Giuseppe leapt to his feet and walked deeper into the cave, his master shaking the shoulder of his uncle, waking him to take the next watch. Giuseppe prepared Marco's bedding then retired himself, visions of crystal demons haunting his dreams, the repeated image of a laughing crystal skull waking him throughout the night.

Wellington Hospital, London, England
Present day, one day after the kidnapping

Professor James Acton held his fiancée's hand as they walked down the hall of Wellington Hospital. His hands were clammy, which was uncharacteristic of him, but he hated being here, not because of a fear of hospitals, but because he felt it was his fault the man they were visiting had been a long term guest of the facility.

Professor Laura Palmer squeezed his hand. "Are you okay?"

She knew him so well she could sense his unease. He squeezed back and glanced at her, her auburn hair loose today and hanging over her shoulders, her alabaster skin brilliantly white and flawless, at least in his eyes. He knew she was showing the odd line around the eyes, the signs of aging unavoidable as she lived the life of an archeologist, her skin baking in the dry heat of desert dig sites, her body exposed to the rigors of running for her life on far too many occasions, bullets, rockets, bombs and plain old knives and spears trying to end her time on this world.

And his too. Their introduction and romance had been a whirlwind, but over the past few years he had finally found true love for the first time in his life, and he had never been happier, despite the innumerable attempts on their lives. The pair of them seemed to be a magnet for danger, but through it they had met each other and made some dear friends despite their ordeals.

And one of those lay in a hospital bed at the end of this hall. Detective Inspector Martin Chaney of Scotland Yard. He had been shot several months ago at Laura's dig site in Egypt trying to protect them and had slipped into a coma due to the massive loss of blood. His former partner, who was also at the dig site, INTERPOL Special Agent Hugh Reading, had held a vigil at Chaney's bedside every spare moment he had, talking to him, yelling at him, bargaining with him, all to no effect.

Until recently.

Three days ago Chaney had awoken, much to the shock and delight of Reading who had been insulting Chaney's choice of football clubs when, according to Reading's phone call Acton had received two days ago, the "most glorious grunt you had ever heard" erupted from their friend and soon after he was talking and moving all his limbs.

Acton had immediately boarded a plane to join Laura who was lecturing at her university in London. She had waited to see Chaney, wanting to give him some time to recover and also to share the excitement with her fiancé.

"I wonder how he's doing?" asked Acton as they neared the door.

"I talked to Hugh last night and he said that other than the memory loss, he seems to be fine, just very weak."

Acton frowned as he knocked on the door. "Hopefully his memory will return."

"The doctors say it's fifty-fifty."

"He's a tough cookie, I'm betting on the odds being better than that."

The door opened and Acton found himself bear hugged by an ecstatic Reading, who then exchanged a more gentle one with Laura.

"'Bout time you two got here!" he cried, waving them into the room. "Look who's here!" he said, turning to his old partner. Chaney was sitting up in his bed, propped up on pillows and the bed adjusted to a near seated position. He had a food tray in front of him with various pale looking offerings, and a huge smile on his face as he saw them enter.

"Hey Buddy, how the hell are you?" asked Acton as he rounded the bed, hand out.

Chaney extended a hand and shook Acton's—rather weakly Acton felt—then exchanged cheek to cheek kisses with Laura.

"Yes, Martin, how are you?"

Chaney pushed the food tray away.

"Apparently much better than I was last time I saw you both, though this food they're trying to force upon me is bloody awful and I'm convinced is designed to put me back into a coma."

Reading roared with laughter, clearly delighted his friend was almost his old self.

"Tell me about the memory loss," said Acton, perching on the side of the bed. "What *do* you remember?"

Chaney frowned. "It's strange. I remember all of you, but not how we met. I don't remember the dig in Egypt, or even deciding to go there which apparently was at least a couple of months before we actually went."

"Are you remembering any bits of it, or is it a complete blank?" asked Laura who had sat in the lone chair.

"I'm dreaming about some stuff that just doesn't make sense that I'm thinking might be memories, but who knows? They could be movies for all I know. Certainly some weird things about glass skulls have to be from a movie." He shrugged his shoulders. "Hopefully it will all come back otherwise they won't let me back to work!"

"Don't you worry about that," said Reading. "If Scotland Yard won't take you back, I'll get you into INTERPOL with me. Much cushier job."

Acton rubbed his chin, debating on whether or not he should ask the question he had been dying to ask. On the dig in Egypt, after Chaney had been wounded, he had said he had something important to talk to him about, and with Chaney being a member of the Triarii, he had assumed it was about that, but he had never found out what the message was, and much to his surprise, no one else from the Triarii had tried to contact him.

And if Chaney had no idea why he was dreaming about "glass" skulls, then he most likely had no idea he was a prominent member of a two thousand year old organization dedicated to protecting and preserving twelve crystal skulls they thought had special powers.

Acton's eyes flitted to Chaney's left inside wrist and noted the tiny tattoo that identified members of the organization to each other. The first time he had encountered these people he had been running for his life, and in a leap of faith, he put himself into their hands. Dozens died, but he and his newly found love, Laura, survived, along with Reading, Chaney's partner at the time at Scotland Yard. Reading had no clue of Chaney's secret life, and at first felt betrayed, but eventually came to accept his partner's alternate existence, if not necessarily agreeing with it.

Acton had been thrust into the secret world of the Triarii when he and his students had discovered a crystal skull at an Incan dig site in Peru. His students were massacred by a Delta Force unit operating under the belief they were terrorists, and he was pursued across the globe before the Delta Force unit disobeyed orders and halted their pursuit. Over the years this group of men that had tried to kill him had helped him on numerous occasions, and he had even stepped in to help them. A bond had been forged between them once Acton realized they had been manipulated, their families threatened every time they questioned their orders by a former member of the Triarii obsessed with possessing the skulls.

He had even found himself thinking of some of them as friends, and he knew they were all eager to make up for their actions. They were good, honorable men, who had been used, and if they had been there the night Chaney was wounded, perhaps they all would have made it out uninjured.

Unfortunately they were too late, and now their friend barely knew who he was. Acton didn't want to say anything about the Triarii because if

Chaney had forgotten something so fundamental about his life, his memory loss must be far worse than anyone either knew, or was acknowledging.

Acton instead turned to Chaney's recovery. "How do you feel physically?"

"Weak. Ridiculously weak. But each day is a little better. They've got me doing physio several times a day, stretching out the muscles and starting to use them again. I was actually able to walk a few paces this morning. Yesterday I couldn't even stand. Hopefully in a few days I'll have the run of the place. I'm climbing the walls here and can't wait to get back to my flat."

Acton smiled, his head bobbing. "I hear ya. I have no doubt you'll make a full recovery in no time."

"Bloody right!" agreed Reading. "He'll be back to his old self and then I can start getting some sleep in my own bed for a change."

The door opened and two nurses entered, both of whom looked like they meant business.

"Time for Mr. Chaney's therapy. I'll have to ask everyone to leave."

Goodbyes were quickly made and Acton, Laura and Reading found themselves in the hallway, walking toward the elevators. Acton turned to Reading.

"What do you think?"

Reading shook his head, his face grim.

"If he can't remember that he's Triarii, he's forgotten far more than he realizes."

"Have you mentioned it to him?"

"No, that was the first hint I had at it. I nearly shat my pants when he called them *glass* skulls." Reading shook his head again as he pressed the button for the elevator. "Only time will tell I guess." The doors opened and he held them for Laura then Acton. "How 'bout some food?"

Acton's stomach grumbled in agreement and plans were quickly made. As they exited the elevator Acton noticed a television flashing to a breaking news report.

Assassinated President's Son Kidnapped.

"Jesus Christ," he muttered and they all turned to see what he was looking at. On the screen footage showed two bodies lying on the ground, covered by sheets, one with the victim's left hand still visible.

Clearly showing a small tattoo on the inner wrist.

"Is that what I think it is?" asked Reading.

Acton nodded. The tattoo was clearly Triarii.

"Why would *they* kidnap him?" asked Laura.

"Until a few minutes ago, I would have said they wouldn't," replied Reading.

"Something's wrong," said Acton. "Very wrong."

And he had a strange feeling that whatever secret message was locked in Chaney's scrambled brain had everything to do with what had just happened back home.

Fleet Street, London, England

Present day, one day after the kidnapping

Proconsul Derrick Kennedy of the Triarii sat at the head of the long conference table, sucking back hard on his favorite vice, a Cuban La Corona cigar, its aromas intoxicating and apparently annoying to some of the younger generation of leaders lining the table. Which was why a special "smoke eater" had been installed during the rebuild after the Delta Force attack on their headquarters. He assumed it worked since he was no longer glared at by some of the more vocal complainers.

On the wall at the far end were a series of large plasma displays, several showing various news feeds from around the world, the panel embedded in the table allowing him full control, the BBC feed of the world's top story currently being listened to.

Behind him, carved in the slate wall was the very symbol he had frozen on one of the screens, though many orders of magnitude bigger. It was the ancient symbol of their organization founded from the surviving members of the third and most experienced line, the Triarii, of the famous Roman Thirteenth Legion, dispatched from Rome by Emperor Nero himself with orders to take a crystal skull found in Judea and exile it to the farthest reaches of the empire, at that time Britannia.

For two thousand years they had kept the crystal skull away from Rome, and when additional skulls had been discovered around the world, they had taken them under their protection. But after a devastating explosion nearly flattened London in 1212 AD when three skulls were placed together, they realized that the skulls could be dangerous and enacted protocols to prevent it from ever happening again.

But today they had been betrayed, as they were once before. There was a split within the Triarii over a decade ago, a small sect at one time agitating from within that the skulls should be brought together to unleash their full potential, the sect's thinking that technology today would allow them to safely do so. The sect was led at one time by a very wealthy and well-connected American named Stewart Jackson. To further his plans of uniting three skulls, he stole the Smithsonian's Mitchell-Hedges skull—the very skull he was assigned to protect—before leaving the Triarii, hiding it away in an unknown location, replacing the genuine article with a fake, unbeknownst to the museum. His power and influence eventually led him to the highest office in his homeland, President of the United States.

Which made him untouchable.

Until he went too far, ordering his elite Delta Force to capture a recently discovered skull under the guise of eliminating a terrorist cell.

He had forced the Triarii's hand and was eliminated by their own man on the inside, a longtime member of the Triarii who had pretended to agree with President Jackson's actions, but in reality was still loyal to the Triarii, staying by his side in hopes of one day retrieving the Smithsonian skull.

After Jackson's theft and departure from the organization, the dissenters had receded into the background, nothing heard again, those who had agitated for unification of the skulls falling silent, denying involvement and disavowing their previous beliefs after such traitorous deeds.

But with today's kidnapping, and the fact Triarii members were clearly involved, it appeared the sect was active again, and there could be only one reason for their actions.

"Clearly they're after the Mitchell-Hedges skull," said one of the twelve others around the table, one for each of the skulls under the protection of the Triarii.

"Clearly," agreed the Proconsul. "The question now is whether or not the son knows where it is, then what we do about it."

"Should we enact The Protocol?" asked the member responsible for the British Museum skull, Maria Thatcher, the very skull under the real-world care of Professor Laura Palmer, who due to Jackson's actions had been drawn into the world of the Triarii, and now knew who and what they were.

"No, I don't think that's necessary at this time," replied the Proconsul. "Be on standby however, as we may need to. At this time there is only one skull I am concerned with."

"We must act on that immediately."

"I had hoped Mr. Chaney would be able to ask for their involvement, but it would appear his injuries are worse than we thought. Though he is out of his coma, his memory is suspect. It appears he has no clue he is a member of the Triarii."

"Then we must act now," said Thatcher, heads around the table nodding in assent as they turned to the Proconsul.

He puffed on his cigar for a moment, eyeing the frozen image of the Triarii tattoo on the wrist of one of the dead kidnappers.

"Agreed. Reach out to the professors immediately. We need their help."

Outskirts of Karakorum, Mongol Empire
March 28th, 1275 AD

Giuseppe lay flat on his stomach, the hard ground cold, his fur coat only protecting him for the first few minutes. It had been over half an hour since they first crawled into position. The others had returned to make temporary camp until nightfall, but his master, Marco, had insisted on staying to observe the city below.

And where Marco went, Giuseppe went.

The city walls were massive, encircling the entire former capital with guard towers at regular intervals, manned each with two men and torches to light the area, some of them already lit and flickering in the winter wind, illuminating little, but the occasional guard could be seen warming his hands near the flame.

"How will we enter, Master?"

"I was thinking through the gates."

Giuseppe hid his surprise, unsure of whether or not his master was once again joking with him, his humor one of his most endearing if not puzzling qualities. He searched his master's face for a hint of the truth, but nothing was revealed to suggest he wasn't serious.

"Then why are we waiting?"

"The guards will be cold and tired near the end of their shift. I would guess they will change near midnight. If we wait until about an hour before then, we shall find our guards eager to let us pass so they can return to their fires. We shall go through the East Gates; they are closest to the Church where our contact is."

"If we are going through the gates, Master, why are you observing the walls for so long?"

Giuseppe shivered as if to emphasize his subtle point.

"I said we'd *enter* by the gates. I didn't say how we'd exit."

Giuseppe nodded, his interest suddenly renewed in the walls. The sun had set behind the mountains now, the entire valley bathed in darkness, the light from fires, lanterns and torches, as well as a quarter moon mostly hidden behind clouds stabbing feebly at the night.

"And now we see their weakness," said Marco, pointing to the guard towers. "What do we know about torches at night?"

Giuseppe shrugged. "I don't know what you mean? They provide light?"

"Yes, but only to the immediate area," said Marco. "If you hold a torch high and peer into the darkness, what do you see?"

And then it dawned on Giuseppe, a smile spreading across his face. "You see nothing! All your eyes can see is the light of the torch!"

"Exactly, my brother. You see better in the dark, when it is dark. Your eyes adjust. But these fools have bright torches on either side of their guard towers meaning they won't be able to see more than ten or twenty paces in either direction. One would be able to scale the wall at the midpoint of two guard towers completely unseen." His master stood, no longer concerned with being spotted. "Let us return to the camp and tell the others of our plan."

"Your plan, Master."

Marco put his arm across Giuseppe's shoulders and squeezed. "You were there when the plan was crafted. We shall call it *our* plan."

Giuseppe was about to protest when a particularly harsh gust of wind had them both gasping for air, their Venetian blood not accustomed to these temperatures. Though Giuseppe was certain he wasn't Venetian, he *was* certain he was of a warm clime, his reaction to the cold seeming to suggest it was completely unnatural to him.

They walked in silence to the camp and dropped near a large fire, sheltered by several large stones and a rock face. Though definitely warmer, it was still ridiculously cold, though Giuseppe kept his complaints to himself.

"We have a plan," announced his master.

"Out with it," said his master's father, Niccolo. "What have you two cooked up?"

Giuseppe felt a surge of pride at the words, along with a few butterflies in the pit of his stomach at the suggestion he had indeed contributed.

"Giuseppe and I will enter through the eastern gates in about two hours with one of our horses, posing as traders for tomorrow's market. There's no reason they should stop us, and we will then make our way to the church which is nearby.

"Once we make contact with the priest, we'll attempt to retrieve the idol, and if successful, we'll escape over the southern wall and join you here."

"And what if you cannot accomplish this tonight?"

"I will shoot an arrow with a message—I will show you the spot where it will land when we leave shortly—and it will tell you when I am expected to return. We should send our party with as many of our supplies as you can back, for I think we shall be pursued. Keep four swift horses and enough provisions for the journey back in case we need to abandon the supply horses."

Marco's father Niccolo nodded, looking at his brother, Matteo. "What do you think?"

"I think your son has thought of everything except what to do should he be captured."

"I did," replied Marco.

"And what is the plan in such an eventuality?"

"To not get captured."

Leroux Residence, Fairfax Towers, Falls Church, Virginia
Present day, one day after the kidnapping

Chris Leroux was pinned to the floor, his girlfriend Sherrie White on top of him. He struggled against her, but not very hard, this a fight he was more than willing to lose. And she knew it, grinding her hips in to his with every move he made.

She was playing to win.

And he was playing to lose.

They both knew what was going on. It had begun as a tickle war on the couch in which he had almost made her sick from laughing, then in a last ditch effort to save herself, she had used one of her CIA Special Operator moves on him that immediately had him on the floor and at her mercy.

He hated being tickled and had quickly stopped his own assault when she began hers, instead focusing on grabbing her hands to prevent any more of the torturous nerve games. He yanked her hands away from her body, pulling her torso toward his so that she now lay on top of him, her hips still straddling his.

"Kiss me," he said, still out of breath.

"No."

He raised his head and tried to find her lips but she jerked back. His head moved to the side, seeking her soft full lips capable of giving so much pleasure, but she continued to resist. Twisting to the right he saw the television, tuned to CNN, display a breaking news graphic.

Assassinated President's Son Kidnapped.

Suddenly he felt Sherrie biting his neck, her tongue flicking out as she starting to suck, the hickey she was about to leave going unnoticed by Leroux as he stopped resisting, his arms dropping to his side.

Sherrie stopped, looking over at the screen.

"What?"

"President Jackson's son was just kidnapped."

"Really? That's too bad."

She turned back and began to kiss his cheek, her pecks travelling over to his ear then down his neck.

"I wonder if we'll be called in." Leroux continued to watch the screen as the kisses reached his chest, then suddenly he felt his shirt get ripped open. His head spun to see a mischievous look on Sherrie's face as she moved down his chest to his stomach, suddenly grabbing his belt buckle with her teeth.

"Probably," she whispered.

"Probably what?" gasped Leroux as the realization of what was about to happen had the news report forgotten.

"We'll probably get called in," she said as she opened his belt then unbuttoned his pants.

"Probably. Especially since the entire story surrounding his assassination was bullshit."

Sherrie stopped, her eyes narrowing.

"What do you mean?"

Leroux looked at her in dismay. "Nothing, I was just joking. Just a theory I have." She continued to stare at him. "For the love of God, don't stop!" She continued to stare at him then suddenly unzipped his pants, yanking them and his underwear down in one motion that left him breathless.

She grabbed him and squeezed.

He groaned.

And both their phones vibrated with urgent messages from Langley.

East Gates, Karakorum, Mongol Empire
March 29th, 1275 AD

Giuseppe didn't need to fake appearing cold and haggard from a long journey. He was. His master, Marco, did have to slouch a little and let his face sag, the man a veritable bundle of energy that seemed without end. As they shuffled toward the eastern gates of Karakorum, the guard towers looming on either side, the torches flickering in the wind, Giuseppe gently led their horse, packs filled with several fine silks from back home for trade.

Two guards stepped out to challenge them, their breath freezing in the frigid air, their noses red and swollen, their eyelashes and brows thick with ice. These were cold, tired men, just as his master had predicted. The howling wind prevented him from hearing much of what Marco said, but the odd word did make it through the gusts suggesting his master was receiving a grilling more detailed than expected. After several minutes Marco waved him forward and he advanced with their horse.

"Get two of the silks," said Marco, his expression one of frustration, no trace of his usual jovial mood remaining. Giuseppe opened one of the side pouches and removed two of the swaths, handing them to his master who took them, turning as a less than genuine smile spread across his face.

"For you and your friend," he said, handing one to the guard he had been talking to, the other to the second who stepped forward eagerly to receive his. "Sell them for a handsome profit, or give them to your special lady friend and she'll be yours to do with as you please!"

The two men grinned at each other, their rotting teeth suggesting any woman would have to think long and hard about giving up anything to these men for mere silk. The first waved at them to proceed as the other called for the gate to be opened. Marco bowed and Giuseppe mimicked him, following his master through the opening gates and into the ether beyond, tomorrow's market empty, the sparse houses at this end of the city mostly dark for the night.

Giuseppe didn't relax until he heard the gates close behind them and didn't dare look back until he saw his master do so. Marco smiled at him, clearly aware of how nervous his slave was. He slowed so Giuseppe could catch up, then they walked side-by-side through the lonely street.

"That wasn't as easy as I had hoped. They all appear on edge, as if they're expecting something. If I had to guess, they're expecting the Khan to send infiltrators before an attack. It's good we went through the East Gates. North or south along the main roads would have been nearly impossible."

Giuseppe merely nodded, his mind wandering to what might happen to them should they be captured as spies for the Khan. It would be one thing to be captured now, before they had caused any mischief, but if they succeeded in stealing the crystal idol, they would be tortured and executed for certain.

He shuddered.

"Are you cold, my brother?"

Giuseppe nodded, not wanting his master to know how terrified he felt at this very moment. He could hide his fear well, it never good to show others when you were weak, but his master knew him so well, he could tell from the expression that Marco was being polite, not wanting to point out the man's true reasons for shivering.

But it *was* cold.

"Where is the church, Master?"

Marco motioned with his chin ahead. "Just up on the left. There's a path between the buildings that leads to a field where the church lies. There's nothing near it, so we'll be exposed as we approach. Hopefully the dark and the late hour will mean no one will notice." He glanced behind them. "No one appears to be following us, but I can't be sure." He looked again. "I feel like we're being watched. Can you sense it?"

Giuseppe hadn't sensed anything seconds ago, but now that his master's words had sunk in, he felt every hair on his body tingle and his heart began to pump faster. He too began to glance over his shoulder, but he too could see nothing but darkened houses and an equally dark street.

The moon suddenly sliced through an opening in the clouds overhead, bathing the entire area in a dull blue light and Giuseppe caught his breath, a shadow in the dark suddenly revealed then lost quickly as it darted between two houses.

"Did you see that?" he hissed, but instead of replying, he felt Marco's hand around his arm, urging him forward, Giuseppe almost coming to a stop.

"Keep moving, we mustn't let him know we've spotted him."

They continued forward, their pace leisurely, that of weary travelers, and Giuseppe tried to relax his constantly tensing muscles, the urge to look back almost irresistible.

Marco turned to the left, a path between two houses barely visible. Giuseppe led their horse into it, but not before his eyes darted down the road as he made the turn, and now that he knew they were being followed, he saw their pursuer plainly, his features indistinguishable, but his movement obvious against the dimly lit stone.

Their pursuer disappeared upon Giuseppe's entry into the gap between the two houses. He looked ahead and could see the walled compound containing the only Christian enclave of the city. It too appeared asleep, the expected glow of a torch or fire somewhere inside not to be seen. The entire situation had Giuseppe wondering if the priest's offer to help them secure the idol had been discovered, and if he had been put to death along with the few Christians the church served.

"Keep walking toward the church. I'll remain behind to deal with our uninvited guest."

Giuseppe was about to open his mouth in protest but was silenced with a glance from Marco, it clear he was determined to be the one to find out what was going on.

Giuseppe nodded and continued forward with the horse, leaving the protection of the two walls on either side, exposing himself to the open fields bordering the path. He turned his head slightly, pushing the fur lining that protected his ears aside, straining to hear against the howling wind.

It was of no use.

His master, the man who called him 'brother', was now alone behind him, waiting for an unknown pursuer in the darkness of a town known to have fallen to the spell of a false idol, and if there was one thing Giuseppe knew, it was how fanatical people could be when it came to their beliefs, especially those not grounded in reality like his own.

A yelp carried by the wind had Giuseppe spinning toward the sound. He could see nothing through the darkness and light snow, but whatever the source of the sound had been, it was silent now. Giuseppe was torn between his duty to obey his master, and his desire to make certain his master was safe.

If he's dead, then you don't need to worry about obeying his orders.

Giuseppe turned, determined to find his master, when a shadow emerged from between the houses, quickly approaching him, but there was something wrong.

The shadow was too big.

Which meant his master was most likely dead, and this behemoth was the reason.

Giuseppe drew his sword, gripping it with both hands as he readied himself for the attack, the massive man continuing forward, straight for him and his beast. He raised his sword high, preparing to defend himself, when the man spoke.

"Put your sword away, my brother, and help me!"

Marco!

Giuseppe sheathed his sword, his racing heart and tensed muscles relaxing as he realized the massive man was actually his master helping another man, supporting him with an arm over the shoulders. Giuseppe rushed forward and took the man's other arm, draping it over his own shoulders, then together they rushed toward the gates of the church, Giuseppe grabbing the reins of their horse as they walked by it.

Within minutes they were at the gates, Giuseppe's untold questions unanswered as they struggled forward in silence. Marco knocked on the doors, quietly as he apparently didn't want the sound to carry.

Nothing.

He knocked a little louder this time, but again nothing could be heard over the howling winds. Marco raised his hand to knock a third time, but as he was about to the sound of the bar behind the gate being removed stopped him. Moments later the left side of the gate swung open and a young man, poorly dressed for the weather, waved them inside. They half carried, half dragged their charge through, the large gate shoved closed behind them as soon as their horse was clear, the wooden bar put back in place.

They were led across the courtyard in silence, the young man who had opened the gate continually looking back at the man they were now almost carrying. As they neared the entrance of the church itself another form emerged from the darkness and took the reins from Giuseppe, leading the horse away and toward a stable to the right. Marco made no mention of it so Giuseppe remained silent.

The doors were pushed open to the church, Marco and Giuseppe carrying the man inside, the young man closing the doors behind him. He led them deeper inside and around the altar to the rectory where they found a roaring fire and wonderful, radiant heat pulsating from the hearth. They lay the man on a bed in a side room, it too having its own fire, then stepped back, the young man going to work, quickly stripping the man of his winter clothing so the fire's warmth could reach him.

As he did so another young man entered with a pitcher of wine and several glasses. Marco took a glass, downing it quickly, Giuseppe doing the same, then they both began to remove their heavy clothing, the fire causing a steady trickle of sweat to run down Giuseppe's back. Within moments they were in regular clothes, sitting out in the rectory office while the young men attended to their pursuer.

In the entire time, Marco and Giuseppe had said nothing. Giuseppe was assuming the man was the priest, the fire light revealing he was quite elderly—far too old to be out in these frigid temperatures.

A thought struck Giuseppe that had him tossing a look of concern over at Marco.

If he should die, how can we possibly find the crystal idol?

Marco poured two more glasses of wine, the bitter brew almost unfit for consumption, Giuseppe used to the fine wines enjoyed in Venice by the Polo family. But it was better than nothing.

Giuseppe grimaced as he took a drink.

"Not up to your standards?" asked Marco with a wink.

Giuseppe shook his head, placing the glass on the table where bread and cheese had been put out for them. He took a chunk of bread and carved himself a thick slice of cheese, folding them together then taking a bite, his hunger ravenous.

"I guess I've been spoiled by *your* good taste," replied Giuseppe between chews, his hand covering his mouth, table manners at the Polo household lax when on the expedition, but not too much so.

Marco smiled, tearing off his own chunk of bread, dipping a corner into the wine. Biting off the now purple portion of bread, he chewed and shrugged.

"It could be worse."

"It could always be worse. Like that camel piss we had in Persia."

Marco began to chuckle then stopped himself with a glance at the bedroom where their hosts were busy with the old man. He lowered his voice.

"That was truly disgusting. I was too nervous to ask what it was made from, but I didn't see any grapes in the area."

"I'm telling you, it was camel piss. I'm willing to bet they only served it to *us* then laughed about it after we left."

Marco laughed aloud this time, jabbing the air with his bread. "I would not be one bit surprised if that were so!"

He leaned in, immediately lowering his voice again. "I fear I may have scared the old man to death when I jumped him in the alley."

Giuseppe moved closer, his own voice lowering. "Is he our contact?"

Marco nodded, his eyes shifting between the door and his slave. "Keep that quiet. I don't know how much these others know, if anything."

Giuseppe nodded. "What will we do if he dies?"

Marco shook his head. "Pray he doesn't, or this errand for the Khan could turn into a fool's one."

One of the young men emerged from the bedroom with a smile. "Father Salvatore will see you now," he said, the relief on his face clear.

Marco rose, as did Giuseppe who followed his master into the small room, two chairs having been placed near the bed where they found the old man propped up on pillows, blankets pulled up to his neck, his arms out and at his sides. Several lanterns had been lit, heavy curtains covering the windows, which Giuseppe thought might explain why there had been no evidence of life from outside. He wondered if it were a function of the cold, or if a Christian church in a Muslim dominated area might need to keep a low profile.

He had heard that within the Mongol Empire infighting amongst the varying religions was not tolerated, and that Christians, Muslims and Jews were free to practice their own religions without fear of reprisals. But with the Khan's influence apparently waning within these city walls, that enforced tolerance may no longer be practiced.

Marco sat nearest the old man, Giuseppe near the foot of the bed, to the side. A nightstand beside the old man's bed held wine and a nearly empty bowl of soup, and judging by the rosy cheeks he was now sporting, it appeared that life had been forced back into him by his dedicated servants.

He smiled at them, the cheeks still betraying his weakened state, but thankfully he appeared no closer to death than any man of his age should.

"Father, I must first begin by apologizing to you. If I had known it was you following us, I never would have jumped you like I did."

The old man shook his head and his hand, waving off the apology. "There is no need to apologize. Like the foolish old man I am, I ignored the pleadings of my altar boys and went out in the darkness like a man twenty years my junior in the hopes of making sure when you did arrive, you weren't followed."

"We weren't, so your mission was accomplished," smiled Marco. He paused, looked at Giuseppe then back at the priest. "Forgive me, Father, but I believe introductions are in order. I am Marco Polo of Venice, and this is my trusted man Giuseppe. Anything you need to say can be said in front of him."

The old man looked at Giuseppe, nodding slightly. "For a master to put so much trust in his slave speaks well of the slave," replied the old man. "Remember that the lower the station, the more God loves him, and for your master to have such faith in you, I think an honored place in Heaven is in your future."

Giuseppe felt his cheeks flush as the praise was heaped upon him by both his master and the priest. His eyes dropped to the floor.

Marco slapped Giuseppe's knee twice, giving it a squeeze then turning to the priest. "I have come to think of Giuseppe as my brother, as opposed to my slave. It is merely a twist of fate that I was born to a rich household, and he to a poor. A man's station shouldn't influence how he is treated and whether or not he be trusted. I trust Giuseppe with my life, and I hope he does mine."

"Absolutely, Master!" exclaimed Giuseppe, his eyes opening wide as he looked at the man who would call him brother. He immediately returned his gaze to the floor, embarrassed by his outburst.

Marco squeezed the back of Giuseppe's neck then returned to the elderly priest. "You know of course why we are here."

"Absolutely," replied the old man.

"Can we speak freely?" whispered Marco, the room currently devoid of helpers.

The priest nodded. "I trust my people."

"Very well. We are prepared tonight to retrieve the idol should you know where it is."

"I do indeed, but I fear it is now out of reach by anything less than an army."

Giuseppe looked at Marco, his concern matching that of his master.

"What do you mean?" asked Marco.

"I mean it now lies at the topmost level of the Red Mosque."

"And where is that?"

"Look out my window, and you will see it."

Marco rose, Giuseppe following, both moving aside the heavy curtain and stepping behind it to maintain the shield against the firelight escaping. When Giuseppe's eyes adjusted he gasped and looked at Marco, whose jaw was set tight, his head shaking slightly at what they were looking at.

A tower, at least ten stories high, it appearing to be a spiral structure ending in a peak that provided a view of the entire city.

And anyone who would dare approach.

1st Special Forces Operational Detachment-Delta HQ, Fort Bragg, North Carolina
A.k.a. "The Unit"
Present day, one day after the kidnapping

Command Sergeant Major Burt "Big Dog" Dawson, BD to his close friends, was in his traditional role of Grill Master Sergeant, manning the grills behind The Unit, his home away from home, or more accurately for him, his home. As the leader of Delta Team Bravo, the toughest sons of bitches ever gathered into one group, he had the distinction of leading, in his opinion, the best squad of operators the US Military had ever put forward. The one dozen men, part of 1st Special Forces Operational Detachment - Delta, were deployed en masse or in smaller teams around the world to put out fires or start them—whatever was needed.

Today the fire was contained in his two charcoal grills, burgers, hot dogs and one veggie burger for an experimental pre-teen were all on the go, buns on the top grill to toast up slightly, a stack of American processed cheese slices ready to be peeled off one-by-one and melted on what he hoped would be perfectly cooked quarter pounders.

It was his favorite job that didn't involve a weapon.

A softball game was underway with the rest of his team and their families, the laughter intoxicating. He normally did this job alone, sometimes pining for the old days when he was just one of the guys, and his old boss would be grilling away.

Command structure was loose in Delta, all of them some type of sergeant. There were no officers here, they were in the building, cooking up and responding to mission requests. But in the field? It was all NCO's—Non-Coms—that did the grunt work.

And he loved it.

There was nothing like being in-theatre, on a mission, living on the edge of life and death, then accomplishing their task and coming back home, all alive, all well. It didn't always work out that way, and just recently they had mourned the loss of one of their own, but they usually made it out with just a few scrapes and the occasional bullet wound, their training and equipment exceptional.

Today however, instead of tending the grill by himself, he had Maggie at his side, chatting him up. She was a hot little number, sporting a t-shirt exposing her flat midriff and shorts that were just a little too short showcasing long, tanned legs. It had taken Dawson a little while to figure out she was sweet on him, and he still hadn't decided what to do about it. He had always thought of himself as a life-long committed bachelor. He'd have the occasional dalliance just to let off some steam, but had never found "the one".

He sometimes envied the family men like his best friend Mike "Red" Belme, his second-in-command, who had a wife and kids. Dawson had a sister with a fantastic daughter who he adored, and he was godfather to Red's son Bryson who was a joy except when he neared Dawson's prized 1964½ Ford Mustang convertible in original Poppy Red with his hands covered in dripping ice cream or worse.

When he was all cleaned up he and Red would take Bryson out for drives, usually ending up somewhere necessitating a cleanup before the drive home.

Red would always admonish him with some variation of "Get a mini-van then you won't care!" Dawson would just give him the evil eye as he supervised the wipe-down.

Cheers mixed with groans came from the game and Maggie motioned toward the group. "Looks like game over."

Dawson nodded, noting her hand resting on his shoulder and the low level of her third bottle of brewed courage. She was a great looking woman, very friendly and intelligent.

But she's the Colonel's secretary!

If it didn't work out, every time he'd have to see the Colonel she'd be there. The level of discomfort would be insane. And if she were to quit because of it? The Colonel would probably tear him a new asshole for losing him a perfectly good secretary.

"Oh, here comes the chaperone."

Chaperone? Are we on a date?

Red trotted over, young Bryson racing behind him, his legs a little too uncoordinated for Dawson's liking.

He eyeballed the boy's hands.

Clean.

"Hey, you two. How're the burgers coming? I think you've got a hungry bunch about to get cranky."

"Almost ready."

"What? You're usually bang on with these things."

Maggie giggled, putting both her hands on Dawson's shoulder and laying her head against him. "Sorry, I guess I've been distracting him."

"I guess so," replied Red, scratching at a few days of stubble, its harsh orange color revealing the source of his nickname.

Dawson motioned toward his nearly bare scalp, a little growth showing there as well.

"Thinking of growing it back?"

Red ran his hand over his head several times. "Nope. Just can't find my shaving knife."

"Huh?" It was Maggie who was surprised by the statement, not Dawson. He knew his friend shaved his head with a Bowie knife. Dawson had asked him once why a knife and not a razor and his response had been typical Red.

"Because I can."

Dawson's car radio, tuned to some generic Top 40 station at the request of the others suddenly went silent, then an announcer cut in.

"We interrupt this broadcast for an important news bulletin. Former President Jackson's son has been kidnapped at gunpoint. Two of his assailants are dead, and his Secret Service escort have been taken to hospital with non-life threatening injuries. At this point in time the identity and motives of the kidnappers is unknown. Grant Jackson, the thirty-three year old son of the murdered President had just given a speech to a partisan crowd announcing his bid for Congress when his car was rammed and he was taken captive. We will update you with further information as it comes in."

The radio flipped back to some pre-meltdown Justin Bieber tune that would normally have Dawson gagging if it weren't for what they had just heard.

"Do you think we'll get called in?" asked Red, holding his son against his side.

"All things considered, probably, since we've already been read-in on the details from before."

"What details?" asked Maggie.

Dawson's head darted to his new appendage and he had to catch himself from saying something that might hurt her feelings. He smiled.

"Sorry, need to know."

She nodded, backing off slightly and patting his shoulder as she took the spatula from him and attended to the forgotten hamburgers. "I've worked long enough for Colonel Clancy to know when to shut my ears."

Dawson gave her shoulder a squeeze which he had the sense melted that half of her body into a puddle of nerves and hormones. "Thanks." He turned to Red just as his phone vibrated, a phone that almost never was called. He answered.

"Speak."

"Mr. Jones, I need you at the flower shop for a delivery."

He frowned. "Five minutes."

He snapped the phone back on his hip then nodded toward the throng now at the picnic tables.

"Tell the boys to lay off the beer. I'll let *you* know what's going on as soon as *I* know."

"These are ready," announced Maggie as she handed the spatula to Red and turned to face Dawson. "It's been fun," she said, then quickly popped up on her toes and gave him a kiss on the side of his mouth. It was so quick Dawson didn't even have time to respond. Instead he stood there awkwardly for a moment then turned crimson when a chorus of "ooohs" erupted from the tables.

He shook his head, a smile creeping up half his face as he turned and headed for his car. As he climbed in Maggie gave him a little wave, a smile on her face that told Dawson everything he needed to know.

She's in deep. And you're in trouble.

Outside the Red Mosque, Karakorum, Mongol Empire
March 29th, 1275 AD

Giuseppe was huddled in the snow, shaking once again, the warmth of the church a quickly fading memory. To his right was his master Marco, his bow in hand, and to his left were the two altar boys from the church. Father Salvatore had been insistent that they be taken along and Marco had reluctantly agreed when his reasoning became clear.

Should they be successful in stealing the crystal icon, the Christians would most likely be blamed.

And slaughtered.

Father Salvatore had sent everyone away weeks ago to seek safety in the south, only his two most loyal altar boys had remained with him, refusing to leave. Fortunately, in the Mongol Empire, even those of the cloth learned to defend themselves or perish, and these two young men apparently were skilled in the use of the bow and adept at swordplay as well.

"They weren't always altar boys."

Marco had smiled at the priest's words, nodding knowingly, and expressed his gratefulness at the two additions to their group. The two men, Roberto, who had opened the gate, and Vincenzo, who had taken their horse, were reluctant to join them at first. Giuseppe had no doubt it was not of fear of the mission, but of not wanting to leave their ailing Father alone.

Giuseppe knew how they felt. Leaving Marco alone, especially if ailing, was something he couldn't fathom. In fact he had been at Marco's side for so long now, he couldn't remember the last time they had been apart for more than a few hours.

Marco pointed at the tower that loomed above them, the exposed stairs inside glowing from torchlight, the howling wind whipping up and down the stairway, lashing at the flames causing them to flicker in the dark. The compound was walled, but not high, perhaps six feet, and from what Giuseppe could see, there were a few guards at the gate but little else.

"I thought he said we would need an army?"

Marco shook his head, pointing at the tower. "They're all inside. Probably trying to keep warm."

"Do we know how many there are?"

"No, but I think I've counted at least six, but there could be dozens."

"Vincenzo and I have been watching for several days now. We believe there are thirteen guarding the idol at all times," offered Roberto.

"Thirteen?" asked Marco.

"Yes," replied Vincenzo. "Father Salvatore believes the number of guards has been chosen intentionally. He says the superstition connected with the number thirteen feeds into their delusion of the idol being something that must be worshipped, and that can easily be offended."

"Hogwash," spat Roberto. "To think these blasphemers would give up the word of God in favor of a crystal idol and some unproven stories of good fortune! It's enough to make one wonder why God hasn't struck them down!"

"Perhaps God has other plans for them. Perhaps tonight is the night His wrath is brought upon them," said Vincenzo, lowering his voice to calm his partner. "Mysterious are the ways of the Lord. Mere mortals shouldn't try to understand His methods."

Roberto's head bobbed, his chin falling to his chest. "I apologize. I just know what this entire situation has done to poor Father Salvatore and it drives me mad. I find I have to pray more and more to control my anger and frustration." He sighed. "I shame myself every time."

Vincenzo put a comforting hand on his friend's shoulder. "Let us put an end to all of this tonight. If we successfully remove this curse from our city, all will return to normal. And should it cost us our lives, we at least die absolved of our sins, and in the service of our Lord."

"Amen," whispered Roberto, making the sign of the cross. Giuseppe did the same, returning his attention to the tower, now seeing the men inside the stairway, mostly through their shadows cast by the torches.

"What do you propose, Master?"

Marco removed the eyepiece he had been looking through and put it in his pocket, turning his head to face his three companions. "I count two at the gate, and they seem to switch frequently to keep warm. We are all skilled with the bow. On the next exchange, we will eliminate all four when they are outside of the mosque. Once you have loosed your arrow, replace it immediately with one from your quiver in case others come out. My hope is the four dead will not be noticed by the others until it is too late. However, should they be noticed, the more we kill from a distance with arrows, the less we need to kill up close with swords. And remember, at that point it could be nine against four." He pointed to the west side of the walled compound then looked at Roberto and Vincenzo. "You two will position on that side and take out the two new arrivals. Giuseppe and I will remain here and eliminate the current guard. As soon as the four are eliminated, we'll climb the southern wall and enter the compound, taking up position at the side of the tower. You should be able to see us. One of you will then return here to help cover our escape. Under no circumstances should you enter the compound. Use your arrows to eliminate anybody you can, but I want you to retreat when you can do no more. Retreat to the west, then make your way back to the church. We don't want anyone discovering Christians were involved. Understood?"

Roberto nodded, as did Vincenzo, though both appeared to do so reluctantly.

"Is there a problem?"

Roberto looked at Vincenzo, then at Marco. "Should the need arise, we are willing to enter the compound and join you. You shouldn't concern yourself with our lives."

Marco smiled. "You are both brave men, and I appreciate that. But should the need arise for assistance from your swords, I fear it will already be too late for us, and by the time you arrived, you would be sadly outnumbered, facing them alone, for we shall already be dead. You must survive so you can try to retrieve the idol another day. Should we fail, more will come, I am certain."

Roberto frowned, but nodded his acquiescence.

Marco lowered his head, gripping the cross around his neck. "Now we pray."

Giuseppe bowed his head, his hand encircling his own cross as his thoughts turned not to his God, but to the crystal icon that had haunted his dreams and reveries since he had heard of it.

And again visions of a laughing crystal skull played over his eyelids, sending a shiver down his spine, the ominous feeling that tonight may very well be his last almost overwhelming.

Wellington Hospital, London, England
Present day, one day after the kidnapping

Detective Inspector Martin Chaney shook in his bed, his hands gripping the rails, sweat pouring off his forehead, soaking his pillow. In fact his hospital robe was sticking to his entire body as perspiration erupted from his pores, his muscles clenching and unclenching, his head tossing back and forth, his face contorted in a mixture of agony and fear.

Suddenly his eyes opened and he gasped, leaping forward to a sitting position. He quickly surveyed the room, finding it empty, momentarily a little disappointed that his former partner and still good friend Reading wasn't passed out in a chair somewhere.

He needs his rest too.

He sat up in his bed for several minutes as he made sense of the flood of memories demanding attention. Skulls, tattoos, secret societies, initiations, a vacation in Egypt, the discovery of an impossible tomb, the attack—

The message!

Suddenly everything was clear, everything that had been forgotten now remembered.

And he knew exactly what he had to do.

Outside the Red Mosque, Karakorum, Mongol Empire
March 29th, 1275 AD

Giuseppe released his arrow, intentionally pausing by counting to three in his head so he didn't mess up his shot in the rush to get his next arrow from his quiver. His master had no such hesitation, already having another arrow in place before Giuseppe even reached for his next. The two targets at the gate collapsed as if felled by the same arrow, the second two freezing for a moment, then they two falling as the arrows of Roberto and Vincenzo proved true.

Marco jumped to his feet, rushing toward the southern wall. Giuseppe pushed himself to keep up, his eyes on the courtyard the entire time. Three of the bodies remained still, but the fourth, one of the new arrivals, had begun to crawl toward the tower. Giuseppe saw a second arrow suddenly embed itself in the man, putting an end to his suffering, and the threat he may attract others.

As they neared the wall their view of the courtyard was blocked, but so far no one had appeared. Marco stopped at the wall, dropping to a knee, cupping his hands. Without slowing, Giuseppe jumped onto the hand then used the push his master gave him to easily grab onto the top of the wall, swinging a leg over and straddling the stone. Reaching down he grabbed his master's left hand and pulled him up then rolled over to the other side, dropping to a crouch, his bow at the ready.

But there was no need. The four bodies still lay in the dark, as yet undiscovered. But those inside would probably be expecting the relieved guard to arrive, and at any moment someone may come looking for the missing men.

Marco rushed to the side of the Red Mosque, its tower looming overhead, at this distance appearing impossibly high. His master's plan might work, but there were so many assumptions he wasn't sure he had the same level of faith Marco at least portrayed. The design of the mosque up close confirmed what his master had suspected—and thankfully it worked to their advantage. The red stone that clad the structure had decorative white stones that jutted out creating a foothold every arm's length, ringing the tower, from top to bottom.

Marco didn't hesitate, removing his gloves, slinging his bow over his back and beginning the long climb to the top. Giuseppe began to follow but was waved off.

"Cover my exit!" hissed Marco, reiterating the part of the plan Giuseppe didn't agree with. The idea his master should execute the most dangerous part of the plan alone was insane, at least in Giuseppe's mind. He returned to the ground and fell back toward the western wall, edging ahead so he could see the main entrance.

Still nothing.

He watched his master quickly scale the side and within minutes he was already halfway up. A change in the light at the entrance had Giuseppe drawing back on his bow, the appearance of a soldier stepping out into the cold triggering the release of his arrow. He readied another as the man dropped in his place, a second arrow hitting him at almost the same time, the knowledge Roberto and Vincenzo were still outside providing him with some comfort.

The body lay unmoving and undiscovered, but that wouldn't remain true for long. A split second decision, perhaps a stupid one, had Giuseppe rushing forward toward the door. He reached it within seconds, peeking inside and seeing no one. He grabbed the collar of the downed guard and pulled him around to the side of the tower, then sprinted back toward his assigned position.

A voice called behind him then cut off with a groan as the thump of two arrows followed by the sound of their victim collapsing to the ground caused Giuseppe to spin only halfway between the tower and wall. As he rushed toward the body in the hopes of clearing it away and out of sight, he glanced up to see his master disappear through the uppermost opening, the speed of which he had cleared the structure impressive.

A shadow in the door and a shout sounding the alarm had Giuseppe arcing to the left, drawing his bow and loosing the arrow as soon as the target was in sight, a seventh guard down, his mental math of the ever evening odds providing little comfort since two of their available swords remained at a distance.

If only we were four! We would stand a chance, especially with God on our side!

Shouts from within were heard followed by the pounding of feet on the steps as the remaining soldiers rushed to their comrade's aid, hopefully numbering no more than the six of the original thirteen they had been promised. Giuseppe drew two arrows, splitting them on either side of his bow, and as the first man came around the corner and burst into the courtyard, he held his fire, a second quickly joining the first.

He loosed the arrows, the first one taking out its target, but the second missing by an embarrassing amount, this shot one Giuseppe had never really tried beyond having some fun.

And it had never worked.

Apparently God does not guide my foolish hand tonight.

He swung his bow over his shoulder, drawing his sword from its sheath as the second man advanced, yelling for the others to join him as he drew his own blade.

He dropped as an arrow pierced his neck, the blood spurting out in a rhythmic pulse as he gurgled an unheard warning to his comrades. Giuseppe still wished the extra two swords were at his side, but for the moment, his Master's plan was working. And if the intelligence provided by the young Roberto and Vincenzo were accurate, there should be only four men left. Again sheathing his sword and retrieving his bow, he fired his final arrow, removing the tenth man, when a chorus of shouts erupted from inside the tower, near the top.

A chorus that sounded like far more than three men.

The sound of swords clashing echoed through the openings of the stairway and Giuseppe felt his chest tighten as he realized his master had been discovered. Cries from above had him frozen, then as the swordplay continued, he realized his master must still be alive, bravely battling his enemy, while his slave stood, doing nothing.

Giuseppe charged forward just as a group of men numbering at least half a dozen poured from the entrance, looking for accomplices. Giuseppe skid to a halt, shooting his final arrow. He was about to draw his sword when he turned to see the first four victims near the gate, not thirty paces distant. Two arrows streaked silently into the courtyard dropping two more of the men as Giuseppe turned and sprinted toward the bodies. As he reached the nearest one, the one who had crawled, he yanked the two arrows from the corpse, spinning as he placed a used arrow in position, taking aim at the first man.

He let his fingers open, the sinew snapping, sending the arrow through the air at an impossible speed, embedding itself in the belly of its unsuspecting victim. As the body crumpled to the ground he fired his second shot as another pair of arrows from his partners outside hit their targets. He scrambled toward the next body, pulling at the arrow buried deep in the man's shoulder, but it snapped.

Roars of anger erupted behind him as he rushed toward the last two men, those originally on guard and eliminated by Marco and himself at the beginning of this entire fiasco. The sounds of swords continued to give him hope for his master, but he was quickly losing it for himself. He pulled the first arrow from a guard's belly, rolling on his shoulder and onto his knee, his bow at the ready as he fired at the nearest guard, four of them now charging at him. He dropped as Giuseppe yanked at the last arrow available to him but it wouldn't give. One final yank failed and he tossed his bow aside, drawing his sword as the first attacker arrived almost immediately joined by two others.

He was surrounded on three sides. He kept his back to the gates of the compound, parrying the first blow from his nearest attacker. An arrow skittered across the stone, missing its intended target, but it was enough to cause all three of his enemy to look up for just a moment.

He swung, slicing the belly of his attacker open, his innards pouring out as the man screamed in agony, dropping his sword and instead focusing on pushing his intestines back inside as he quickly bled out. Enraged, his two remaining friends charged forward. Giuseppe parried, shoving the first attacker's sword upward then dropping to a knee as his blade swung wide and high, then forcing it down and below the man's guard, slicing his leg in two just below the knee as the final guard rushed in from behind. Giuseppe looked over his shoulder and saw the man's sword held high over his head begin to drop for the death blow.

Giuseppe leaned forward, still on his knee, his sword carrying through the down stroke interrupted only by the leg it had just sliced through. He twisted his wrists, redirecting his weapon up in a desperate attempt to parry the final blow, when he heard a thump and saw the man's eyes bulge wide in shock as he fell on Giuseppe's blade, his own flying from his hands and clattering to the ground. Giuseppe shoved the now twitching corpse off him, freeing his sword with a yank, the body rolling to its side then stopping, an arrow protruding from the back.

Giuseppe jumped to his feet, sword at the ready, but found himself alone, surrounded by corpses, the swordplay at the top of the tower continuing. He pushed himself forward, exhausted from the battle he had just endured, but determined to reach his master before it was too late. As he stumbled toward the entrance to the mosque he readied his sword, trying to catch his breath as best he could.

Plunging through the entrance, he found it empty save the bodies of those eliminated earlier. The stairs that wound around the outside wall of the tower were to his right. He mounted the first step and began the long climb, the sounds above him getting louder as he neared the battle. The stairs were narrow, barely a man wide, which was probably why his master had been able to survive for so long, but the sustained battle must have him exhausted.

As he rounded the stairs he readied his weapon, uncertain when he might encounter the first of the enemy, or how many there may be. It was when he saw the back of the first that he heard the footfalls on the steps behind him, and the realization that he was now surrounded with no hope of escape set in.

CIA Headquarters, Langley, Virginia
Present day, one day after the kidnapping

National Clandestine Service Chief Leif Morrison sat behind his desk, reading something on his computer screen as Chris Leroux and Sherrie White sat quietly, waiting to find out why they had been called in. It was strange that they were both here. Leroux was an analyst and Sherrie was a field agent. Usually the two domains didn't mix enough to be in the same briefing, and with Sherrie being a junior agent, her active status not even a year old, Leroux had to wonder why just the two of them were here.

The Assembly?

The thought of some breakthrough on the mysterious organization he had been hunting for longer than he cared to admit with no success had his heart race a few extra beats. It was his side project, known only to him, the Director, Sherrie and his best friend, Special Agent Dylan Kane. It was Kane that had exposed the organization that he was now under orders to identify the members of, but they were so secretive he had had no success to date.

Except for that one damned message that I'm not allowed to open!

Morrison pushed his keyboard away and turned to the pair of lovers, something Morrison knew of and thankfully permitted. Leroux quite often wondered what he would do if Morrison ordered them to end their relationship since it was against Agency policy.

He glanced at Sherrie through the corner of his eye. He could never ask her to give up her dream. She loved it too much and he had no idea what she would do if she were forced to give it up.

I'd quit.

He could get a job elsewhere easily enough. His computer skills would have him in high demand. In fact he'd probably double or triple his salary almost instantly. His eyebrows climbed slightly at the thought.

Triple?

"I'm sure you're dying to know why you're both here."

They nodded in unison.

"President Jackson's son was kidnapped today."

"We saw the news flash," said Sherrie, exchanging a look with Leroux as he knew damned well she was remembering what had happened after that, just as he was.

"You're going to be read-in on a file that is above Top Secret. Once you know what's really going on, Mr. Leroux, you'll be our lead analyst on this. I'll want you to hunt for anything that will lead to the recovery of Grant Jackson. Agent White, you'll be our liaison with the Special Forces team that has been assigned should they be needed since you've worked with them before."

"Delta Team Bravo?"

Morrison nodded.

"Now you are all aware that President Jackson was murdered by his Chief of Staff, Lesley Darbinger. Here's what you didn't know."

Fifteen minutes later Leroux knew exactly why he could never quit this job, even for triple his salary.

Inside the Red Mosque, Karakorum, Mongol Empire
March 29th, 1275 AD

Giuseppe, surrounded with enemy guards ahead of him and reinforcements arriving from below, decided it was best to attack up and perhaps save his master, rather than try to save himself with the easier downward attack. He thrust forward with his sword, embedding it in the back of the unsuspecting soldier ahead of him, swiftly withdrawing the blade. Pulling the body with his left hand down the stairs, he plunged forward with his blade at the next guard, then the next, their bodies collapsing, the final one with a surprised cry that had his compatriots farther up the stairway turn, finally realizing they were under attack from behind.

As they turned, Giuseppe, blade soaked in blood, thrust again, but this time was parried by the now prepared guards, guards who had the advantage of being higher on the stairs. Giuseppe could hear the swords continue to clash above him, though they seemed to have slowed, his master obviously tiring. He could only imagine Marco's exhaustion, his own tremendous, though the total time of his own engagements far shorter.

His master's persistence only inspired him more. He rapidly ceded several steps, and as his closest opponent rushed down after him, Giuseppe suddenly stopped and shoved forward, catching the man off guard, the sword sinking several inches into his stomach. The guard grabbed for the wound with his free hand, his sword slashing down onto Giuseppe's blade before he could remove it from the man's flesh.

The man cried out in pain as his stomach opened from his own mistake. He collapsed forward, causing Giuseppe to cede several more steps then spin as he heard the footfalls of the reinforcements reach him.

An arrow flew past him, embedding itself in the approaching guard's neck, another swiftly following, slicing into a man's shoulder causing him to drop his sword. Giuseppe smiled, his relief palpable, as it was the two altar boys, Roberto and Vincenzo, who had been rushing toward him, disobeying their orders.

Thank God!

Words weren't exchanged, Giuseppe instead raising his sword over his head, his energy renewed at least momentarily, dropping it rapidly, cleaving the man's other shoulder. He collapsed with a cry and Giuseppe pressed their advantage. As the next guard rushed forward to attack, Giuseppe ducked and one of the two new arrivals fired an arrow into the man's chest. They continued forward, this method working as the staircase was so tight, the guards behind couldn't see how their compatriots were being felled.

Within minutes they were near the top, the clash of swords continuing ahead, but the shouts and grunts of their enemy far fewer than earlier. Thirteen had been the estimate, but Giuseppe was certain it was closer to thirty.

Suddenly he heard his master cry out in pain, his voice unmistakable above the fray. Giuseppe charged forward, thrusting his sword into the back of the next soldier, all having turned to press their apparent renewed advantage above. The man cried out as Giuseppe ran him through, reminding the others of the continued threat, but as Giuseppe rounded the corner he found only two men opposing him, one swinging his sword toward Giuseppe, the other about to plunge a sword into Marco.

"No!" screamed Giuseppe, sidestepping his attacker and ducking under the blow, the thump-thump of two arrows taking the man out ignored as Giuseppe rushed forward, his sword extended in front of him as the final guard's blade swiftly swung toward Marco's prone body. Marco looked over at his servant, his expression one of shock at seeing him, then rolled away from the stairs, the upper level of the tower a floor containing nothing but a pedestal in the center of the room.

The guard's blade smacked hard into Giuseppe's, sending it clashing to the stone floor, his hands shaking from the blow. The man's hands were skilled, his own recovery almost instantaneous as Giuseppe stumbled forward, hitting the floor along with his loose sword. He looked over at Marco as the man raised his weapon high above his head. Marco slid his sword across the floor toward Giuseppe who rolled, grabbing the weapon and swinging it across his body, batting the rapidly descending death blow aside.

The man suddenly groaned, his eyes bulging as he dropped to his knees, then flat on his face, an arrow embedded in his back, Roberto rushing onto the topmost level along with Vincenzo. Giuseppe scrambled across the floor to his master.

"Are you okay?" he asked, searching for a wound, but finding none.

"Yes, I'm fine."

"But you screamed. I thought you were wounded!"

"The behemoth stepped on my foot and nearly broke my toe," replied Marco, getting up. "I fell backward and they almost got the best of me before you arrived. It's good to know you can't follow orders."

It was said with a smile and Giuseppe took it for what it was. "Would you rather I wait for you down in the courtyard?"

Marco put his arm around his servant, then pointed to the center of the floor and the pedestal. "This is what it is all about."

Giuseppe turned and gasped, a feeling of terror and uncertainty gripping him at what he saw.

In the center of the pedestal, surrounded by candles whose light seemed to pool together in the idol's eyes, sat a crystal skull, exactly as he had imagined it in his dreams.

Colonel Thomas Clancy's Office, The Unit, Fort Bragg, North Carolina
Present day, one day after the kidnapping

With Maggie at the barbecue, Colonel Thomas Clancy's outer office was empty. Command Sergeant Major Burt Dawson rapped on the closed inner office door, still dressed in his Bermuda shorts and gaudy Hawaiian shirt with genuine bamboo buttons. He glanced down and quickly buttoned it up, covering his rock hard abs and chest—exposed to impress Maggie, but he figured the effect would be wasted on the Colonel.

"Enter!"

The Colonel didn't sound happy. Dawson opened the door and stepped inside, closing it behind him.

"Good afternoon, Colonel," he said, sitting in one of the two chairs in front of Clancy's desk, the orders of the day always casual within the Colonel's office unless brass or Washington were present.

"What the hell's good about it?" muttered Clancy, jabbing his finger at a file on his desk. "Do you realize I'm supposed to be fishing right now? Fishing! Just me, a boat, a hat, a damned fishing rod and a cooler of beer. And some damned fine cigars my wife doesn't want me smoking!" Both their eyes darted to the empty space on his desk that used to be occupied by his humidor.

"Sorry to hear that, Colonel," replied Dawson, knowing the man too well to be worried that he was actually upset at him. Clancy was a soldier's soldier. Dawson knew he always had his back, regardless of what politics might make him say publicly. He believed in "no man left behind", he believed that The Unit was a family, and that to lose a member of the family was unacceptable.

"You heard about the kidnapping?"

"Just did."

Clancy pushed the folder toward Dawson. "Take a look."

Dawson took the file and flipped it open.

"Skip to the photos," said Clancy, grabbing a pencil and sticking it in his mouth, the placebo a poor substitute for the real thing.

Dawson flipped through the file and found several crime scene photos. A Caddy with a dented front end and crushed rear end. An SUV that had rammed it. Two bodies and then something that had him stop, his chest pounding.

"Are we sure about this?" he asked Clancy, still staring at the enlarged photo of a man's wrist, the symbol tattooed on it far too familiar for his liking.

"Absolutely. Both bodies have the tattoo on the inner left wrist. It's identical to London. And their MO is the same. Non-lethal force, using tranquilizer darts instead of bullets."

Dawson pursed his lips, flipping back to the two men. "Should have used bullets by the looks of it."

"Agreed."

Dawson flipped the folder closed. "So why am I here?"

"Because you're one of the few in the Special Ops community who knows what really happened. The powers that be think this is going to get ugly, and our type of expertise might be needed, so they want people who already know the truth, rather than have to read-in more that don't."

"My team?"

"Take only those who were there from the beginning."

Dawson nodded. "And where are we going?"

"Get your asses to Langley, you'll liaise with one of their people and deploy as necessary."

"Posse Comitatus?"

Clancy pushed another folder toward Dawson. "By order of the President of these United States, suspended. You are free to operate on American soil so long as it relates to the recovery of former President Jackson's son."

"Understood."

Clancy waved his hand toward the door. "Now get out of here. I just might be able to squeeze a few hours of fishing in."

"Yes, sir," said Dawson, standing. "Good hunting."

"You too, Sergeant Major," replied Clancy as Dawson opened the door. "Oh, and Sergeant Major?"

"Yes, sir?"

"Try not to blow up half of London this time."

Dawson snapped his sandaled heels together and gave the Colonel a Sergeant Bilko salute.

"Yes, my Colonel!"

"Piss off!"

Dawson stepped out and closed the door as a roar of laughter erupted from the other side. The smile on his own face quickly faded however as he recalled the events that had ended with dozens dead, all innocent, due to the manipulations and obsessions of one crazed man.

The President of the United States.

Stewart Alfred Jackson.

And he couldn't help but wonder if his son was another innocent, caught up in his father's affairs, or a willing participant.

All he could say for sure was that this time they wouldn't be manipulated into doing anything.

Outside the Red Mosque, Karakorum, Mongol Empire

March 29th, 1275 AD

Giuseppe's arms pumped, his chest heaving from exhaustion. Never would he have thought he'd long for the simple hand-to-hand combat they had just experienced. At least it involved little running. But now the four of them were sprinting across the city in the darkness, hoping to not be spotted and praying the massacre at the mosque wouldn't be discovered until they were long gone.

Marco led the way, his level of energy remarkable. Giuseppe was gasping, sucking in lungsful of air and near collapse. The two young men appeared none the worse for wear.

Who would have thought the life of a slave would leave you weak?

He couldn't remember the last time he had run so hard for so long. Thankfully Marco suddenly came to a stop at the side of a building. Giuseppe dropped to the ground, lying on his back, gasping for air as the others gathered around, all taking a knee.

"Try to slow your breathing, my brother," said Marco calmly, placing his hand gently on Giuseppe's chest.

It didn't help.

Marco turned to their companions. "This is the end for you two. We will continue through the nomad's camp to the southern wall, then once over, will make haste to the south, and eventually safety." Vincenzo opened his mouth to protest, but Marco cut him off with the raising of his hand. "Your duty now is to Father Salvatore. All I ask is that you remain here until we are out of sight to cover our escape, then return with caution to the church. I suggest you leave your weapons here then burn your clothes once you return as they are soiled in blood." Marco looked from man to man. "There must be no evidence you were involved. If you are questioned, and someone says they saw us enter the church, confirm this. Don't deny it. Simply tell them that we sought sanctuary then left shortly after, claiming we would be back, but never returned. Remember our horse is there. When things have calmed down, you may sell it and our belongings and donate it to the church."

Roberto and Vincenzo reluctantly agreed, stripping themselves of their weapons as Marco rose, holding out a hand to Giuseppe, his gasps shallower, but exhaustion still his master. Giuseppe reluctantly took the hand and let himself be hauled to his feet.

Marco smacked him on the back. "Do not fear, my brother. We will walk most of the way. Two people running past tents won't go unnoticed. Two men strolling toward the south gate shouldn't attract any attention."

Giuseppe smiled in relief as Marco turned to their companions, shaking their hands. Giuseppe did the same, still thankful for their ignoring orders and following him inside the tower. If it weren't for them, he and his master would surely be dead now.

With one final expression of gratitude, Marco stepped onto the road and set a brisk but reasonable pace, Giuseppe casting a final wave over his shoulder and following. To their right were the large round tents of the nomads, the Bedouins, occupying the entire south-western quarter of the city. As he continued to catch his breath from their ordeal, the southern gates slowly increasing in size as they neared, he wondered if those in the tents were permanent residents or merely travelers. And if travelers, what was their purpose here? Was it the crystal skull now slung over Marco's shoulder, or were they merely traders? All he was sure of was if they were at cross-purposes with them, he and his master would surely die, for the Bedouin's penchant for and ability to fight was legendary.

The gate continued to get closer as their pace remained brisk and he began to wonder if his master intended to walk right through them, but as they neared the final tent, the gate only five hundred paces ahead, if that, Marco suddenly veered off the road and into the snow covered field.

With the city still bathed in darkness Giuseppe was certain anyone manning the gate or the towers could not have seen them, however his master was cutting it awfully close. Almost fifteen minutes had passed since they said goodbye to their companions in this endeavor, and Giuseppe stood with his master between two guard towers on the southern wall, their torches casting a blinding glow just as his master had predicted.

"How will we scale *this* wall? It's far higher than that at the mosque."

Marco jerked a thumb at his pack strapped to his back. "There's a length of rope with a hook in my pack. Get it for me."

Giuseppe undid the straps holding the pack closed and found the rope in question, coiled at the top. He removed it, handing it to his master as he retied the pack. Marco began to approach the wall, wrapping a portion of the rope around his arm, leaving the rest in his right hand with the hook. They were within ten paces of the massive stone and mud barrier when footfalls in the distance, rapid and heavy, had them spinning.

A robed figure was rushing down the road.

Followed by at least a dozen men, giving chase.

As the figure approached, Marco turned and rushed to the wall, spinning the rope with the hook several times then tossing it in the air and over the wall as Giuseppe continued to watch the figure, hand on his sword, ready to draw it should it become necessary.

"Climb!" hissed Marco.

"You first, Master. I will hold them off while you make your escape."

"Brother! Go! Now!"

The voice was still low but insistent. But it was time to make a stand, the first figure too close. "Master, I insist. Go now, I will follow you immediately!"

Marco shook his head in frustration then grabbed the rope, quickly scaling the wall. Giuseppe saw him reach the top then grabbed the rope himself, taking one last look at the robed figure. The man tossed his head covering back and Giuseppe gasped.

It was Roberto.

Laura Palmer's Flat, London, England
Present day, one day after the kidnapping

"They must be after the Mitchell-Hedges skull," said Laura, sipping a glass of ice water, she having indicated to Acton she had had enough wine for the evening with a wave of her hand over her glass when he had tried to fill it.

Reading hadn't been so quick, holding his own out. Acton's friend's cheeks were flushed and his voice a little louder than normal, he on his fourth glass, but with the bottle now empty, a third bottle had already been ruled out by everyone.

Acton, himself a little buzzed, finished his own fourth glass with a flourish, placing it down a little harder than he had intended, shooting a quick apology with his eyes at Laura who winked at him then toasted him with her water, she having stopped at two.

"It doesn't make sense though. The Triarii are usually non-violent—"

"They did use tranquilizers like last time," interjected Reading.

"True," agreed Acton. "But why now? They've had years to try and get it. It just doesn't make sense."

"Nothing makes sense to me about those people," muttered Reading. He jabbed at the air. "Think about it. Perfectly sane people, well educated, well balanced—like Martin—believing in magical crystal skulls with magical powers that will magically save mankind in some magical way in some magical future."

"You're drunk."

"Bollocks."

A noise from the front of the apartment had them all jumping to their feet, it so loud it was as if someone had tried to knock down the door.

"Stay back, I'll check it out," said Reading, his police instincts immediately kicking in.

"It's times like these I wish you guys carried guns like back home," said Acton as he followed Reading to the door, Laura close behind—Acton knowing better than to tell her to stay back.

Reading crept to the door and looked through the peephole.

"No one there," he whispered. He stood to the side, the others mimicking him, and he placed his hand on the doorknob. Exchanging glances with the others, he suddenly yanked the door open and they all gasped.

Lying on the floor was their friend, Martin Chaney.

"Bloody hell!" exclaimed Reading, grabbing his friend by the shoulders and pulling him inside. Acton closed the door as Reading helped the moaning Chaney to his feet, Laura rushing back into the apartment. Acton slung one of Chaney's arms over his shoulder, Reading doing the same, and they both carried him into the apartment. Laura had cleared off the couch, propping several pillows at the end and moved anything breakable out of the way.

Carefully placing him on the couch, Laura went to the bathroom and returned with several wet cloths and knelt beside him, applying the cool compresses to his face as she wiped away the sweat he was drenched in.

"James, grab a blanket, would you? He's shivering something fierce."

Acton went to the hall closet and grabbed a blanket and a duvet just in case. Returning to the living room he put the duvet aside and tossed out the blanket, covering Chaney from chin to toe as Reading removed the man's shoes.

"Should we call 9-9-9?" asked Laura.

Reading shook his head. "Not until we know why he's here. For all we know he was escaping someone."

Chaney continued to shiver and Laura motioned for the duvet. Acton and Reading folded it out and put it over him while Laura left the room. She returned a few minutes later with two hot water bottles. She placed them at the foot of the couch, positioning the bottoms of his feet on both. Within minutes the shivering stopped and their friend began to rest comfortably.

"What was the daft bastard thinking?" whispered Reading. "He could have got himself killed!"

"He was pretty confused when we saw him," said Laura, kneeling beside their unexpected guest. "Maybe he just wandered off?"

"And came here?" Acton's skepticism was easily read.

"Maybe he's remembered the message he was trying to deliver from the Triarii?" suggested Laura.

Acton nodded. "That has to be it; why else would he come here?"

"How about we ask him?" suggested Reading, motioning toward Chaney. Acton looked and saw their patient's eyes were now open, color returning to his cheeks.

"Where am I?" he asked, his voice weak.

"You're at my flat," answered Laura as she wiped his damp hair off his forehead. "We found you on the landing outside the door."

"I feel like shite."

"You look it too, mate," replied Reading. "What the bloody hell were you thinking?"

Chaney pushed himself up on his elbows and Laura helped reposition the pillows so he could sit up. He smiled his thanks then looked at Acton.

"I remember everything now."

"So you know what the message was you were supposed to give me in Egypt?"

Chaney nodded. "They want you to return to the Vatican and find the Thirteenth Skull then bring it to London."

Acton felt a pit form in his stomach at the thought of getting involved with the Triarii once again. The last time they had been called to the Vatican a worldwide religious war had almost broken out, and the time before, he and the Pope had been kidnapped.

The Vatican was not his favorite place.

"Why can't they just get it themselves?"

"His Holiness trusts you."

Acton frowned, dropping into one of the chairs. "He's Triarii for Christ's sake! He doesn't trust his own people?"

Chaney shook his head. "No."

"Does this have something to do with yesterday's kidnapping?" asked Laura as she handed Chaney a glass of water.

"What kidnapping?"

"President Jackson's son was kidnapped today, and it looks like the Triarii are involved."

Chaney sipped the water and handed the glass back to Laura. "How?"

"We saw the tattoo on one of the dead kidnappers," replied Reading.

Chaney seemed to pale slightly. "Then it's even more important that you retrieve the skull."

"Why?"

Chaney sighed. "There's a split in the Triarii."

"A split?" asked Reading, perching on the end of the couch. "What kind of split?"

"We call them the Deniers. I call them bloody daft maniacs. They deny that there is any danger in uniting the skulls, and they are demanding that we unite at least three of them—under controlled conditions with modern technology of course—to determine if the Great Fire of London was actually caused by the union of the skulls. If nothing happens, then they want to unite all thirteen skulls to trigger what they believe will be a new age of enlightenment."

"And if the three skulls blast the shit out of everything?" asked Acton.

"They believe with modern technology they'll be able to harness the energy created, and mankind will benefit regardless."

Acton pursed his lips. "You know, Martin, no offense, but I don't believe in the skulls, their power, whatever. I don't think any of us really do with the possible exception of Laura"—he winked at her and she shrugged her shoulders—"but why is this *our* problem? Don't you have any Triarii you can trust?"

Chaney swung his feet to the floor, sitting up. He spotted the hot water bottles and placed one behind his back, the other on the floor where he rested his feet on it.

"Of course we do, but the problem is we don't know who we can trust. I was given the message by the Proconsul himself. Only the counsel and His Holiness know of this. We want someone from outside of the organization to retrieve the skull, someone who wouldn't raise suspicions at the Vatican, and then transport it to our headquarters here in London, where it will then be placed in safekeeping until a permanent home can be found for it."

"Why not just leave it where it is?" asked Laura.

"Because we have no control in the Vatican," replied Chaney.

"Umm, isn't the top man there yours?" asked Reading.

"For now. But maybe not tomorrow. And once he's gone, we'll never be able to gain access to it." Chaney leaned forward and picked up the glass of water. "Remember, our goal is to have the skulls circulated through society so they may have their effect on mankind as we believe they were designed to do. And by having them in public, we too have access to them should they need to be protected. But in the Vatican? It's not circulating, and it's out of our reach should it need protection."

Acton waved his hand in the air, cutting off the line of conversation knowing full well there was no way they would change Chaney's mind, the man clearly a true believer.

"Okay, so you need me to go to the Vatican and find the skull, then bring it back here. Why is it more urgent now that this kidnapping has happened?"

"The Triarii would never have kidnapped President Jackson's son. His father was a member of the Triarii for most of his life and betrayed us in the end. In fact he is the founder of the Deniers and they were thought to have given up after his death, but clearly they're back. If they have his son, they're after the Mitchell-Hedges skull that his father stole. With one in their possession, they might be bold enough to try and break into the Vault of Secrets at the Vatican to get a second. Then all they would need is one more skull to have an incredibly destructive power at their disposal."

"So you believe," said Acton with a frown.

"Yes, so I and many others believe."

Acton looked at Laura. "What do you think?"

She shook her head. "I think I know you well enough to know we're going to the Vatican."

"And I'm coming with you," added Reading. "You two will need someone to watch your backs."

Acton smiled at his friend then turned to Chaney. "Anything else we should know?"

Chaney nodded, his face grave.

"Yes. Trust no one."

Southern Wall, Karakorum, Mongol Empire
March 29th, 1275 AD

"It's Roberto!"

Giuseppe tried to keep his voice as low as possible, but it was clear Marco couldn't hear him over the wind, and yelling louder would risk the guard towers hearing him. Instead he waved for Roberto to run faster, hoping his master would get the message without putting an arrow through the man's chest.

Roberto hit Giuseppe hard, pushing them both back into the wall, the young man's gasps reminding Giuseppe of his own exhaustion not so long ago. Roberto's pursuers were only a couple of hundred paces away now, the heavy blanket of snow slowing them down only slightly. Giuseppe grabbed the rope and gave it to Roberto.

"Go! Climb now!"

The young man nodded and took hold of the rope, pulling himself up, Marco above straddling the wall, hauling on the rope, speeding up the process. But Giuseppe already knew it would be too late for himself. He turned to face the pursuers, drawing his sword, the wall at his back providing no hope of retreat. He glanced over his shoulder and saw young Roberto now straddling the wall with Marco, the latter pulling his bow and taking aim.

I won't die without a fight!

He took position, rear foot back, perpendicular to the front, sword held over his right shoulder, both hands gripping tightly, but not too tightly, his eyes focused on the closest man.

Who dropped from an arrow embedded in his chest.

Another fell, then another, and Giuseppe quickly glanced over his shoulder at the top of the wall and felt his chest swell with hope and pride as the situation turned, for atop the wall perched Marco's father and uncle, bows in hand, Roberto now with one of his own, as all four men evened the odds. Giuseppe looked back at the horde and smiled. Only two remained and they had turned to flee. He grabbed the rope and felt strong hands above drag him up as his feet scrambled to help. Seconds later he was on the top of the wall, looking back at the battle that hadn't involved a single swing of his sword to see all were dead, including the two who had tried to flee.

Without a word they dropped to the ground on the other side, sprinting away from the city, the older brothers leading the way to where they had hid the horses. The Polo's jumped onto their steeds, Giuseppe onto his, holding his arm out for Roberto to climb on behind him. The pace set by the brothers was brisk and Giuseppe soon found himself falling behind, his horse carrying an extra passenger. Within minutes the Polo's were out of sight, the snow and darkness making things even worse.

He glanced behind him as did Roberto.

"I don't think we're being followed," said the young man.

"Neither do I," agreed Giuseppe, easing off on the demands he had been putting on the horse. "Let's not break our necks. We'll catch up with my master eventually." They traveled in silence for several minutes, the only sound the wind and the clopping of the horse's hooves on the trail. Giuseppe continued to peer into the darkness for any sign of the Polo's and saw nothing but shadows playing tricks on him. He cursed his bad luck and for a moment resented his passenger.

But only for a moment. The look of terror in the poor boy's eyes had been genuine, and were a memory he wouldn't soon forget. And he had to realize that this young man was but a boy. Eighteen at best, and living under the protective umbrella of the church, his maturity compared to most young men his age was probably severely curtailed.

He glanced over his shoulder, curiosity finally demanding an answer as to what had happened. "What went wrong?" he asked of his passenger.

"It was terrible. As soon as you were out of sight we returned to the church to find Father Salvatore dead in his bed, stabbed. Two men attacked us. We fought them but Vincenzo was struck down almost immediately. I managed to flee, but not before more joined in. The only thing that saved me, besides you and your friends, was their apparent lack of horses!"

Giuseppe's eyes narrowed as he stared at their path ahead.

No horses? That's odd.

"Why wouldn't they have horses?" he finally asked, their own now at a trot, Giuseppe having given up in catching his master and elders. As they passed a bend in the canyon, his eyes caught sight of a shadow to their left. He reached for his sword when a voice called out.

"Giuseppe, is that you, brother?"

His heart leapt in relief as he let go the breath he had been holding. "Yes, Master. I have Roberto with me."

"Good, good! Dismount now so I can tell you of our plan."

Roberto jumped down, as did Giuseppe, Marco's father taking the reins of their mount and walking it over to a sheltered area where the other horses were resting, Marco's uncle feeding and watering them.

"What happened?" Marco asked Roberto, who then relayed the story Giuseppe had already heard. Giuseppe took several swigs from a skin of water, then chewed on a small pouch of dried meat and fruits tossed to him by Marco.

"No horses?"

He was happy to hear his master was as surprised at that point as he was. It almost sounded to Giuseppe as if they intentionally didn't capture

Roberto in hopes that he would lead him to those who had stolen the skull. And it had worked, only thankfully none had survived to tell the tale.

Which might explain why no one is following us?

The thought was comforting, but only fleeting.

"More will come," said his master, echoing his subconscious.

"Agreed," said Marco's father, Niccolo. "We must act quickly."

"Agreed." Marco turned to Giuseppe. "You will take the idol ahead, rejoining the caravan. You should reach them by morning. We will stay behind to intercept any who may follow you."

"But, Master, there could be dozens!"

"Hundreds!" piped in Roberto.

"There could be, but I doubt it. We have no choice but to chance it otherwise we shall fail in our mission. Should the numbers be overwhelming, we shall know so in advance, and retreat to join you," assured Marco. "Don't worry, brother, I have no intention of sacrificing myself needlessly."

"Nor I!" piped in his father with a smile. "Now, take a good horse and make haste. We will join you most likely mid-afternoon."

"Let me go with him," said Roberto. "Speed is not of the essence for his journey, but it may be for yours, and we've already seen how two on one mount doesn't work."

Marco looked at his father who nodded. "Very well. The two of you shall take my horse. She is the strongest and fastest. If I rode her hard, I'd just leave these two old men behind which I would end up regretting."

"You're damned right you'd regret it!" his father replied, punching his son in the arm. "Castration comes to mind!"

His father and uncle roared with laughter, Marco grinning but turning his private parts slightly away from the elders. Giuseppe grinned, taking another drink then handing the skin to Roberto. He strode over to the horses, taking the reins of his master's beast and swinging atop the mighty steed. He held out his hand and pulled Roberto on with him as Marco soothed the creature, gently stroking its face and neck, rubbing his cheek on the long snout.

"You treat my brother well," he whispered. "Be fleet of foot, but sure of it too. They need you to be steady for a few hours. Be their eyes and ears. Warn them of dangers, guide them through those dangers, and tomorrow you will be rewarded with apples and sugar, I promise!"

The horse neighed, as if it understood, and Giuseppe silently hoped it did. Marco handed him the bag containing the idol. "Be careful with this. A lot of people have died because of it."

Giuseppe nodded, tying it at his waist. "I won't let you down."

Marco grinned. "I never thought you would. Now go, we have wasted enough time," he said, stepping back.

Giuseppe nodded to the Polo's, then gently nudged the horse with his feet, the creature tossing its head then complying. Within moments the family he had lived with most of his remembered life was left behind to defend against an enemy of an unknown size, to perhaps be massacred, all because the great Kublai Khan had "requested" they retrieve a crystal idol worshiped by citizens of his northern capital.

It was ridiculous.

Why should he and his masters risk their lives for this man? He wasn't even their liege, ruler over any of their lands. If anything, he was a rival to the mighty Venetians, though a distant rival. Giuseppe was no fool. Should the Khan turn his attention to Venice, he knew it stood little chance of withstanding a foe so powerful.

But it still didn't justify, in his mind, the family putting themselves at risk over something so trivial as a crystal skull worshipped by a bunch of crazies of so little faith that they'd toss the real God aside and worship some carving.

It disgusted him.

If it were up to him, he'd smash the idol right now against the rocks they were rushing past, but alas, it wasn't up to him. He had no doubt the Khan wanted proof the idol had been retrieved, and for now his mission was to obey his master's wishes.

To safely deliver the idol to their caravan and await the arrival of the family.

The horse was guiding itself, there little choices for it to make in the mountain pass they found themselves. Giuseppe barely held the reins, letting the beast do its own bidding. They were making better time than if he were in control, the animal able to judge for itself the speed at which it was safe to travel. Giuseppe kept an eye on things, ready to pull on the reins at any moment, their pace one far faster than he would have been comfortable with, but with the sky cloud-covered, and the night not yet over, he could see little regardless.

No horses.

The thought had been nagging at him, and with his mind free of guiding their transport, he returned to them. He retold the story in his head, breaking it down into the facts. They watched he and Marco head for the wall, leaving once they were out of sight. That at most was five minutes. They then returned to the church via the main streets, probably not running. That would be at least ten minutes. They found the father, fought the enemy. Another minute or two, perhaps three. Roberto then ran, full tilt, from the church to the wall. At that pace, still a ten minute journey.

Giuseppe's eyes narrowed at the mental tally he had just calculated.

Almost thirty minutes!

Their walk to the wall had been about fifteen minutes, at most twenty.

Yet Roberto reached us before we had a chance to climb it!

It didn't make sense.

"Is something wrong?"

Giuseppe almost jumped but caught himself. Roberto's body was pressed against his back so he didn't fall off the horse, and also to share body heat in the frigid cold.

So he definitely would have felt the muscles tensing in Giuseppe's body.

"No," replied Giuseppe hastily. "I just keep seeing things in the shadows."

It seemed a reasonable reply, one that would explain his tenseness. He glanced over his shoulder to flash a smile when he caught something glinting in the moonlight above and behind his head. He threw his elbow back, catching Roberto in the nose then pulled on the reins, bringing the mighty beast to a halt as he threw his elbow again, knocking Roberto off the back. The horse reared on its hind legs, catching Giuseppe unprepared, tossing him off as well, the impact with the hard ground cushioned by the body of Roberto.

Giuseppe quickly rolled away, drawing his sword, Roberto leaping to his feet, wiping the blood from his nose, the dagger he had been about to stab Giuseppe with held out in front.

"What the hell is going on?" demanded Giuseppe. "You never had time to return to the church!"

Roberto smiled, approaching him, the much smaller blade still a danger if he could counter Giuseppe's first thrust. Instead, Giuseppe kept his distance, knowing full well the risk if he committed.

"You're right," replied Roberto, continuing to circle. "There was no need. You had the idol. I merely had to gather some worshippers to help me." He feigned a quick attack, but rapidly fell back when Giuseppe pointed his sword directly at him.

"What happened to Vincenzo?"

"I killed him of course."

Giuseppe felt his chest tighten as he pictured the young man who had risked his life to save complete strangers only an hour before, now dead. It enraged him that this young altar boy should die such a senseless death over something as trifling as a crystal idol with a grinning face.

"Then I shall kill you," said Giuseppe, advancing, his sword held high, the muscles in his arms flexing as he swung the blade. Roberto easily sidestepped the blow and lunged forward with his dagger, Giuseppe letting the blade continue as he used the momentum to swing him away from the attack, the blade arcing around his body as he spun on his toe. Roberto cried out in pain as the tip of the blade, not even a fingernail in length, sliced open the murderer's belly.

Roberto dropped his dagger as he fell to his knees, gripping his stomach. Giuseppe flipped his sword, blade down, ready to thrust it into the exposed nape of his opponent's neck when the sound of horses filled the canyon. He backed away, readying his sword to defend himself, when three men burst onto the scene, quickly coming to a halt and expertly jumping from their mounts.

"Brother, are you okay?"

Giuseppe dropped the tip of his blade to the ground, his shoulders sagging as he nearly cried in relief at the sound of his master's voice. He was so tired of fighting, of running, of fearing for his life, that the sight of these three men, the Polo family, was like a font of warmth springing in his heart as hope returned.

"He killed Vincenzo," he gasped, exhausted physically and emotionally from the day's events. "And he tried to kill me."

"We suspected as much," replied Marco, circling the kneeling Roberto.

"You did?" Giuseppe knew his voice sounded incredulous, and there was also a tinge of anger. *If you knew, why didn't you tell me?!*

"Didn't you wonder why we went on ahead and left you two behind after we scaled the wall?"

Giuseppe shrugged as Marco's father lit a torch so they could see each other. "I figured you didn't notice we weren't behind you."

Marco shook his head, a smile on his face. "Oh brother, how I thought you knew me better than that." He looked at his father and uncle. "We went far enough ahead so that we could talk for a few minutes before you arrived. I knew right away it was impossible for Roberto to have returned to the church then make it to the wall in the time he had. I figured if he were innocent, then Vincenzo had been killed by their pursuers as they returned to the church, and Roberto had been able to run away. In which case you were perfectly safe.

"On the other hand, if he had betrayed his God, he would have killed Vincenzo, found some of his compatriots, then staged his escape. And again you would be perfectly safe since you didn't have the idol."

Giuseppe looked at his master, not totally convinced that he had been safe on that first leg of their escape, but certain he hadn't been on this final portion.

"And now? Despite your misgivings you let me travel alone with him, with the idol?"

"We had to be sure. I honestly didn't expect him to make his move so soon. You must have figured it out yourself."

Giuseppe nodded. "Just before he attacked me."

"So you were ready for his attack."

It was a statement of fact that happened to be true to a point. But his being ready didn't mean he wasn't covered in bruises and scrapes from his fall, or exhausted from one final bout of swordplay.

"Yes," was all he could manage, and it was barely a murmur.

"Then all is well!" pronounced Marco's father. "We have the betrayer, he has been incapacitated. We have the idol, and we have escaped our pursuers. I think the day has been a success!"

"You will never escape," muttered Roberto, wincing as he tried to straighten himself to glare at his foes. "You will be pursued to the ends of the earth until either the idol is retrieved, or you are all dead. Your victory today shall be short lived."

Marco eyed their prisoner, then looked at his father. "What do you think?"

"I think he's right. The sooner we get to Khanbalig the better."

"I say we destroy it, leave it here to be found, and then there's no reason to pursue us," said Giuseppe, sheathing his sword.

Marco's head bobbed in agreement. "That's a good idea."

"But it isn't what the Khan wanted," replied his uncle. "We must obey his wishes."

Marco frowned. "Then we must move forward, and quickly. We will be safe in Khanbalig."

"You may be safe there, but the moment you set foot outside its walls, you will be pursued once again," said Roberto, his eyes filled with hate.

Giuseppe turned to Marco. "You could be in hiding for years. Decades!"

"If that is God's will, then so be it," replied Marco. "We have rid a city of its false idol and freed a people to worship the true God once again. When this idol is safely hidden away, it matters not what happens to us. Should we die, we die. But the idol will never disturb another soul again."

"You will spend the rest of your lives in exile for your actions today."

They all turned toward Roberto.

"Do we need him for anything?" asked Marco's uncle.

Marco shrugged. "I can't think of anything."

His father plunged his sword into Roberto's belly, twisting the blade. "Neither can I."

Unknown Location

Present day, one day after the kidnapping

Grant Jackson lay on a cot, his left hand cuffed to the frame, his right free to pull at it uselessly. He had woken here several hours before and determined that "here" was a basement of some type, it seemingly old, the beams over his head solid wood that clearly showed its age, and if he knew his home renovation shows from television, they hadn't made them like that in decades, if not nearly a century.

No laminated beams here.

The musty smell and tiny windows set high in the walls had him thinking a century old home, perhaps even a farmhouse. His head had pounded for the first couple of hours, now it was a dull ache that had him closing his eyes and massaging his temples with his free hand. No one had come to check on him yet, but he had heard muffled voices and footsteps overhead the entire time.

He wasn't alone.

And with his hand cuffed, the windows tiny, and the only set of stairs probably leading directly into the room where his captors were, there was no hope of escape.

What the hell am I supposed to do?

He had debated this for much of the past hour after his racing heart had settled and he could begin to think clearly. *Don't panic!* had become his mantra, something he repeated over and over every time he felt a twinge of fear begin to settle in again. He knew he had to keep a cool head if he were to survive this.

Survive!

What were their intentions? They had killed his security detail, so he knew they had no qualms about murder. He was still alive, so this wasn't an assassination attempt, though why anyone would want to assassinate him was beyond him. Then again, why anyone would want to kidnap him was equally so.

What would Dad have done?

Asking this question was how he solved most problems where the answer wasn't immediately evident. The outcome however wasn't always to his satisfaction, either he misjudged what his father would have done, or he was naïve enough to think his father had never been wrong.

He got himself assassinated by his best friend. How on the ball could he have been?

He mentally kicked himself for insulting his father. He knew Darbinger wasn't himself, the brain tumor having affected him to the point he didn't even know who was who, the doctors saying he most likely was suffering from extreme paranoia, in the end thinking everyone around him was an enemy. He had cried tears of sorrow and anger when they concluded that Darbinger most likely had acted in what he thought was self-defense, Grant's father his final victim.

The state funeral had been impressive, the outpouring of emotion from the country moving to say the least, but none of it was any comfort to him. He had lost his father in a most violent and unexpected way, decades before he expected it to happen, and it had crushed him. He had hated Lesley Darbinger with every fiber of his being, even shunning Nora, Darbinger's wife, when she had tried to see him to apologize for her husband's actions.

He felt guilty about that now, but had never made amends. Perhaps if he made it out of this nightmare he now found himself in, he'd do so. It was obvious Darbinger wasn't in control. There was nothing he could have done since he had no clue about the tumor and the effect it was having on him.

It wasn't his fault.

But if it wasn't his fault, then his father died for nothing.

The thought of a useless death for the greatest man he had ever known pissed him off even more.

"Hey! What the hell do you want with me?" he screamed in fury, in frustration, in desperation. He wasn't sure if it was what his father would have done, but he was certain the man wouldn't have lain there feeling sorry for himself. He would have confronted his captors, even if it meant his death.

But probably would have done it more eloquently.

He heard chairs scrape and footsteps, then a door creaked open at the top of the stairs. A light switch was flipped and several bulbs began to burn brilliantly, no moronic mercury-laden overpriced compact fluorescents here. He sometimes wondered whether or not the powers that be who banned the incandescent light bulb realized that millions of CFLs would end up in landfills and in the future contaminate our water supplies with mercury leading to birth defects and mental handicaps. But of course that was the worst case scenario—which never happens.

Two men descended the stairs, their faces uncovered, and to his surprise, both smiling—not sneers, but genuine smiles.

And they appeared unarmed.

The first approached him with a key in hand.

"Here, let me get those off you," he said as he bent over and unlocked the cuffs. Grant's mind immediately began to run through his options, all involving him miraculously incapacitating the two unarmed men, when a third man walked down the steps, an occupied holster evident on his hip.

His options suddenly boiled down to one.

Do nothing.

The cuffs were removed and he swung his legs off the cot, sitting upright.

"There, that must be better," said the man. "It was necessary so you didn't hurt yourself when you woke up." He motioned toward the stairs. "Now how about we all go upstairs and have a little chat. Get to know each other, so to speak."

To say Grant was confused would be an understatement. None of it made any sense. These men had killed his escort, shot him with something, obviously not a bullet, kidnapped him against his will, handcuffed him in a basement, and now wanted to be friends?

The third man climbed the stairs, the man who had done the talking motioning for Grant to follow. He warily complied, certain something sinister awaited him at the top—perhaps a bullet or a beating. He cleared the steps and entered a kitchen with a small dining area. A fourth man was sitting eating a Subway foot long. He smiled, waving at him with one hand as he took a sip from his large fountain drink. Grant waved back, half-heartedly, his confusion growing.

The third man led them into a living area and he pointed at what appeared to be the most comfortable chair available, some sort of La-Z-Boy. He sat, sinking into the soft cushions as the diner emerged from the kitchen with a large drink and a still bagged Subway sandwich and handed it to him.

"Eat up, I'm sure you're starving," he said. "I got you a ham with just lettuce, tomatoes and mayo, just to be safe since I wasn't sure what you'd like. And a Diet Coke."

Grant took the drink and sandwich, still uncertain as to what was going on. He put the drink on an end table to his left, the sandwich on his lap.

"What the hell is going on here?" he finally asked. "Who are you?"

The first man smiled. "We're friends of your father."

Grant's jaw dropped as almost every muscle in his body slackened. He reached for the drink blindly, sipping the ice cold liquid as his eyes darted about the faces in the room.

"Bullshit."

The first man laughed. "You're a lot like your father, you know that?" He pointed at his chest. "My name's Mitch Reynolds." He pointed at the second man. "That's Chuck Holder"—he nodded toward the third man with the gun—"that cheery fellow is Ben Cowan and finally, your waiter is Chip Schneller."

"Pleased to meet ya!" said Chip with a wave. "Don't be afraid of that sandwich, it won't bite."

Grant nodded, looking down at the still bagged meal. His stomach grumbled.

To hell with it. If they poisoned it, then they mean to kill me anyway.

He pulled the sandwich out, unwrapped it and tore the two halves apart. He took a bite and chewed as the others looked on, his eyes still wandering the room. He noted the curtains were all closed, the furniture mostly dated if not worthy of an antique shop, the walls plaster with deep cove molding usually only seen in older homes.

Definitely very old.

His stomach growled again in appreciation as he swallowed his first bite, and after a few more, he began to feel his old self.

"How do you know my father?" he asked between chews.

"Tell me," said Mitch, "did your father ever mention the Triarii?"

"Tree what?"

"Triarii. It's Latin."

Grant took a drag on his drink, shaking his head. "Never heard of it."

"That's too bad. It would have made this a lot easier," replied Mitch. "What I'm about to tell you will probably sound like BS to you, but I assure you, it's all true, and your father believed in it deeply."

"Okay."

"Have you ever heard of the crystal skulls?"

"Sure, who hasn't? Indiana Jones, Stargate SG-1 before that. They've got some in museums, don't they? But they're all fake. Carved in the nineteenth century."

"That's what the Triarii want you to believe."

"Huh?"

"Almost two thousand years ago a crystal skull was found near the site of the crucifixion in ancient Judea."

"You mean where Jesus was nailed to the cross?"

"Exactly. It was shortly after his death that it was found. It was brought to the Roman Emperor Nero as a gift. Nero became obsessed with the skull and convinced it was speaking to him, filling his nights with torment and his days with whispered warnings of doom to the empire. To rid himself of the torture, he ordered his finest legion, the Thirteenth, to take the crystal skull as far from Rome as possible.

"The legion made their way north, to Britannia, the farthest outpost of the empire. Along the way they encountered several bands of barbarians and the first and second lines of the Thirteenth were mostly wiped out. By the time they reached Britain, all that remained was the third line, their most experienced troops, the Triarii. They settled in Britain, keeping the skull hidden, and over the next thousand years integrated into their adopted country, but never forgetting their duty, a duty handed down generation to generation.

"In time a second skull was found in ancient Greece. Word of it reached the Triarii, who at this point had spread out around the known world, and it was immediately taken back to Britain where it too was protected. Then in 1212 a third skull arrived in Britain. When it was placed with the other two, it began to hum, then after a few hours a massive explosion wiped out most of London, burning over half of it to the ground, killing thousands."

"I call bullshit on that."

"It's well documented. It's the original Great Fire of London. Look it up if you want to—it's part of history. Once we realized the danger of having these skulls together, we made it our mission to keep any two skulls apart."

"What does any of this crap have to do with my father?"

"Your father was a member of our organization, and some time ago he stole the Mitchell-Hedges skull that was at the Smithsonian."

"I've heard of it. Didn't know it was stolen."

"Nobody at the Smithsonian knows it was. What they have is a fake."

Grant swallowed his last bite. "So my Dad was a thief. Wonderful."

"No, your Dad was a patriot. He believed, like we do, that our technology is advanced enough now to harness the power of the skulls. He wanted to join three of them together, and if able to do so safely, harness the power of all the skulls."

"How many are there?"

"Twelve, possibly thirteen."

"Lucky thirteen."

Mitch smiled, nodding. "Yes indeed. The twelfth skull was discovered in Peru a few of years ago while your father was president. He ordered its capture and sent in the Delta Force. Unfortunately things didn't go as planned, and the international incident blamed on Lesley Darbinger was actually your father's doing."

"You're hardly winning me over to your side," muttered Grant, sucking on his drink.

"Perhaps this will. Lesley Darbinger did not have a brain tumor. He was perfectly healthy, perfectly sane when he shot your father in cold blood, under orders from the Triarii."

Grant stopped sucking on his drink. "Come again? I thought *you* were Triarii."

"We are, but we're what you might call an offshoot. A breakaway group. The Triarii like to call us the Deniers, but we prefer to call ourselves the True Believers. We believe in the power of the skulls, and we believe it is time that this power was harnessed."

Grant shook his head in disbelief.

I've been kidnapped by a bunch of wackos!

Crystal skulls with magic powers? It was complete and utter nonsense. And there was no way his father was part of this bullshit organization either.

"I can tell you don't believe me," observed Mitch as he removed his watch. He held up his bare wrist, revealing a small tattoo. Grant gasped, immediately recognizing it. He had seen the exact same tattoo years ago on his father. He had asked him about it and his father had brushed it off as a stupid fraternity dare during Rush Week. Mitch smiled. "I see you recognize it."

Grant nodded.

"Where have you seen it before?"

Grant didn't want to admit to it, but he had to, the sudden realization his father was indeed associated with these nuts a truly shocking, disappointing discovery.

Maybe my father was the crazy one, not Lesley?

"My father had the same tattoo."

Mitch nodded in satisfaction, putting his watch back on. "And there are thousands of us spread across the globe, at every level of society, even as high as the President of the United States a few short years ago."

"So my dad was a nut."

Mitch laughed, exchanging smiles with the others. "No, he was just a believer. If you read our history, the detailed accounts of our organization, you would realize the devotion is not misplaced. But regardless of whether or not *you* believe, your father did. And that's why we are here today."

"Why?"

"Because we believe you know where the Mitchell-Hedges skull is."

Exiting the Karakorum Pass, Mongol Empire
April 13th, 1275 AD

"At last!"

It was his master's cry of joy that snapped Giuseppe from his reverie. He looked up at the sight before him and smiled, exchanging grins with all those around him in the Polo caravan. It had been a long, hard journey through the pass, with half his time spent looking over his shoulder, certain more would be pursuing them. But none had come. The occasional messenger on horseback, their load light, had sent their hearts racing but other than a wave and a shout of greeting, they had all continued on their way.

Emerging from the mountains and to the lush greens and golds of the plains he breathed a sigh of relief. Stretched out in front of him, as far as the eye could see, were infinite escape routes, unlike their journey through the pass where they could only retreat one way.

"We'll set up camp by the river and rest," said Marco's father. "I think we've all had enough travelling for the day. In the morning we'll continue our journey east."

Giuseppe followed the caravan down to the river that cut a swath along the south of the mountains, the land on either side nourished by its waters, providing the thick vegetation they now found themselves surrounded by. As they reached the river's edge Giuseppe dismounted and immediately began to strip down his horse.

"Brother."

The voice was a whisper, barely audible. Giuseppe turned to see his master standing behind him, his own horse blocking the rest of their group from sight.

"Yes, Master?"

"I need to ask a great favor of you, one only you can be trusted with."

"Anything, Master."

Marco stepped closer, lowering his voice further.

"I need you to take the idol to Rome."

Giuseppe's chest tightened and his heart raced as the muscles in his face slackened. The thought of travelling for so long with the idol that still haunted his dreams was overwhelming. So overwhelming he found himself shaking his head, something that shocked him to his core.

You're refusing your master!

"I'm sorry, Master," he finally managed, forcing his head to stop shaking. "I of course will do whatever you require."

Marco smiled, his face one of understanding and compassion. "I knew you would." He sighed. "I fear this may be the last time we see each other. Our journeys are long and in opposite directions. When you reach the Holy See, this letter"—he handed him a scroll with a wax seal—"will give you an audience with the Holiness himself. It is from the Khan explaining the idol, and his wishes concerning it."

"I will guard it with my life, Master," said Giuseppe, looking briefly at the seal then back at his master.

He fetched another scroll from his bag, handing it to Giuseppe, but before letting go, he looked deeply into his eyes. "This is the most important thing you carry."

"Yes, Master."

"These are the papers granting you your freedom, and your Venetian citizenship as a freeman and member of the Polo family."

Giuseppe's heart nearly stopped. "I don't understand."

"Undertake this mission for your family, brother, and you will be free, an equal to all those you once served. And should you choose to—for you are free to make your own choice—I would be honored if you would take Polo as your name, and join me in China as my brother."

Marco's eyes were glass, as were Giuseppe's. The gesture was overwhelming, and rare. He had met several freemen in his life, but had never considered it for himself, his life with the Polo's far better than what many slaves endured. He was confused, emotions conflicting with each other, excitement and sorrow amongst them. Freedom, but without his master, his friend, his brother.

He looked up at him. "Should God will it, I will do everything I can to return to your side as I was always meant to be." His voice cracked and he looked away.

Marco's hand found his shoulder, providing comfort. "And I shall wait for you as long as it takes, for should you fail in your mission, then clearly what Roberto said is correct and we are not safe without the Khan's protection."

"Should I fail, you will remain? What of your life and family in Venice?"

"My remaining may very well protect that life and family," replied Marco. "But not to worry. You will succeed, you will journey back to join me should you wish—"

"I demand it!"

"—and we will enjoy the Khan's hospitality, side-by-side, for as long as it is ours to enjoy and desire. Then we will return to Venice, brothers, and richer than the Doge himself!"

"I think I would like that," managed Giuseppe. The mood changed almost instantly when Marco handed him the bag containing the crystal idol.

"You will take this now, and mention it to no one. After all have gone to bed, I will wake you on my watch as usual. You will pack your horse and leave. I will say we had a fight and that I sent you back to Venice as punishment. Only my father and uncle will know the truth. We will pretend we still have the idol and that we are bringing it to the Khan. This should hopefully buy you time to escape those who might pursue us."

"I understand, Master."

They stood in silence for a moment, Giuseppe fearing to say anything that might put him over the edge. What his master had offered him was incredible, but to claim it he must give up that which he loved most for years, and perhaps forever—his master.

Marco suddenly embraced him, Giuseppe standing in shock for a moment, then returning the embrace as it was given.

As a brother.

Papal Office, Apostolic Palace, The Vatican
Present day, one day after the kidnapping

Professor James Acton had always accepted that his would be a plain life from a materialistic point of view—you didn't become an archeology professor if you wanted to be rich. The riches you might find would go to the university or whoever might be funding the expedition, and with funding rare, much of his own hard earned money would be spent supplying some of the essentials that others felt weren't.

Like mosquito netting or finer brushes.

But Professor Laura Palmer, his fiancée, who he was certain had similar ambitions to his own—the glamorous life of globetrotting after trinkets—was rich. Filthy stinking rich some might describe her as. When she had been kidnapped he had become privy to just how rich when they were looking at paying her ransom.

Over one hundred million British Pounds rich. And that was just the slice he had seen and he had no doubt there was more. Her brother had been an Internet tycoon, selling his company for massive amounts of money, then dying at one of her dig sites several years before Acton had met her. Her brother had left her everything.

She hadn't asked to be wealthy, nor did she flaunt it, but she did use it to fund her own digs when necessary, to pay for students who couldn't afford to go—always as an anonymous benefactor—and to make their lives a little easier.

Like today, on a private Gulf V jet, that had them to Rome within hours in exquisite comfort. And a few quick phone calls while in the air had them now sitting before the main man himself, His Holiness the Pope. Acton had to admit it was nice having a girlfriend with mountains of cash, but he also felt weird about it, he a bit of a traditionalist when it came to money, thinking he should be the breadwinner. Laura was slowly bringing him over to her way of thinking in that it shouldn't matter who made the money, it only mattered that they were both able to enjoy it by making their lives a little easier.

Neither could see themselves living in some mansion, but why not have air conditioners at desert dig sites. Why not fly first class or private? Why not jet across the Atlantic twice a month to see each other? He knew eventually a decision would probably have to be made as to where they would live. Either she would have to move to his home and join him at St. Paul's University, or he'd have to leave home and join her in London. Neither really struck him as a great option. They'd figure it out eventually, he just knew that getting their hands dirty at dig sites was their true love, and whatever decision would ultimately be made would have to guarantee that for both of them.

We should just go independent!

Permits however were hard to come by when you were private. Attach yourself to a university or museum and you were gold. Attach yourself to something with "Inc." at the end, and you were almost guaranteed to be shutout unless you were willing to grease a lot of palms, which was something he hated doing beyond the odd small denominations designed to smooth a checkpoint or traffic "infraction". Bribing big government? Never.

His life before meeting Laura had been fantastic, but lonely. He had a few friends, one good friend—his Dean and friend since college, Gregory Milton—but other than that his life was his parents and his students, and he loved it. After the events in Peru then London, his life had changed forever. Laura entered it, removing any loneliness he might have felt, but it also had become much more violent. They just seemed to be a magnet for trouble, but they managed to survive their encounters with the help of friends and acquaintances made along the way.

And today they sat in front of one of those acquaintances—how can you call the Pope a friend?—along with an actual friend, Mario Giasson, the Inspector General for the Corps of the Gendarmerie of Vatican City State—essentially the head of security—and someone who Acton knew he could trust, their bond forged under fire during a terrorist attack on the Vatican.

A knock at the door interrupted the casual talk of the weather and the idea of having winter Olympics at essentially the same latitude as Rome. Giasson rose and opened the doors. Two priests entered carrying an old wooden chest Acton knew to be almost two thousand years old. Engraved with a Saint Peter's Cross with a prostrated pope in front, the only words on the entire chest were Unos Veritas, or One Truth in Latin. The two priests placed the nearly fifty pound chest on a nearby table, then left.

"This is my cue I guess," said Giasson. "Come see me when you're ready. I'm sure Hugh is going mad by this point." He nodded to the room, bowed to His Holiness, then exited, closing the doors behind him.

"It is unfortunate he and your friend Special Agent Reading must be excluded, but even letting you two see the contents of the Unos Veritas Chest is a breach of protocol. It was necessary before, and unfortunately, it is necessary once again. And should you find what we all hope you will, I shall never see that abomination again."

Acton watched the old man shiver, it truly affecting him to his core. Acton sometimes found it hard to reconcile the fact that someone could be Triarii, but also believe in a mainstream religion. In this case, the Pope was Triarii, groomed for decades to rise in the Roman Catholic Church so he could one day become Pope to gain access to the rumored Vault, a secret chamber under the Vatican that stored its greatest secrets. It was known to almost no one, knowledge of it passed down from Pope to Pope in a secret ceremony the first night of their inauguration that according to His Holiness, changed most men.

For the Vault of Secrets didn't hide tawdry gossip of who slept with who—those types of documents would be in the Vatican Secret Archives, open to the public with the proper credentials—the Vault contained secrets that the Vatican wanted to protect the *world* from. Blasphemous texts and objects. Unexplainable artifacts, preserved mutations, accounts of evil and horrors beyond imagine.

The Vault of Secrets, a massive underground complex, was filled with the very things that would shake the faith of the most devout Christian.

He and Laura had read the catalog of what it contained, and it was horrifying. They had never spoken of it since, and neither cherished the thought of reviewing it again. It had tested their own faith, given them both nightmares, especially once they had started to search the Vault and confirmed that what was catalogued in the Unos Veritas Chest was actually real.

The Pope's words repeated themselves in Acton's head. *I shall never see that abomination again.* He turned back to His Holiness. "What do you mean?"

"It means, my son, that once you have retrieved the Thirteenth Skull, I will step down. Though I am a true Christian, a true Roman Catholic, and I cherish the role I was blessed to be chosen for, every day I pray to God for forgiveness, for abusing this station, and using it for ulterior motives. Though I believe I have performed my duties humbly, and ably, the mere fact that you are here, for the second time, under false pretenses, tells me I am not worthy of this position.

"Man's conduit to God on Earth should *not* be sneaking around, attempting to find false idols for an organization that worships blasphemous icons."

His voice had slowly risen. Not to what anyone would consider loud, the man very soft spoken, but almost to a normal level, and the passion in what he said was clear, his cheeks flushed, his eyes wide and glistening in their pain. Acton couldn't help but feel for him, and a glance at Laura, whose hand was gripping his hard, showed a tear rolling down her cheek unnoticed.

"I don't know what to say," began Acton, "except that we shall try to finish this business as quickly as possible so that you can find the peace you so desperately crave."

His words were carefully chosen, far more eloquent than his normal speech, but the moment felt like it needed sophistication rather than a casual reply. He felt Laura's fingers squeeze his own three times, their secret "I love you" code.

At least she's *pleased.*

The Pope nodded, a sliver of a smile creeping into the ends of his mouth. "I appreciate your words, and pray to God you shall be successful." He glanced at the chest. "And now I must take my leave of you. Merely being in the presence of the Unos Veritas Chest I find disturbing." He rose, as did Acton and Laura, both bowing slightly as the old man rounded his desk. The doors opened, the Pope's private secretary, Father Morris, standing there as if he had been listening, holding the doors.

How does he do that?

The Pope removed his ring.

"You will of course need this."

He handed it to Acton, who took it and bowed again as the Pope left his office. Acton looked at the hardwood floors as the doors closed behind the elderly Pontiff, then retraced the steps, hearing a creak as he approached the door.

"What are you doing?" asked Laura, already setting up her laptop beside the chest.

"Trying to figure out how Father Morris knows to open the doors."

"He can hear the floor creak from outside," replied Laura, not bothering to look at her fiancée bouncing up and down on the floor.

Acton stopped, flushing as he realized his fiancée was far ahead of him, his fantastic discovery apparently not so much so. He joined her at the table with the chest, sitting down. He looked at her and she nodded, all joy in their souls shoved aside by the evil they were now about to immerse themselves in.

He pressed the Papal ring against the lock, and turned.

Near Jericho, Kingdom of Jerusalem

June 4th, 1277 AD

Two years since leaving Marco Polo

To be tired would be a blessing. Giuseppe was instead exhausted. Almost from the first day of his journey back home he had been hunted. It was as if the Karakorum Pass had belched an endless number of soldiers searching for their stolen idol the next day. Giuseppe assumed it had taken that long to organize themselves, or that God had somehow given them all a head start, one just long enough to stay alive should they keep their faith.

And Giuseppe had kept his faith. He had been determined to fulfill his master's wishes, and to reunite with him someday, as a brother. But it appeared that God had other plans for him. It had been over two years and he was now near death. Constant hiding, constant vigilance. The journey had taken its toll, the searchers having spread out across the empire and beyond, searching for a lone man of European descent, something rare for most of his journey.

And he was still nowhere near home. He had been forced south, toward the Holy Land, instead of his desired northern route. It had bought him a slight reprieve in that his hunters had spread north, thinking his final destination was most likely Venice.

It was clear they had been watched. Closely. He had heard no news of the caravan or of the Polo's. There was no way for a message to be exchanged, but he held out hope that should something have happened to such a noble family, word would have spread of it.

Then again they wouldn't be the first explorers to have disappeared without a trace.

The fact the pursuit seemed to have targeted him all along suggested someone had witnessed his departure with the idol in the night, which he hoped meant the caravan had been left alone. And the longer it was left alone, the deeper into the Khan's territory they would find themselves, and the safer they would be.

As he journeyed, mostly at night, he found his thoughts often drifting to Marco and the others, to the stories, the laughter, the hearty meals around the campfire.

His stomach rumbled.

He was weak, starving, and worse, thirsty.

He lay on the rock covered ground in the shade of a large boulder, his horse nearby, it nearly as gaunt as he. He didn't have the heart to kill it, to put it out of their shared misery, but he knew it was only a matter of time when the poor beast would collapse and he'd be forced to end its existence. And if he didn't have his mission to fulfill, he would gladly lay at its side, and die together, master and beast.

But he had his mission and he must go on, but he wasn't sure how he could possibly manage. The gems his master had given him had long run out, much of it stolen when he was accosted in Persia. He had been relying on scraps, begging his way from town to town since then, and it was remarkable how far he had actually come, surviving on will alone and the charity of strangers for the most part.

As he drifted in and out of sleep, his thirst overwhelming, he thought he heard voices, but as he struggled to stay awake, to listen for what the wind had carried him by chance, he was finally overcome by his exhaustion, the world finally going black.

Unknown Location

Present day, one day after the kidnapping

Grant Jackson finished his soda, then shook it, there still a fair amount of ice in the cup. The sandwich had hit the spot, though he missed the onions and cucumbers. And Diet Coke was definitely the right choice. Chip had done well. And if it weren't for the meal he knew there was no way he would be able to keep himself together enough to respond to Mitch, the revelations about his father and his past, this insanity about magic skulls, all too much to take in at once.

"I can assure you I have no clue where this skull of yours is."

Mitch smiled, batting away the words with his hand. "Of course you do, you just don't know it."

"Huh?"

"Your father never told you he was in the Triarii."

"Correct."

"So why would he tell you where his greatest possession was? Eventually he had planned to tell you the truth and let you decide whether or not you wanted to join him."

"He did?"

"Yes." Mitch leaned forward. "Grant, your father and I were friends. I'd known him almost twenty years before he was killed. We spoke often, met often. I was with him when we stole the Mitchell-Hedges skull from the Smithsonian. But it was useless without two others, so he had it hidden away so that someday his dream of uniting them could be fulfilled. It was his intention, Grant, that should he become too old, that you would take over for him, that *you* would fulfill his destiny."

Grant felt his chest tighten. He loved his father, but with him always being so busy, a distance had grown between them over the years. And the discovery of this secret life had made that distance seem to grow into a chasm so deep, there was really no connection between them at all.

But Mitch's words seemed to fill that void, the chasm gone in the knowledge that his father had believed in him, and was just waiting for the right time to bring him into the fold, to trust him with his greatest secret, and his ultimate goal in life.

"How can I help?" he asked, not quite yet ready to believe the stories he had been told of the power of the crystal skulls, but with the realization of how important this was to his father, he was ready to help complete the mission of the most important person in his life.

Mitch beamed a smile around the room, sitting back in his chair. "When your father died, did you receive anything in the will?"

Grant's eyes popped slightly, reaching for his drink then stopping, remembering it was empty. "I received a letter."

"And what did it say?"

Grant shrugged. "I don't know. I didn't read it."

"You didn't read it?" The surprise in Mitch's voice was plain. "Why not?"

Grant shook his head. "When I received it I hated the world. I hated my father for never being there and for getting himself killed. I hated my mother for refusing to grieve with me, instead locking herself in her room. I hated everyone who tried to console me who I barely knew. A letter from my father with some platitudes was the last thing I wanted to read. I wallowed in my own self-pity and bile for the better part of two years. By then the letter became something I said I would open only when I had no more negative feelings about my father. If it were truly heartfelt, then I wanted to be in the right frame of mind to read it." Grant shrugged. "I guess I haven't been yet."

"And how about now?"

Grant shrugged again. "After all that I've heard in the past few minutes, perhaps it's time."

"Great," grinned Mitch, slapping his hands together in anticipation. "Where is it?"

"In my nightstand at home."

"You moved back in with your mother after your father's death, didn't you?"

Grant frowned. "I didn't think she should be alone. Hell of a lot of good that did anyone."

Mitch threw his hands up, looking at his compatriots. "Which means it's surrounded by police by now."

Grant agreed. "You guys are wanted for murder, and you've kidnapped the former President's son. I would expect the place is swarming."

"Murder?"

"You killed my detail."

Mitch waved his hand. "No, we didn't kill anyone. We used tranquilizers. The Triarii doesn't kill unless it absolutely has to."

"Even you guys?"

"We're still bound by the same principals, just different end goals."

"Well, if you're not willing to kill, you're never getting in there," said Grant. "But I do have an idea."

Monastery of St. Gerasimos, Kingdom of Jerusalem

April 17th, 1281 AD

Six years since leaving Marco Polo's caravan

Giuseppe stared at the parchment in front of him. He had been working on it for the better part of two years, dozens of drafts had been made, and in the past several days what he had settled upon had completely changed again, for he knew he was near death.

The voices he had heard four years ago had belonged to a pair of monks returning to their monastery. A desperate whinny from his horse had drawn their attention and he had been rescued, along with his faithful beast. Days of recovery turned into weeks then months. His strength had returned gradually, but never did he recover to be his old self. The damage to his body was too great internally. Something to do with his body failing, his urine over the years getting darker and darker, he now knocking at the gates of Heaven he was sure.

These men of the monastery had taken care of him, provided for him, asking nothing in return. He had been nothing but a burden to them, but they had become his friends. About the only contribution he had been able to make was to tell them of his brief adventures on his journey with his master, and how he had finally arrived thanks to God delivering him into the hands of Angelo and Bartholomew, now two of the best friends he had ever known.

"Is it ready?"

Giuseppe looked up from the simple wood table at Angelo as he approached, Bartholomew immediately behind him.

"Not quite," replied Giuseppe. He picked up a small knife then carefully sliced the parchment in two, almost down the center, careful to cut around the letters rather than through them, then directly through the drawing of the skull he had put in the center. He carefully rolled the first half, tying it with string, and then the other, applying hot wax from a candle to seal each. He handed the left half to Angelo. "This is for his Holiness in Rome." He then handed him the scroll his master had given him containing the message for his Holiness. "This will get you an audience with the Pope. Tell him what went wrong and where the second half of this scroll is. He can send a force to retrieve it and my master, and then the idol." He handed the second scroll to Bartholomew. "This is for my master, my brother, Marco Polo, who I believe still resides in Khanbalig. I fear you have the hardest part to fulfill. It will be a long, difficult journey, but when you reach your destination, my master will take good care of you, and you will see wonders that will never cease to amaze you. Tell him where the second half of the scroll is, and that I am sorry."

"Why not tell us where you have hidden the idol?" asked Angelo. "Why the need for all this secrecy?"

Giuseppe smiled weakly.

"I have intentionally not told you where it is to protect you. Death follows this secret, and the less you know, the better. With half the scroll safely in the Holy See, my master will be able to retrieve it to get the entire message and locate the idol with Church forces to protect him. Should either of you be captured, the half scroll is useless, in a code that is hopefully gibberish, but should it be decoded, of no value since you need both parts to find the location. This will protect both of you, and protect the idol from falling into the wrong hands."

"Will Marco know how to decipher it?" asked Angelo.

Giuseppe nodded, a smile spreading across his face as his eyes gazed into the past. "It is a simple code we used when we were younger. He will recognize it immediately, and decipher it readily, of that I am certain. And with the drawing of the idol on the document, he will absolutely do so with haste."

A sudden jabbing pain up the side of his back had him grabbing at it with his hand, his body breaking out in a sweat and his strength, what little of it he had, immediately draining from him. He collapsed on the table and the two brothers immediately rushed to his aid, carrying him to his small bed in the corner of the room and lying him down.

Water was brought, broth as well, but Giuseppe was too weak to drink much of it, the pain continuing to rack his body. Finally too weak to even react to that, he felt himself beginning to slip away. As the world grew dark around him, he reached out for the hands of his friends. Angelo took his left, Bartholomew his right.

"Fulfill my wishes," he managed, and he felt his friends squeeze his hands, their assurances before God that they would, filling his ears. His head lolled to the side and his eyes met Bartholomew's. "When you see my brother, tell him I loved him, and that my deepest regret was failing him."

The reply wasn't heard, a mere distant echo of a world he was no longer part of. And as the darkness of the sweet relief of death enveloped him, he swore he heard the singing of angels, and a light in the distance, beckoning him toward it, whispering a promise that he would see his brother again.

The Vault of Secrets Entrance, Apostolic Palace, The Vatican

Present day, one day after the kidnapping

Acton stepped inside the large, plain wardrobe that occupied much of the wall of the small sleeping quarters off an unfrequented hall of the Apostolic Palace. They had been here before, and it hadn't ended well. With the knowledge however that the unknown entrance that had allowed the Keepers of the One Truth to ambush them the last time was now sealed permanently, they were confident they were now alone.

But secrecy must be maintained.

They had slipped down the hallway successfully, it usually kept vacant due to its distance and lack of renovation, and entered the room unseen. Acton flicked on his flashlight as Laura climbed in, closing the wardrobe doors behind them. He pushed up on the second hook from the left and he heard a click. Pushing on the back panel of the wardrobe, it swung open, revealing a long stone corridor. He stepped out of the wardrobe and down onto the floor, then helped Laura down.

"I hate this place," whispered Laura, her voice low yet still echoing, the walls unforgivingly solid.

"You and me both," replied Acton, the hair on his arms already standing on end. "Let's just find this damned thing and get the hell out of here."

"And never come back."

"I can live without ever seeing the Vatican again," said Acton as they reached a set of spiraling stairs that led down to the vault.

"I'm thinking Rome."

"Whatever you say, dear."

Acton quickly descended the tight staircase, Laura close behind him. When they reached the bottom they stepped out into a massive chamber they already knew extended for hundreds of meters. To their left was a pulley system used to transport large objects, and as he played his flashlight about, he could see their footprints in the dust from their last visit here.

"Let's hurry," urged Laura. "This place is freaking me out."

Acton grinned at her in the dark, wondering if she noticed she was speaking more 'American' all the time. Occasionally he caught himself using some of her British idioms, especially when he was visiting her and was surrounded by it. It didn't bother him, it was natural. It wasn't like Madge faking a British accent.

"It was the sixteenth row, wasn't it?"

Acton nodded in the near pitch black, the only light their flashlights. "Yeah. A little farther than we got last time. Hopefully the damned thing is in plain sight."

The catalog of items contained in the Vault had been converted electronically during Pope John Paul II's reign, and since they had already gone through it the last time they had been asked to help the Triarii, they had known what they were looking for. In the partially reconstructed texts, some of them almost two thousand years old, they had found an obscure entry that read, translated from Latin, "…referencing crystal icon in form of human skull…", the rest of the description apparently unsalvageable.

Laura marched ahead, her flashlight flipping from one row of shelves to the next, the Roman numerals engraved at the end of each counting up the deeper they went. Acton hurried to catch up, his fiancée's eagerness to finish the job evident.

"Here it is, sixteen!"

Her voice echoed throughout the chamber and Acton found himself playing his flashlight around, looking for any evidence of unwanted company.

Finding none, he breathed a sigh of relief and joined Laura who was already scanning the shelf with her flashlight. Acton strode to the other end to save time, and after several minutes, they found themselves both in the middle, empty handed.

"Could we be wrong?" asked Laura.

"In the description? No. Maybe somebody found it first?"

"Considering almost nobody knows of this place, and the only people who would want it would be the Triarii, who sent us here, I doubt it."

Acton bit his cheek. "I wonder…" His voice trailed off in thought as he went through the Latin translation again.

"What?"

He shone the flashlight up at his face so Laura could see him. She did the same. "Well, it did say 'referencing'."

"So?"

"So maybe we're not looking for a skull."

Laura pursed her lips, nodding. "What 'references' something?"

"It has to be a document."

"I definitely saw some of those," said Laura, excitement in her voice. "Let's start from the beginning and gather any documents we find." She immediately began scanning the shelves, reaching up and carefully lifting a scroll off a high shelf. "These things are pretty old, so be careful."

Acton nodded, picking up a sheaf of papers from the bottom shelf, then continuing on. Within minutes he had about a dozen scrolls, and reaching the end of the line, he rejoined Laura to find she had about the same.

She looked about. "Barmy idea, but how about we look at these upstairs?"

Acton nodded. "You don't have to ask me twice." Laura led the way to the staircase and they quickly wound their way up and into the corridor leading to the wardrobe entrance. Once through, they placed all of what they had found on the bed in the small room, keeping them in the order they had been found so they could be returned to their proper places.

"Leave anything too fragile to the end. We may have to have them analyzed in a lab."

"His Holiness isn't going to like that," said Acton with a grin, examining his first document. It turned out to be an account, in Latin, of a demon birth. *Next!*

"Oh my God!"

"What?" asked Acton, looking over to see his question answered as he stared at the scroll Laura had opened before her. At first he had thought she had torn it in half, but instead realized it was already like that before she opened it.

"This has to be it!" she exclaimed, barely able to contain her excitement.

It was a document that appeared to be gibberish, with a small drawing at the center showing half a skull. Acton lay his document aside, shuffling over to get a closer look.

"What the hell does it mean?" he asked, the Latin lettering appearing random.

"I have no idea. But I can tell you one thing."

"What?"

"I know where the second half is!"

Jackson Residence, Potomac, Maryland
One day after the kidnapping

Louisa had kept herself busy upstairs most of the day, the men with guns and questions below scaring her, reminding her too much of her native Columbia. *Never trust anyone with a badge or a gun.* Most of the men and women downstairs had both and she found herself shaking so much that her boss, Katherine Jackson, had sent her away, thankfully recognizing her discomfort.

She is a good woman. A very *good woman.* Louisa had cried for days when Señora's husband was killed. *And to be killed by a friend like Señor Darbinger!* It had crushed them all, but mostly Señora. She had locked herself in her bedroom for weeks, only letting Louisa in after she begged her to open the door so she could eat. Then it was only once a day that the door would be unlocked. Louisa would clean the room, bring in food, and urge Señora to get out of bed and walk around.

After almost three weeks Louisa was stunned to find her downstairs sipping coffee, acting as if nothing had happened. She had refused to mention her husband again. Her son Grant moved back into the house several weeks later which seemed to buoy her spirits, but she still refused to talk of her husband, despite how much Grant was clearly grieving.

And Louisa had cried.

She tried to provide comfort to Grant, a young man she had helped raise since he was a newborn, Louisa having served the Jackson family for almost thirty-five years. Grant had eventually moved on, and during the years since the murder, Louisa had never once heard her or her son speak of Señor again.

And now he had been kidnapped.

How much can one family take?

Señora was beside herself, but under the eyes of so many downstairs, she was keeping herself together better than Louisa was. If it weren't for her work, being done again for the umpteenth time today, she knew she'd collapse and sob as if her own child were missing.

Her phone vibrated in her apron pocket and she grabbed her chest, the unexpected not what she needed today. She looked at the call display but the number was blocked. She answered.

"Hola."

"Hi Louisa, it's me, Grant. Don't say anything! Nobody can know I'm calling."

Louisa wanted to shout out, to let everyone know that Grant was okay, and she almost did, his words lost on her, but before she did, her brain caught up with the moment and kept her silent. She instead sat on the edge of Señora's bed.

"Are you alone?" he asked.

"Yes."

"Good. I need you to do me big favor."

"Are you okay, Señor Grant? Have they hurt you?"

"I'm okay, they haven't touched me. In fact, they're not bad people, they are—rather were—friends of my father."

Louisa's chest collapsed in relief as a long sigh escaped her. He sounded fine, excited even, and to her it didn't sound like anyone was forcing him to say what they wanted him to.

Which had her confused even more.

Friends of his father?

"Are you sure, Señor Grant? The police are downstairs, I can tell them and maybe they can trace the call and rescue you."

"No, don't do that, Louisa. I'm okay, believe me. No one must know that I called you."

Louisa shook her head, not sure what to do. "If you say so Señor Grant."

"Good. Now I need you to go to my bedroom."

Louisa stood, her legs shaking. She looked into the hall and found it thankfully empty—she was certain she wouldn't be able to keep things together should she encounter someone. She quickly walked to the other side of the large house and opened Grant's bedroom door, stepping inside and closing it behind her.

"I am in your room, Señor Grant."

"Good, now in my left nightstand, top drawer, there is a letter from my father. Get it for me."

She walked over to the nightstand and pulled open the drawer. She frowned at some of its contents, blushed at others, but soon found the envelope in question, the envelope with "Grant" in the center in his father's handwriting.

"I have it."

"Okay, now here's what I need you to do."

When Louisa heard what Señor Grant wanted her to do, she nearly fainted.

The Holy See, Rome

September 23rd, 1282 AD

Over one year after Giuseppe's death

Angelo sat on the steps in front of the Lateran Palace, pilgrims and the faithful streaming around him, desperate to receive the blessings of the church to free their dead loved ones from Purgatory and into the dominion of Heaven.

But freedom and eternal bliss were only available to the faithful with money. That was the corruption of the Roman Catholic Church, an institution bastardized from its founder's vision, and instead now merely another kingdom with a ruler who demanded to be obeyed through adherence to a faith whose creator would have probably damned what it had become.

But Angelo was blind to all the desperation and suffering around him. He had received his audience with the Pope, which was a miracle unto itself, only the name of Marco Polo and the scroll provided him by Giuseppe left to him by his master, getting him through the door. But it was a new pope who now ruled, and Pope Martin IV had no interest in forging ties with Kublai Khan, and owed no favors to the Polo's, it being his predecessor who had been interested in pushing Catholicism to the Far East.

"I have enough problems in Europe to deal with. The Far East is of no interest to me now."

The words had shaken Angelo, and he had wondered how he could possibly complete the mission he had undertaken at Giuseppe's request. But the letters had been delivered, and his Holiness had taken the carefully wrapped and sealed half-letter, written in code, and promised should any Polo return to the Vatican someday to claim it, it would be delivered.

Then he had been ushered out.

The meeting had been less than ten minutes. A journey of over a year for ten minutes with a man who could care less.

He had dropped onto the steps, his mind awash in grief and self-doubt, only moments after leaving. It had been over an hour of sitting, his emotions overwhelming him, tears pouring down his cheeks, then rage gripping him. He was angry at the Pope for his indifference, at himself for leaving the document with the man, at Giuseppe for dying and not fulfilling his own duty.

It was this thought that had him racked with guilt.

And this thought that had him determined to reach Marco Polo in the Far East, and ensure he knew what had happened.

He just wished Giuseppe had let him in on where the crystal idol was actually hidden so he could tell Marco himself, but only the head of their order knew Giuseppe's wishes, and he would die with the secret never crossing his lips.

Angelo rose from the steps, wiped his cheeks, and strode forward, determined to deliver his message, when a scream rose above the din of the crowd behind him. He spun toward the sound, as did those around him, to find a man, blade held high, striking the neck of a guard. The blade sunk deep into the man's neck, nearly cleaving his head clean off.

Screams of terror erupted from almost everyone as they turned to run away. Angelo stood frozen, uncertain of what to do as the man roared his anger into the air, his head held back, his sword raised high, shaking in defiance.

"I demand to be heard!" he screamed. "I demand forgiveness for my wife's sins!"

He lowered his head and sword, looking about him, the steps now empty save Angelo. Their eyes met, then the man's gaze took in Angelo's attire, the robes of a monk. His eyes then fixated on the plain wood cross around Angelo's neck.

"You!" challenged the man, his sword pointing at Angelo as he stormed down the steps. "I demand you bless my wife so she may rest in peace!"

Angelo's jaw dropped, uncertain of what to say.

"I-I can't," he murmured. "It's not my place. I'm only a monk!"

"Then you are no good to me."

Without missing a beat, the man continued down the steps and buried his blade deep into Angelo's stomach, twisting it before pulling it free. Angelo collapsed onto the steps, blood pouring out onto the stone, his hands gripping his stomach as he felt the life drain from him as soldiers rushed toward them. In the faint distance he heard yells and a cry, his assailant felled, too late to help Angelo, but at least providing him a small comfort in knowing no one else would be hurt.

As he continued to weaken, he felt hands on him and he was flipped over on his back, and as the world faded to nothing, he heard the distant echo of the last rites being recited, and he passed with the comfort of knowing he would be going to Heaven, and the distress of knowing he would soon face Giuseppe without having satisfactorily fulfilled his promise.

Outside the Jackson Residence, Potomac, Maryland

Present day, one day after the kidnapping

Command Sergeant Major Burt "Big Dog" Dawson sat behind the wheel of a standard issue government SUV—big, gas guzzling, with souped-up engine, tires, suspension, the works—and tinted windows. Beside him sat Carl "Niner" Sung, the funniest man he knew—a Korean American who could be relentless in teasing his comrades-in-arms and himself, his own nickname a variation on a racial slur delivered in a bar by someone whose nose was never the same afterward.

Niner was a good friend and a fantastic soldier and a lot of fun on a stakeout. Eight of them had survived the London incident, four good men lost—Smitty, Spaz, Clint and Marco all having lost their lives for nothing—a madman's quest for a damned piece of carved crystal. Not to mention the dozens of innocents they had killed believing they were attacking a terrorist cell.

Not a day went by where Dawson didn't regret his actions, but with terrorists coming so young and from every part of the world including home, they couldn't go by their feelings anymore when seeing college students and assuming they were innocent. Their intel said it was a terrorist cell of American kids, and that's what they found. Their orders were to interrogate and eliminate, the names on the President's Termination List. They had eliminated countless terrorists this way before, and just because they were Middle Eastern Muslims, did it make it any more right or less wrong?

That day it had, these kids merely students unfortunate enough to have been there when some stupid sculpture had been found, a sculpture his handler had told him was a stolen top secret experiment belonging to DARPA, the military's research wing.

It had all been bullshit, and it was now something he and the others had to live with. His vow at the end of the mission to kill President Jackson had turned out to be unnecessary, one of the Triarii doing it for him. And now they found themselves back in the thick of those memories, the son of the very President responsible for it all now kidnapped by those his father had tried to kill.

It had him seeing red every time he thought of it.

"Penny for your thoughts."

Dawson grunted, glancing at Niner. "Huh?"

"You seem deep in thought. If you don't share, my feelings might get hurt."

Dawson grabbed his water bottle from a cup holder and took a swig. "London."

"Keep that to yourself. I don't want to be reminded." He sighed. "Okay, remind me."

Dawson returned his water bottle. "It makes no sense. Why would they go after Jackson's son?"

"That's what doesn't make sense to you? What doesn't make sense to me is why these guys don't use bullets! Did you know nobody in that truck in London that we hit had a bullet on them?"

Dawson frowned, his chest tightening slightly. "Not at the time." He shuffled in his seat, suddenly uncomfortable. "You're right, maybe we shouldn't talk about the past. I still have trouble sleeping at night sometimes."

Niner, more subdued than usual, nodded. "Me too. When I think of those kids…" His voice drifted off and he turned his head to look out the window.

Dawson nodded, understanding the pain his friend was feeling. Many a tear had escaped, many a beer had been drunk not for pleasure but to dull the pain over those events, and he knew he wasn't alone.

Niner shook his head, sighing. "So, what do you think we'll find out by sitting here?" he finally asked, thankfully changing the subject.

"Probably nothing. I'm just waiting for the next move by somebody. But something's not right. The Triarii kidnapped Jackson's son. Why? There've been no demands, no claims of responsibility, and they used non-lethal force, losing two of their people because of it. They wanted to make sure nothing happened to the son."

"Which means he's more valuable to them alive than dead."

"Exactly. Since we know the Triarii are loaded with more cash than Fort Knox, it can't be ransom, so they're either after something he has or something he knows."

"So if it's something he knows, knowing them they'll interrogate him then let him go but—"

"If it's something he has, then it's most likely in that very house that's swarming with every agency you can name, and surrounded by every news outlet in the world."

"There's no way he or they are getting in there, so why are we really here?"

"Because I read the file."

"So did I."

"And what did you read in there?"

Niner shrugged. "The usual. Name, address, phone number, standard bio. Nothing really."

"He moved out when he was eighteen to go to college and never came back home, instead getting a place of his own in Atlanta, becoming a criminal lawyer. Became decent at it then gave it all up to move back in with his mother after his father died."

"Loyal son?"

"Absolutely. But did you read the will?"

"The will?" Niner shrugged. "I skimmed it."

"Well, if you read the will, you would notice that the son was left a letter by his father."

"So he left a letter. Lots of people do that."

"Yes. Even I've got letters to be delivered in my will—"

"One for me I hope."

"Top of the list, Sergeant, top of the list," said Dawson, chuckling. "What's odd here though is that there was no letter left to the wife. Just the son."

Niner frowned. "That *is* odd. What do you think it means?"

"I think old dad was telling his son something important that had nothing to do with sentiment, and everything to do with the family's dirty little secret."

"That Dad was Triarii."

"Exactly. And the only reason you'd tell your son that is if there was some unfinished business he needed his son to complete."

Niner turned slightly toward Dawson. "But since the Triarii killed his father, then maybe it's not Triarii business. And since the Triarii killed his father, there was obviously a rift there. Maybe he wasn't acting alone, and there's actually a split in the Triarii."

Dawson pursed his lips, thinking. "Interesting idea. So that would mean that these kidnappers might not necessarily be playing for the home team. They might have their own agenda."

"And didn't the professor say once that the entire purpose of the Triarii was to keep the skulls apart because in the past three had been put together and blew the shit out of London?"

Dawson nodded. "So?"

"So, maybe this splinter group wants to do that again. Join the skulls together and create some sort of weapon."

"You're assuming it works."

"*I'm* assuming nothing. *They're* the ones who have to believe it's going to work."

Dawson nodded slowly as he looked out the front window. "So a splinter group of the Triarii are trying to get their hands on as many skulls as they can so they can create a weapon. That's so thin it's science fiction thin."

"No shit. But we are dealing with wackos who believe in magical crystal skulls."

Dawson let out a deep breath. "So, if President Jackson was Triarii, he obviously left them since he sent us in to wipe them out, but the Triarii had the presence of mind to have Darbinger, one of their own, remain with him all those years, then Jackson must have been part of the splinter group. And if we assume the splinter group's goal was to unite the skulls, and the Triarii had a plant with him the entire time, and now the splinter group is after something the son either has or knows, there can be only one thing they're after."

"A crystal skull."

Dawson nodded, his heart picking up its pace slightly. "President Jackson must have stolen a skull from the Triarii, and now either they or the splinter group want it."

"Super thin," muttered Niner. "Do you think the son has it?"

"Christ, it could be sitting on his bookshelf for all we know."

"Maybe we should go inside, take a wander."

Dawson shook his head. "No, if it was that easy the Triarii would have taken it back years ago. I think we can be certain that if there is a stolen skull, it's hidden away somewhere other than here."

"But where?"

"Well, there's no way the Triarii didn't have the son under constant surveillance if his father had stolen a crystal skull."

"Splinter cell or regulars?"

Dawson scratched his neck. "Probably both. And if we assume that both groups had him under surveillance, then both would know if he had tried to retrieve the skull, and would have intercepted it then."

"So we can assume that the son hasn't retrieved the skull."

"Exactly!" Dawson turned toward Niner, resting his left arm on the steering wheel. "If we assume that the father's instructions would have been to retrieve the skull and hand it over to the splinter group, or perhaps just pass the information as to where to find it on to the splinter group, and we assume it's the splinter group that kidnapped him today, then we have to assume the son either never read the letter, or didn't follow through on his father's instructions."

Niner's head bobbed with enthusiasm. "And if I were to have hidden away the skull from one of the most ingrained secret societies I've ever heard of, the instructions on retrieving it probably wouldn't be something easily remembered, and would most likely at a minimum involve some sort of key."

Dawson pointed at the upper floor of the house. "A key placed inside an envelope with a letter from dear old Dad that his son probably never opened, too pissed off his father was dead, blaming him for his own pain."

Niner whistled long and low. "Wow, that's thin, but with the shit I've seen over the years, it's a lot more solid than some of the intel we go off of."

Dawson pointed at the driveway. "And now we have what we've been waiting for."

Niner's eyes narrowed as he watched an old but well-maintained Honda Civic inch through the reporters, the poor old Hispanic woman driving it holding up one of her hands to try and shield her eyes from the glaring camera lights and the flashes from dozens of smart phones. Finally clear, she turned away from where Dawson and Niner were parked.

Dawson started up the engine and pulled out into the street, following the car at a reasonable distance. A quick check of his rearview mirror showed him no one else in law enforcement had had the presence of mind to put a tail on her.

"Do you really think the maid has it?"

Dawson pointed at the car. "Right signal light."

"So?"

"She lives to the left."

"Man, you really read that file," said Niner. "But for all we know she could be picking up dry cleaning."

Dawson nodded as he made the turn. "Or she could be delivering that envelope to Junior."

Approaching Khanbalig, Mongol Empire

July 14th, 1291 AD

Ten years after Giuseppe's death

Bartholomew felt even weaker than the skin and bones he had been reduced to suggested to those staring at him. His clothes were threadbare, if there at all, his feet unclad, hard callouses his soles. But the sight of the city walls that towered above him, mere steps away now, had fueled him these last few hours. The knowledge that his promise, his pledge to his friend Giuseppe was about to be fulfilled lifted his spirits to heights they hadn't seen for ten long years.

Ten years!

His journey at first had been uneventful. It had been long, monotonous and tiring, but that was expected. But when he reached India after over a year of travel, the caravan he had settled in with was ambushed and anyone who survived taken as slaves. He managed to hide his message from Giuseppe in the bedroll he was allowed to keep, and over the years of his captivity he had broken the seal and memorized the seemingly random letters that composed the coded message to Giuseppe's master.

It had taken him almost two years of effort but he could now rewrite the message from memory should the precious scroll be lost. But it hadn't been. Through good fortune and a meticulous routine surrounding the safeguarding of the scroll, he had managed to keep it hidden during the nearly five years of his captivity. It wasn't until, by chance, they encountered a large group of Christian missionaries that he had managed to tell one that he was a Christian monk being held against his will.

Swords had immediately been drawn and his outnumbered captors forced to flee. He had been nursed back to health by his rescuers as they travelled south, deeper into India, and within weeks he felt well enough to resume his trip.

Six weeks ago he had been robbed of all he had except his clothes and the scroll, tucked up his sleeve where no one would notice it. His food became scraps discarded by others, his water rain or the occasional stream he managed to cross.

As he neared the gates he extended an emaciated arm toward a guard.

"I have a message for Marco Polo," he whispered, then collapsed in the man's arms, his mission nearly over.

Mario Giasson's Office, Corpo della Gendarmeria

Palazzo del Governatorato, Vatican City

Present day, one day after the kidnapping

INTERPOL Special Agent Hugh Reading examined the copy of the scroll Acton and Laura had found. He shook his head, handing it back to Laura then tugged on his shirt, all of them uncomfortable, the HVAC apparently malfunctioning and forcing heat into the security offices instead of air conditioning.

"What the bloody hell does it mean? Looks like gibberish to me."

"It's obviously some kind of code," replied Acton, using his own copy as a fan. "And without both pieces, we have no hope of deciphering its complete message."

"But you're certain this is what you've been looking for?" asked Giasson, wiping his completely bald head with a handkerchief.

"Pretty certain," replied Laura who appeared as cool as a cucumber. "Completely certain? No. But I *have* seen the other half of this document, so it's worth a try."

"You've seen the other half?" asked Reading, wiping his forehead. "Where?"

"About ten years ago I was contacted by a private collector in Munich who said he had something that might interest me. I flew down and he showed me an ancient scroll he claimed belonged to Marco Polo."

"Why did he think it would interest you?" asked Giasson, redirecting a fan slightly.

Laura held up the copy, pointing at the partial drawing of a skull. "Because of this. He knew I was considered an expert on the skulls, and he felt that the drawing looked like a crystal skull rather than something human."

"And what did you think?"

"I thought it was rather curious, and the lines shooting out from the skull"—she pointed to several of them—"seem to suggest light, so it was possible."

Reading leaned forward to look at the drawing closer. "Did you have any luck deciphering it?"

"No, the collector wouldn't let me even take a copy. It was quite disappointing in the end." She sighed. "To tell you the truth, I had put it out of my mind until now. But there is one thing he did say."

"Which was?" asked Giasson, shoving his face into his desk fan.

"He said he had figured out the code, and if I were to bring him the second half, should it ever be found, he would translate the entire text and share it with me."

Acton slapped both his knees as he looked at the others. "Sounds like we're heading to Munich."

Reading shook his head, exchanging knowing looks with Giasson. "And if I know you two, after Munich we'll end up somewhere I *really* don't want to be."

Khanbalig, Mongol Empire

July 17th, 1291 AD

Ten years after Giuseppe's death

Bartholomew heard whispered voices around him speaking in a language he didn't understand. His skin pressed against luxurious bedding under him, a silk sheet caressed above. A soft pillow cradled his head and the aroma of fresh incense filled his nostrils. He opened his eyes and blinked several times as he tried to bring the sights before him into focus.

Almost instantly he felt hands on him, helping him sit up, adjusting his bed covers, and before he could ask, a glass with cool water was pressed against his lips. He drank rapidly but the glass was soon taken away as a man approached. His skin was dark, not as dark as those he had seen from the African continent, but close to a deep tan he was used to seeing amongst his Christian brethren. His eyes were pinched, his mustache thin and long, and his beard merely at the chin, the whiskers long and shaped into a point.

It suddenly struck him that he was looking at someone from the Far East. He had never seen anyone from so far away, and he couldn't help but stare as the man began pressing various parts of Bartholomew's body with his fingers, finally ending with several taps on his chest then a long look into his eyes.

He stepped back and nodded with apparent satisfaction, motioning for one of the women standing to the side to bring water. This time Bartholomew made certain he took the glass and held it to his own lips rather than let the nurse, otherwise it might be taken away.

He drained it, motioning for more.

The nurse looked at what was apparently the doctor then she brought him more. It took at least half a dozen glasses before he found himself begin to be quenched.

He felt a twinge in his stomach.

"My name is Chan. Can you understand me?" asked the man.

Bartholomew nodded. "You speak Italian?"

The man nodded. "I was taught it by a young man, though not so young now. His name was Marco Polo."

Bartholomew shoved up on his elbows, his heart slamming against his chest in excitement. "That is who I seek! Do you know where I can find him?"

The man frowned, shaking his head. "I am sorry to hear that. It would appear you have had a long, arduous journey."

"Ten years."

"So long, so close, and yet so far."

"What do you mean?" Bartholomew could feel a knot in his stomach begin to form as he sensed bad news was about to be delivered. *Could Marco be dead?*

"Marco Polo, his father and his uncle, left several months ago to escort a princess to her wedding in Persia, then they are to return home to Venice."

Bartholomew collapsed into his pillows, all strength leaving him. Ten years of hardship. Ten years of pain. And if he had just travelled with Angelo, stopped in Venice and waited, he would have had more success.

Ten years wasted!

Tears welled in his eyes as self-pity swept over him, his mind cursing Giuseppe for this promise, Angelo for getting the easier part of the journey, and Marco Polo for having forced his slave to deliver the crystal idol to the Pope in the first place.

The thought of the Pope had him awash in shame just as quickly as he realized his self-pity had twisted everything. Giuseppe loved his master, and his master apparently loved him, even having given him papers granting his freedom. Giuseppe had become too ill to fulfill his final mission and had entrusted that responsibility to his two best friends.

I'm sorry, Giuseppe!

Tears rolled down his cheeks as he realized he had failed. He turned his head in shame, burying the side of his face in his pillow as his chest and shoulders heaved in sobs.

"What is it that troubles you?"

Bartholomew sucked in a breath and held it, fighting off the sobs through sheer willpower, finally exhaling then wiping his cheeks dry with the sheet covering him. He turned back to the doctor, his eyes burning from the tears.

"I have failed."

"Failed? How?"

"I have a message for Marco Polo from his former slave. It was essential that he receive it."

"You mean that?" asked the man, pointing at a nearby table. Bartholomew looked and saw his carefully preserved scroll sitting on it. It was everything he could do to not leap from the bed and take it.

"Yes."

"And it was from Giuseppe?"

"You know of him!"

"Of course. Marco and I became very close friends over the seventeen years he spent with us. He spoke very often of Giuseppe with great fondness. He was deeply saddened when he never heard back from him, and eventually he came to accept that Giuseppe must have failed in his mission and died. He held a memorial for the man he called his brother and wept in his honor." The man wiped a tear from his own eye. "It was very moving."

Bartholomew motioned for some water and it was immediately brought to him. He quickly gulped it down as both men composed themselves. Before he could speak, the doctor continued.

"It occurs to me that you have not failed in your mission."

"I don't see how."

"Your mission is to deliver the message to Marco. Just because Marco is no longer here does not mean you have failed."

Bartholomew sank back in his pillows slowly as he realized what the man said was true. Even if he had to travel all the way back to Venice to deliver the message, as long as it was eventually delivered, he would have succeeded. A smile spread across his face.

"Do you have any suggestions as to how I might accomplish this feat?"

The man nodded, his own smile stretching across his face. "Kublai Khan himself has asked to meet with you. I am certain if we asked him, he would fund an expedition to return you safely to Venice."

"We?"

The smile broadened even further. "Yes, *we*. I have every intention of coming with you so I can see my friend once again."

Horseshoe Lane, Potomac, Maryland

Present day, one day after the kidnapping

"This must be it," said Niner as the car they had been following for the past fifteen minutes pulled off the road and into the drive of what appeared to be an old farmhouse. Dawson continued to drive without slowing down as Niner punched a button on his phone, marking the GPS location.

A large stand of trees at the corner of the next neighbor's property provided good cover and Dawson stopped. Niner already had his binoculars trained on the house when Dawson retrieved his from the backseat.

"She's getting out now," said Niner.

Dawson followed the driveway to the house and saw the Hispanic woman standing uncertainly, her purse clutched tight to her chest. A door opened and a man stepped out.

"Gun."

Dawson nodded. "This is it. Call it in."

Niner tapped his comm. "Control, Bravo Eleven. Possible location on target at GPS coordinates I am transmitting now." He pressed a button on his phone. "Requesting immediate backup—"

"And eyes in the sky," said Dawson.

"—and aerial surveillance, over."

"Bravo Eleven, Control. Request confirmed, standby, over."

"There he is," said Dawson as he saw Grant Jackson step out onto the porch, urging a reluctant servant inside. As soon as the woman saw him she ran to him, hugging him hard as they were ushered inside by the armed man.

"He's alive," said Niner, activating his comm again. "Control, Bravo Eleven. Confirmed sighting of target and at least one armed hostile, over."

"Bravo Eleven, Control. Units are rolling your way now, ETA fifteen minutes. Drone has been retasked, will be on your location in five, over."

"Roger that, Control, out."

Niner swung their tactical computer, mounted to the dash and punched up the feed from the UAV. Within moments they had an overhead shot rapidly speeding by as the UAV acquired the target.

"Fifteen minutes," repeated Niner. "This could be all over by then."

"Agreed," said Dawson. "But that place could be crawling with HT's and there's only two of us."

Niner nodded. "If only there was two of *me*, then we could go in."

Dawson laughed then stopped as he saw a curtain move and a set of eyes looking directly at them.

"We've been made."

Horseshoe Lane, Potomac, Maryland
Present day, one day after the kidnapping

"We've got company!" called Chuck Holder as he stepped back from the window. Grant's heart leapt, not sure of how he felt. He was after all a hostage to these men and was quite certain, though he had decided to cooperate for the moment, they had no intention of letting him go, even if he asked. He eyed the front door. All he had to do was cross the room, open it, then run outside. He knew they wouldn't shoot him, that much was already obvious to him. And if Louisa had brought the letter, they wouldn't need him regardless.

You'd be free!

"Are you sure?" asked Mitch, immediately stepping to the window and peeking outside. "Where?"

"Stand of trees, just down the road."

"Shit! I see them." He turned to the room. "Let's go, now!"

Grant's grand plans of escape had one flaw. Louisa. She was still hugging him hard, gripping him like a vice, as if he were the one piece of dry land in a sea of insanity, and if she were to let go she'd drown.

Grant could barely move.

Mitch grabbed him by the shoulder. "Let's go, now!"

Grant removed his arms from Louisa. "We have to go," he whispered. She released her grip from around his waist and instead grabbed his arm as he followed his captors, or partners—he wasn't sure which—to the basement, which to him seemed an odd choice.

Once down the narrow stairs, Mitch stepped over to a wall and pushed against a shelf that to Grant's surprise swung inward. Mitch motioned everyone to hurry and as Grant entered this hidden room, he gasped. Inside were two full-size SUVs at the head of what looked like a fairly long tunnel. Mitch opened the rear door of one of the vehicles, motioning Grant and Louisa inside.

"You've got the letter, right?" he asked Louisa.

Louisa nodded, pulling it out of her purse and handing it to Grant. He knew exactly why Mitch had asked again—Louisa was in such a panic, she might have left it in her car, or worse, back at the house. Grant looked at the envelope, confirming it was indeed the one he had received from the lawyer when the will was read.

"This is it," he said. Mitch slammed the door shut in acknowledgement, then jumped in the passenger seat, Chuck already at the wheel. The SUV surged forward and into the tunnel. Grant glanced back and saw the headlights of the second SUV bouncing behind them.

He wasn't sure how long it was before they suddenly angled up then skid to a halt, but it felt like a significant distance to him, easily hundreds of yards. Chuck reached up and pressed a button and a garage door opener kicked in, opening the doors blocking them. As soon as the doors stopped Chuck hammered on the gas, sending them hurtling toward the entrance.

"Easy," soothed Mitch. "Remember, we want to look like we're out for a Sunday drive."

Chuck eased off on the gas as they emerged from the tunnel. Grant looked back to see the other SUV right behind them, the garage door of a small farmhouse closing behind it. He turned back to face the front as they pulled onto a road, their escape made.

"What the hell was that?" he asked, having to admit he was impressed.

"Tunnel. Most of our safe houses have at least one. Gets us out of a lot of jams."

"I guess so."

Mitch turned in his seat.

"Now, how about we see what's in that envelope."

Grant nodded, his chest tightening as he eyed the envelope for a moment, then tore open the end. Tipping it, a key fell out on his lap. He picked it up and looked at it.

Mitch held out his hand. "How about I take that."

Grant refrained from frowning, knowing he had no choice but to comply. He handed over the key then pulled out the letter. He looked at Louisa and he knew she understood his pain. She squeezed his leg and nodded, her lips pressed firmly together to prevent them from trembling, her eyes glistening with tears ready to escape down her cheeks.

He unfolded the letter and began to read. Almost immediately tears poured from his eyes and he had to wipe them dry to focus.

My son,

If you are reading this, then I am dead. But more importantly, an essential undertaking of mine is incomplete. I know this may seem heartless, but the fact I am entrusting this most important task to you should demonstrate how important you are to me, how proud I am of you, and how much I trust you.

I am a member of a secret organization called the Triarii. I won't explain it here to you now, and it is critical you mention it to no one. After following my instructions, those you will meet will explain it to you. I have, in my possession, an important artifact that must be delivered to my friends in the Triarii. Below is an address for a storage unit where I have left important documents, and most importantly, the artifact.

You must, using a burner phone, or some other means that can't be traced, call the number below and arrange to meet one of the members of the Triarii. If he's lucky, my friend Mitch Reynolds will still be alive. Ask for him personally. When you meet him, you will note that he has a tattoo on the inside of his left wrist, exactly like the one I have, and a scar across the top of his right hand.

Give him this letter, and follow his instructions. And ask him any questions you may have about me and the Triarii.

I love you, son, and have every faith that you will carry out my final wishes as ably as I know you are capable of.

Yours,

Dad

Grant dropped his hands to his lap, looking out the window as the farms whipped by. He held his breath, trying not to sob as he struggled for control of his emotions. He felt Louisa's hand on his shoulder, squeezing gently, infusing some level of comfort into him.

Wiping his eyes, he turned back to the others. "Here," he said, handing the letter to Mitch. "I was supposed to contact you. The address for a storage locker is at the bottom."

Mitch smiled, a genuine smile Grant felt, his eyes conveying sympathy for what Grant had just gone through. "I told you we were friends." He turned to face the front, grabbing the GPS and punching in the address from the letter.

"Good," said Chuck. "We've been heading in the right direction. Should be there in ten."

Mitch turned back and looked at Grant then Louisa. "Don't worry, it's almost over."

Grant nodded, his feelings mixed. Simply handing over his father's life work, no matter how insane it might sound to him right now, just didn't feel right. He looked at Louisa, terror still written all over her face, and he knew he had to get her to safety, his decision made for him.

Horseshoe Lane, Potomac, Maryland

Present day, one day after the kidnapping

"Here they come," said Dawson, pointing ahead at two black SUV's racing toward their position. He activated his comm as he started the engine and pulled a U-turn back onto the road. "Bravo Two, Bravo One. I want team one on the front of the house, team two to the rear, enter through the front on my mark. Unknown number of hostiles, two friendlies on site—one Grant Jackson, the other a Hispanic female, mid-fifties. Remember, we're here to rescue hostages, shoot to kill is authorized, over."

Dawson brought the SUV to a halt and jumped out as Red acknowledged the instructions, his SUV rounding the house as the other, Sergeant First Class Will "Spock" Lightman at the wheel, quietly came to a halt behind them. The doors opened, Spock, Trip "Mickey" McDonald and the massive Leon "Atlas" James exiting, leaving their doors open so no one inside would hear them slamming shut.

Using hand signals, Dawson directed Mickey and Atlas to the corners as he, Niner and Spock rushed the porch. Over the comm he heard Red's voice. "Bravo One, Bravo Two. In position, over."

"Bravo Team, Bravo One. Execute in three-two-one-Execute!"

Niner yanked the screen door aside and Dawson booted open the front door. Spock rushed in followed by Niner then Dawson, Spock breaking left, Niner right, Dawson advancing straight forward.

"Clear!" called Niner, quickly followed by Spock. Red and his team announced the all clear as well as Dawson advanced up the stairs to the second floor, Spock and Niner joining him. Within minutes the above ground floors were cleared. The team congregated at the entrance to the basement.

"The element of surprise is no longer ours," said Dawson. "Let's try to negotiate their release." He turned to Red. "Secure the perimeter. I don't want somebody escaping out a storm cellar." Red nodded and immediately headed out the rear with two of the team. Dawson opened the door and listened.

Nothing.

Something's not right.

"Federal agents. You're completely surrounded. Drop your weapons and send up the hostages, and you won't be harmed."

He listened and there was no response. He looked at Niner and motioned for him to follow as he took the first step, his weapon and flashlight extended in front of him, the light off for the moment, not wanting to present a perfect target as there seemed to be lights on in the basement. Each step creaked painfully loud and Dawson knew they were sitting ducks if this turned into a firefight.

But he was going on instinct. He knew something wasn't right, and he had a gut feeling that this was London all over again. As he reached the floor he found an empty basement, just as he had suspected. A shelf to his left was at an odd angle and he rounded it then shook his head.

"What is it?" asked Niner.

Dawson stepped into the open area behind the fake wall and shone his flashlight down the long tunnel to the right as Niner stepped through.

"Aww for Christ's sake," cried Niner. "How the hell do you dig a tunnel that big and that long without anyone noticing!"

Dawson pointed at the aging timbers supporting it. "You do it a century or two ago." He pointed down the tunnel. "You and Mickey see where it comes out. Radio when you get there. It can't go too far. I'll check to see if our eye in the sky spotted anything."

Niner and Mickey took off at a run down the dark tunnel, their flashlights bouncing off the walls as Dawson examined the basement for any clues. All he spotted out of the ordinary was a cot with a pair of handcuffs sitting on it. Returning upstairs he updated everyone over the comms to stand down, then contacted Control with an update. Colonel Clancy's voice responded.

"Bravo One, Control Actual. Review of the footage shows two black SUV's exiting a garage about three hundred meters to your due east, turning north. We're redeploying our bird to track them. FBI should be on your scene within three minutes. Redeploy to the north, we will feed you directions as we have them, over."

Dawson motioned for those within sight to rally the troops and join him outside. "Roger that, Control Actual. I have two men on recon down the tunnel. Will retrieve them and redeploy north, out."

Dawson's comm squawked and Niner's voice came in, slightly breathless. "Bravo One, Bravo Eleven. Nothing here. We're at a farmhouse a few hundred meters to your east." There was a pause. "Are you picking us up? Over?"

Dawson grinned, as did the others as they climbed in their vehicles.

"Bravo Eleven, Bravo One. You sound kind of winded. Extra PT for you when we get back to Bragg. In the meantime I'll pick you up, out."

Dawson gunned his vehicle around the house and across the field behind it, Niner and Mickey in the distance waving. The first set of directions appeared on the tactical computer mounted to the dash. Dawson glanced at it, frowning.

Wherever they were going, they're probably there already.

Eagle National Storage, Potomac, Maryland
Present day, one day after the kidnapping

Mitch was the first to exit the vehicle leaving Chuck to open the rear doors, the child locks apparently engaged as Grant discovered when he tried to open the door himself. By the time he and Louisa were out, Mitch had already pulled open the door of the storage unit. Grant looked around before entering. They appeared to be alone, nobody at this time of the evening apparently interested in storing or retrieving anything, at least not down this long lane of units.

As Grant stepped inside the neatly organized storage unit, shelves with bankers boxes full of documents lining all three walls, there was one box at the back that appeared different. Shabbier than all the rest, stuck in a corner with two other boxes stacked on top. Mitch pointed.

"If I know your father, that would be it. He'd want to make it unappealing to any thieves."

Mitch motioned for the others to retrieve the box as he pulled out his phone. Chuck and Chip opened the box, moving some packing material aside then exchanged grins, giving Mitch the thumbs up.

"We've got it…okay, two minutes." He ended the call and put the phone in his pocket. "Transport is here in two. Transfer it to the case."

As Chip opened a metal sided case with what appeared to be a custom formed interior, Chuck carefully removed a felt wrapped object from the box and, removing the covering, placed it inside the case—a perfect fit.

Grant gasped.

"It's beautiful!" he gushed as he approached it. Chip held the box out, still open, so Grant could enjoy his first ever exposure to a genuine crystal skull.

"Yes it is," agreed Mitch. "This one hasn't been seen in almost a decade. Feel it."

Grant's hand advanced tentatively, almost afraid to touch it. Chip gave him a reassuring nod, and Grant finally made contact, running his fingers over the skull and down the brow.

"It's so smooth!"

"No detectable tool marks, one piece of crystal, cut across the grain. Impossible even with today's technology."

Grant continued to run his hands over the skull, captivated, and as he stared into the eyes, he felt a strange sensation come over him. Every hair on his body seemed to stand on end, a tingling sensation rolling through him as he found himself holding his breath. Staring into the eyes, the world around him lost focus, then suddenly Chip stepped back, snapping the case closed and Grant back to reality.

Outside the sound of a helicopter approaching could be heard.

Mitch extended his hand to Grant as they walked outside.

"Thank you for your cooperation. Your father would have been extremely proud in how you handled yourself."

Grant shook the man's hand. "What now?"

"Now we leave you. The keys are in the ignition," Mitch said, nodding toward the vehicle they had arrived in. He handed Grant the letter. "This is yours. Treasure it. It came from a great man. And if you ever want to talk about your father, call that number."

"You're just leaving us here?"

Mitch nodded as the chopper began to land about thirty yards away. "Yes, our job here is done."

"But what about the plan? To unite three skulls and see what happens?"

"That's next."

"We've got company!" yelled Chuck. He pointed to the end of the row of containers as two SUV's pulled up, blocking the lane. Grant spun his head to the other end and found a third SUV coming to a stop, men, all in black, stepping out.

Mitch and his team ran to the chopper and Grant found himself chasing after them. Mitch climbed in and looked down at him.

"I'm coming with you!" yelled Grant, trying to be heard over the rotors.

"What?"

"I'm coming with you!" he repeated. "I want to see my father's work through!"

Mitch smiled, almost as if he were proud of his own son for stepping up and doing the right thing. He extended his hand and pulled Grant inside, sliding shut the door, leaving Louisa standing by the entrance of the storage unit, her hands on her cheeks, her mouth agape, stunned at the turn of events.

Grant waved at her and smiled.

Leesburg Executive Airport, Leesburg, Virginia

Present day, one day after the kidnapping

"I got the distinct impression that our hostage was playing for the other side," said Niner as Dawson hurtled their SUV toward a private airstrip the helicopter had been tracked to.

"I noticed that."

"Stockholm Syndrome?"

Dawson shook his head. "I've never heard of it happening that fast."

"Me neither, but I'm just an exceptionally handsome warrior, not a psychiatrist."

"You're something," muttered Dawson as they careened around a corner.

"There it is," said Niner, pointing to an airstrip just ahead and to the left, a private jet taking off as they watched. "Do you think that's them?"

"Could be," said Dawson as he tried to shove the gas pedal through the floor. "What I'd give to have my 'Stang right now!"

Niner gave him a look. "Are you kidding me? You'd be babying that thing so much we'd still be sitting out front of the Jackson residence while you buffed out an imagined handprint."

Dawson chuckled as he turned into the airport, rounding the terminal and racing onto the tarmac, the rest of the team following close behind him. He rolled down his window and using hand signals directed the others to split off in two directions to cover the entire field. Dawson aimed them directly at the helicopter that sat halfway down the field with the same tail number as the one that had carried out the escape.

He hammered on the brakes, the ABS kicking in, shuddering them to a stop as Niner jumped out then Dawson, weapons drawn, advancing on what he knew would be an empty helicopter. But if they were lucky, perhaps the pilot might still be nearby.

"Clear!" announced Niner, the first to look inside.

"Shit!" cursed Dawson, spinning around, quickly surveying the airport. "Check your six!" he ordered as he focused his weapon on the driver of a car approaching at high speed. Niner stepped forward, doing the same.

The car screeched to a halt almost immediately, the two men inside raising their hands. Dawson flicked his weapon, motioning for them to get out as he and Niner advanced.

The two men, clearly terrified, climbed out of their car and stood, hands in the air.

"Federal Agents! Identify yourselves!" barked Dawson.

"I-I'm Victor Keith, Airport Manager," said the passenger.

Dawson lowered his weapon as did Niner.

"You can lower your hands," said Dawson. The driver lowered his, but Keith kept his up for a moment, then looked at them as if he had forgotten they were there. He lowered them.

"Are you here about what just happened?"

Dawson's eyes narrowed. "What just happened?"

"We had a private jet take off without a flight plan. They just taxied out and took off. Almost hit a Cessna that was on final approach!" Keith was getting himself into a frenzy, his adrenaline still pumping through his system and making him jumpy.

"Calm down, Vic, you're gonna have another heart attack," whispered the driver.

Keith, his entire body shaking, turned to the driver. "Y-you don't th-think I know that! I-I can't stop sh-shaking."

Dawson pointed at Keith's eyes then his own. "Focus on me. You're not in danger, you've done nothing wrong. I need you to take slow, deep, steady breaths, okay? With me." Dawson took several deep breaths, Keith soon matching him, the shaking slowly stopping. "Better?"

Keith nodded. "Much. Sorry, I've just never had a gun pointed at me. In fact, I don't know if I've ever seen one out of its holster."

"Consider yourself lucky," said Niner as he turned to brief Red and the others who had returned from opposite ends of the airfield.

"You said a plane left without a flight plan. Was that the one we just saw leave?"

Keith shook his head. "No, that one was fine. It was about five minutes ago."

"I'm going to need everything you can get me on that plane," said Dawson, pointing at their car and climbing in the back seat. As Keith and his driver climbed in he found himself questioning the entire situation.

How stupid can they be? They have to know we'll be able to track them.

Most Serene Republic of Venice

September 2nd, 1296 AD

Five years after Bartholomew arrived in Khanbalig

Chan hammered on the outer door of the large home in the richest quarter of Venice. His knock echoed in the courtyard beyond, and footsteps could be heard scurrying across cobbled stone. Bartholomew sat in a carriage, paid for by Kublai Khan's purse, still weak. He had never recovered from his trip, and knew his days were numbered. His jaundiced eyes and dark urine apparently marked the failure of his organs according to Chan. It was his determination to see this through that was keeping him alive now. He was quite certain he would never return to his monastery to die surrounded by his brothers, but if he fulfilled this last promise, he knew he would die in peace, his soul otherwise fated to eternal unrest should he fail.

A small opening was revealed and a servant, a shriveled old man who appeared barely able to see, poked his head forward, the look of shock on his face obvious as he took in the features of the Oriental standing in front of him.

"Who are you?" he asked curtly, apparently not impressed by the finery Chan was sporting, or the carriage that had brought him.

"Is this the Polo residence?"

"Yes it is. Who are you? What do you want?"

"I am a friend of your master, Marco Polo. I have an important message for him, and an important guest." Chan motioned toward the carriage.

"Your name?"

"Chan Wei. He will know who I am."

"One moment."

The small window slammed shut and the man could be heard hobbling across the courtyard, and several minutes later far more youthful legs covering the distance between the house and gate in seconds. The gate swung open and before them stood a man in his early to mid-forties, slim, distinguished, but with a smile so genuine it buoyed Bartholomew's heart.

"Wei my friend!" he cried as he extended his arms and the two men embraced. "It is so good to see you!" They held each other for what seemed to Bartholomew to be an eternity, finally placing some distance between themselves but still holding hands. "What brings you to Venice?"

Chan motioned toward the carriage. "I bring an important message." He beckoned with his hand for the carriage door to be opened. Bartholomew stepped down carefully, forcing a smile on his face as he painfully stepped toward the two friends.

"This is Bartholomew, a monk from the Monastery of St. Gerasimos. He has an important message for you, but is very ill."

"I can see that," said Marco, his eyes filled with concern for this new arrival. "St. Gerasimos. That's in the Holy Land, is it not?"

Bartholomew nodded, his head feeling heavier than it ever had, his body spilling its strength as the end of his journey, the end of his duty, neared. He reached into his robes and pulled out the scroll, its seal long broken out of the necessity to memorize its contents.

"A message for you from your faithful servant, Giuseppe," whispered Bartholomew as he held out the scroll.

Marco's eyes instantly filled with tears and his jaw dropped. He took the scroll and opened it, staring at the jumble of letters, puzzled.

"Why is there only half?"

"The other half, God willing, was delivered to the Vatican for safekeeping fifteen years ago, by my brother Angelo. Giuseppe said you would recognize the code, and with the two pieces, would be able to determine where the crystal idol had been hidden. He died entrusting his final task you asked of him to us, his friends. His journey after leaving you was hard and when we found him he was nearly dead. We nursed him back to some health, but he remained weak, dying several years later."

"Did he die in peace?" asked Marco, his voice cracking. "Did he say anything?"

Bartholomew nodded. "I was there when he passed. He said, 'When you see my brother, tell him I loved him, and that my deepest regret was failing him.' Those were his last words before he passed, surrounded by friends who cared about him, and who were determined to carry out his final wishes."

Marco dropped to his knees, the scroll tumbling from his hands and onto the street as he covered his face with his palms, sobs erupting from within, his shoulders shaking in agony as the news of the loss of the man he called brother sank in. Chan and Bartholomew watched quietly, Bartholomew continuing to weaken. He tried desperately to hang on, but soon the world began to spin and he felt the sensation of falling, but had passed out before he could feel the impact with the ground.

Montpellier Airport, France

Present day, two days after the kidnapping

Captain Pierre Lapointe of the Sûreté Nationale watched as the Bombardier Challenger 605 taxied toward the far end of the tarmac. The four Mirage 2000 fighter jets that had escorted the plane in from the Atlantic seaboard still circled overhead, their massive engines filling the air with a throbbing roar that made it hard to hear.

At least one hundred law enforcement officers from various agencies including several American representatives that had just arrived were swarming the area. There was no way Lapointe was going to risk this operation going south, so he had called in everyone he could think of to help.

As he eyed the near chaos, he began to question his wisdom.

If this turns into a gunfight, over one hundred weapons will be firing back.

He activated his radio.

"This is Lapointe. No one is to fire under any circumstances, even if fired upon!" He received some looks, but didn't care. He couldn't risk the plane being blown up by a stray bullet, or worse, the cameras lining the outside of the airfield capturing the shooting of an American President's son by French police.

The plane came to a stop about fifty yards away and the engines began to power down, the ground vehicles escorting it peeling away. Security immediately blocked the wheels then fell back as the mass of forces began to advance, surrounding the plane.

"This is Lapointe. Everyone fall back fifty meters. Primary team advance with me."

The sea of men fell back as if a pebble had been dropped in the middle of them, the ripple pushing them back. Lapointe and his team of six heavily armed and armored men advanced toward the nose of the plane. He had a clear view of the pilot who had his hands raised, his expression clearly one of fear. Lapointe pointed at the door and the man nodded, unstrapping himself from his seat then getting up and disappearing from view.

This isn't right.

None of it was right. Lapointe knew from the moment he had received the call that it wasn't right. Who in their right mind would kidnap a former President's son, then get on a private jet and think they'd get away by going to Western Europe, let alone France? If they had stuck to the roads they might have been able to continue to evade the authorities in the United States, perhaps even escaping to Canada or Mexico. But to get on a large plane that has limited landing options, then point it toward Europe?

This doesn't make sense!

Then the pilot, when intercepted, cooperated completely, pleading ignorance and a bad comm. Now here he was, apparently terrified, about to open the door.

Suicide by cop?

Could that be their idea? They didn't care if they were captured because they were willing to die? Perhaps dying was their plan all along? It would definitely fit the terrorist profile, so many of these pathetic men ready to commit suicide to further prove their cause was worldwide insanity. Was young Mr. Jackson about to become the latest innocent victim?

As the door opened, he patted himself mentally for pushing the bulk of the security back, his own team now deployed to cover the door. The small metal stairs dropped and the pilot appeared in the doorway.

"Come down slowly, with your hands up!" ordered Lapointe.

The man, his face as white as his dress shirt, nodded, carefully taking the few steps to the ground, his hands raised high, fresh sweat stains rapidly expanding.

"Lie down on the ground with your legs spread, your hands on top of your head!"

The pilot complied, and once in position, two of Lapointe's men rushed forward, one cuffing the man's hands behind his back, the other searching him. Finding nothing, they hauled him to his feet, bringing him to Lapointe.

"Your name?"

"Frank. Frank Carey. Is my family okay? Have you found them?"

"I'm asking the questions!" snapped Lapointe, the man's own giving him a sinking feeling. "How many are onboard?"

"Nobody! But what about my family? Are they okay?"

Lapointe's blood pressure went up. "I have no time for games. How many men are onboard? Is the hostage okay?"

Carey blanched and his knees nearly gave out. "Hostage? What are you talking about? There's nobody onboard, I swear to God!"

Lapointe motioned for his men to advance. Two took up positions at either side of the door from the ground, the other four rushing up the steps and into the fuselage, shouting orders for everyone onboard to freeze.

Moments later one of his men appeared in the doorway, shaking his head.

"There's nobody here."

Lapointe grabbed the man by his shirt. "What the hell is going on here?"

Carey tried to back away but was blocked by one of Lapointe's men who had no plans to budge. "Listen, I don't know what you think is going on here, but all I know is I was told to take off without a flight plan and head for France or they'd kill my family. Are they okay? I refuse to answer any more questions until I know my family is okay!"

Lapointe stared directly into the man's glistening eyes, searching for the truth, and after a minute stepped back, convinced he was telling it. He raised his mike to his mouth. "Search the plane, check the onboard computer, and tell the Americans their missing person is not aboard, and never was."

He pointed at the pilot. "Take him in for questioning."

"What about my family?" cried Carey.

Lapointe looked at him for a moment.

"And let him call his family."

Lapointe walked up the steps into the plane just to see for himself, it already filled with a large crew of investigators pulling open floor panels and searching luggage compartments for any stowaways, but Lapointe already knew the truth.

This plane was a decoy from the beginning, buying the hostage takers almost eight hours to make their escape.

Oberpfaffenhofen Airport, Germany

Present day, two days after the kidnapping

Grant Jackson felt a hand on his shoulder, shaking him. He scrambled in his seat, fighting to wake up, the unfamiliar surroundings sending a surge of panic through him. He opened his eyes and suddenly reality and his situation came into focus and he stopped struggling, smiling sheepishly at Chip.

"Sorry, I'm not a good sleeper."

"No worries, bud. We're about to land."

Grant nodded, straightening his chair and himself. He glanced around and saw the others all strapped in. Looking out the window he began to have the same second thoughts that had tormented him most of the flight. He had at first wondered how they could possibly get away, but was assured they would be safe, a decoy plane having been sent just before them that would have everyone occupied long enough for them to land and make their getaway safely.

He had grilled Mitch on his father, finding out as much as he could about the Triarii, their history, their current status, how his father had become involved, and what he had done while a member. He had even scraped together enough courage to ask about his father's death, managing to hold back the pain he felt in hearing the answers.

But in the end he still felt he had become part of a cult.

Crystal skulls? Explosive powers? The ability to influence the evolution of man?

It was all nuts. And the more he thought about it, the more he realized he had made a mistake. Staying with these men was not only stupid, it was dangerous. It had killed his father, and from the history, especially recent events he had been told about, it sounded like crossing paths with the Triarii or the crystal skulls could easily lead to your death, as dozens if not hundreds of others had found out the hard way.

But he was here, and as far as he could tell, committed to a path he wasn't sure of.

He was certain of one thing, however.

He had no idea how to get out.

These men were crazy, and he no longer served a purpose. He had given them what they wanted, and now if he were to betray them, how long could he expect to live? There was a very good chance they might just let him go, perhaps even with a handshake and a slap on the back. But there was also a chance they might decide he had seen too much, or knew too much. And he didn't trust Ben Cowan to not put a bullet in his head if he felt Grant were putting them at risk.

He would have to play it safe for now and go along with their plans.

But if he saw the opportunity for escape, he'd take it.

But they know where you live!

His heart sank as the plane touched down. There was no escape. Not permanently. The only way he could survive for certain was to play along.

Perhaps forever.

He turned to look at Mitch sitting across the aisle.

"Where are we?"

Mitch turned to face him.

"Munich. We've got some unfinished business here."

Teufel Residence, Munich, Germany

Present day, two days after the kidnapping

"So good to see you again, Professor Palmer!" cried the elderly man who had opened the door, his accent thick but his English near perfect. "I was surprised to hear from you last night. I am of course delighted to show you the scroll again," he said with a smile, then added with a little jab of the elbow, "but I have a sneaking suspicion you have something to show me as well, heh?"

Laura smiled with a nod. "You are a very perceptive man, Herr Teufel. We're sorry for the early hour, but time is of the essence."

"Of course, of course. I have the scroll already out for you and your friends to see."

Laura slapped her forehead. "Forgive me, Herr Teufel. My manners!" She motioned at her fiancé. "This is Professor James Acton from St. Paul's University."

"A pleasure, Herr Teufel," said James, shaking the man's hand.

"Professor Acton, there's no need for an introduction. I have followed your career for many years. I understand you two are engaged?" asked the little man with a twinkle in his eye. "To be married? Soon perhaps?"

James laughed and winked at Laura. "Yes, we're engaged. Haven't set a date yet, things seem to keep getting in the way."

Teufel batted the air. "You must never let things get in the way of love. You should set a date now, get married and make lots of babies!"

Laura blushed, something she rarely did, then beamed a smile at her beloved James as he too seemed a little taken aback by the man's forthrightness.

Awkward! as James might say.

"And this is Special Agent Hugh Reading of INTERPOL," said Laura, changing the subject and finishing the introductions.

"Ach! Your bodyguard!" cried Teufel as he shook Reading's hand vigorously. "Too wonderful! Too wonderful!" He motioned down the hall. "Now follow me and I will show you what you have come to see."

Their journey to Herr Teufel's house had been uneventful. A quick plane ride from Rome then overnight in a nice hotel had refreshed them for what was sure to be an exhausting day. Matching the two halves of the scroll would be one thing, but decoding them a completely other. Hours if not days of laborious mental work could be ahead of them even if Teufel had broken the code as he claimed.

But it would be fantastically exciting work!

To say she adored her job would be an understatement. She had only ever met one person whose passion for their work rivaled her own, and his hand she now held as they walked deeper into the large home by urban European standards.

She loved James, even more than her work, which was something she would have found unfathomable a few short years ago. But the bond that had been formed since they met was so strong, she ached every time they were apart. It was approaching the point where she was considering leaving her job in London and moving to be with James in America. She could take a position at one of the colleges in the area, perhaps raise some children.

Children!

The thought sent chills racing up and down her spine, the idea titillating and terrifying at the same time. She had never really considered children and felt she had at least another five to ten years to consider them. With the way they worked now, children weren't a possibility, and if they were to have them, they definitely would need to be in America. She had no family, and James' parents were still alive and healthy to help out.

Children!

She sighed.

Perhaps we should see if we survive until the wedding day first.

"Something wrong?" asked James, apparently hearing her sigh.

She shook her head with a smile, squeezing his hand. "No, everything's perfect."

He squeezed her hand back, three times, as they took in the home. It was modest appearing from the outside, but inside it was quite ornate, old timber beams crisscrossed the ceilings, plaster walls were trimmed with large carved moldings, delicate frescoes painted directly on many of the walls. The furniture was mostly antique, and the surfaces were filled with artifacts and collectibles of impeccable taste and, Laura had a feeling, of questionable pedigree in some cases.

There was easily millions of pounds worth of items here, most of which she felt belonged in a museum.

After descending a set of steps into the basement, they entered the same room she had years before but gasped at the significant upgrades. It was still a large room but now had a glassed in smaller room in the center that appeared to be environmentally controlled for temperature and humidity—clearly Teufel had money, a setup like this well into the six figures.

"I won't ask you to put the bunny suits on," said Teufel with a chuckle. "There is nothing needing that sort of protection in here today."

Laura exchanged a surprised glance with James as they each stepped through a clean-room entrance, air mixed with various gasses blasting any loose debris off them. She was the second into the lab, Teufel the first. She approached a table in the center of the room, already lost in the moment.

Carefully laid out on it was the scroll she remembered from years ago, unwrapped and contained within a vacuum sealed glass to preserve it for future generations. Alongside the genuine article was a replica, on modern day paper so it could be handled without fear of its destruction.

"And I believe you have something for me?" asked Teufel after they gathered around the table.

Laura nodded and produced the ancient scroll from her satchel. "This I believe is the second half."

Teufel rubbed his hands together in anticipation, bouncing up and down on his toes as his eyes, wide with anticipation, locked onto the scroll as Laura gently placed the case on the table, beside its partner, having used the Vatican's own preservation tools to protect it from destruction.

"It's a match," whispered James as they all leaned forward, Laura carefully pushing her piece of the document toward Teufel's, the precise cut down the center of each, seemingly designed to split certain words so they couldn't be decoded without the other half, clearly a perfect fit.

"But it's still gibberish," observed Reading.

Laura slapped his arm. "Of course it is. It needs to be decoded."

"Okay. How?"

Reading was right, it *was* just gibberish. An apparent mass of scrambled Latin lettering with no indication of how to decipher it, or even what language it might be written in, the Latin alphabet being used by dozens of languages including English.

"That is no problem," replied Teufel. "I deciphered the other half years ago. With the second half, all we need to do is scan it into the computer and it will put the two together and give us the translation. Perhaps five minutes."

"Five minutes?" exclaimed Reading. "What is it, some child's code?"

Teufel chuckled, wagging a finger at him. "Never underestimate a child's code! It can provide many challenges."

"So it *is* a child's code."

Teufel positioned a camera over the scroll and took a photo with the computer. "No, it's a *slave* code."

"Huh?"

"To be exact, this is known as the Venice Code. It was used by the ancient Venetians to pass messages between themselves that they didn't want their slaves to understand. Most couldn't read, but some could, which could make private communication difficult, so they came up with this code. The slave would hand over the message, and as I learned through my own trial and error, the day of the week the message was written was the offset for the cipher."

"So how does it work?" asked Laura as she watched the two halves being matched up on the computer by Teufel.

"It's really quite simple. The message is written down, then each letter is moved alternately forward and backward by a set number of letters, the offset. Remember, it was meant for quick communication and they didn't have computers back then. The code ended up breaking down eventually when slave owners too lazy to translate their own messages taught their slaves how to do it, thus defeating the purpose."

"So how did you figure it out?" asked James. "I've never heard of this code."

"And neither had I until I stumbled upon a piece of text purportedly written by Marco Polo that referred to a slave of his, someone named Giuseppe, and how he had taught him the Venice Code when they were children, not realizing slaves weren't supposed to know it. He was severely punished, but it was too late. Marco and his slave then used it to exchange secret messages between themselves."

"Not the typical master-slave relationship I've heard of," commented Reading.

"Indeed," agreed Teufel. The computer beeped. "Ahh, finally!" he gasped as he hit a button and the decoded text appeared on the screen, still a jumble of letters, but words could be made out though no spacing or punctuation seemed to be included.

"Is that Latin?" asked Laura.

James nodded. "Yup. How's your Latin, Herr Teufel?"

"I assure you, much worse than yours even if you can't speak it!" he said, laughing. "It took me days to translate the few words I managed to retrieve from my half of the scroll."

James smiled, exchanging a glance with Laura. She could read the excitement on his face and it rivaled her own. This was a mystery he had been living with for a day. She had been living with it for years. A seven hundred year old scroll, perhaps about the crystal skulls, found amongst the possessions of Marco Polo upon his death.

Goose bumps covered her body.

"Okay, here goes, it will be a little rough. Somebody writing this down?"

"I've got it," said Laura as she pulled out her smartphone, activating the note taking feature. Her thumbs hovered over the keyboard in anticipation.

"Okay, it says, *'I am sorry I failed you master. After relentless pursuit, I am near death.'*"

"It must have been written by a slave to his master," said Teufel, his voice barely a whisper.

"Perhaps to Marco Polo?" suggested Laura.

"Translate the bloody thing and we'll find out," suggested Reading with all the subtlety of a hammer.

"Don't take the fun out of our work, Hugh," admonished Laura with a smile. "Continue, hon."

James looked back at the screen, a grin stretching across his face. "'*I have been unable to deliver the idol as promised, and in my weakened state have been forced to hide it.*' That has to be the skull!" exclaimed James.

"Skull?" asked Teufel. "You mean this *is* about one of those crystal skulls your fiancée is so eager to research?"

Nobody said anything, fearing perhaps too much had already been said. Instead James said, "Let's find out. *'I will have trusted friends deliver this scroll in two parts, one to the Holy See, one to Khanbalig.'*"

"Khanbalig? Where's that?" asked Reading.

"Modern day Beijing," replied Laura. "Kublai Khan built it to be his capital city."

"Really? I always thought it was Chinese."

"Very different world back then, Hugh. You should attend some of my classes," said Laura with a wink.

"Like I've got bloody time for that," muttered Reading. "Though it might be a good place to catch up on my sleep."

"Touché!" said Laura, tapping James' shoulder to continue. "Continue on, hon, I think our profession just got insulted."

"Yeah, I heard that. Somebody could be catching their own plane ride home."

"I know where you live," reminded Reading.

"Uh huh." James turned back to the screen. "*'I know you will immediately recognize the code to decipher this. When both parts are put together, you will see the location where I have hidden it below.'*" James' head dropped and Laura knew he was as eager as she was to get to the end and find the location, but his head quickly popped back up, realizing that jumping to the end of the book was never a good idea. "*'Should my new friends have followed my wishes, and been successful in their tasks, then you are reading this now. The idol is near Jericho in the crypt of the St. Gerasimos monks with my remains.'*"

Reading grunted. "Jericho. Isn't that in Israel?"

James shook his head. "Sort of. It's in the West Bank."

"Bloody hell, of course it is," cursed Reading, throwing his hands up in the air. "What is it with you two?"

"I don't know," replied James. "My life was pretty good until I met you. Then all this shit starting happening to me."

"I think that's the other way around, mate."

"Shall I finish?" asked James.

"Please."

James winked at Laura then returned to the screen. "*Forgive me brother for having failed you. Your faithful servant, Giuseppe Polo.*"

Acton straightened, glancing at Laura's phone. "Did you get it all?"

She nodded. "Yes."

"Giuseppe?" murmured Teufel. "That must be the same slave he taught the code to, the one mentioned in the letter I read. And for a slave to call his master 'brother'! Why, it's almost unheard of!"

"They must have been very close," agreed Laura. "We know from Marco Polo's will that upon his death he granted freedom to a Tartar slave. Perhaps he treated his slaves well."

"But 'brother'? That's an equal. That's familial. And to use the family name? Very out of the ordinary," said Teufel. He pointed at the phone. "You will of course send me a copy of that," he said, handing her a business card with an email address.

Laura nodded. "But I must ask that you not share its contents with anyone until you hear from me."

"Who would I have to share them with but you?" asked Teufel, his shoulders up, palms facing upward.

Laura had an odd feeling, as if there was some hint of deception on Teufel's part. She quickly swiped her thumb and put the phone in airplane mode, killing its communications capabilities, then sent the email containing the text, leaving it in the Outbox.

"I've sent it but it looks like I have no signal in here. I'm sure you'll receive it as soon as we get outside," she said, smiling. She picked up their half of the scroll, returning it to her satchel and extended a hand to Herr Teufel. "Thank you so much for seeing us on such short notice."

Teufel smiled, clasping her hand in both of his. "You have no idea how happy you've made me today, Fräulein. A decades old mystery for me, and a centuries old mystery for the world, has been solved."

As they headed for the front entrance, Laura leading a slightly brisk pace that had the men scrambling to keep up, Teufel offered them tea.

"On any other day that would be delightful," she said as she opened the door, "but today we're on a tight schedule."

Suddenly James grabbed her arm and yanked her inside, slamming the door shut. Her hand jumped to her chest in an attempt to calm her suddenly racing heart.

"What's wrong?" she cried.

"We're not alone."

The Holy See, Rome

September 9th, 1296 AD

One week after Bartholomew delivered his message to Marco Polo

Marco Polo sat in his carriage outside the gates of the Holy See, his meeting with Pope Boniface VIII cancelled, and not to be rescheduled. It was made quite clear to him that any letter delivered almost fifteen years ago to Pope Martin IV was either disposed of or lost, there having been five Popes in that span of time. He had argued, pled, even threatened, but it had been no use. He was shown the door and sent on his way, his half of the scroll never to be married with the other half, the secret his beloved Giuseppe died protecting never to be revealed.

He ordered the coachman to proceed, and with a flick of the reins they began to roll forward, the cobblestones shaking the carriage slightly, their rhythmic clacking lost on Marco as he settled into a deep depression. He stared out the window at the masses, then closed his eyes, his head resting against the padded side, tears pouring down his cheeks as he pictured his beloved brother, Giuseppe, and how heartbroken he must have been failing in his mission, a mission that he had sent him on.

If it wasn't for you, he'd be alive.

He shook his head, gripping the cross that hung around his neck.

No, if it weren't for that blasphemous crystal idol, he'd be alive!

And at that moment, he swore to God that if he ever laid hands on it, he'd destroy it himself, it already having taken so much from him. Death followed the skull, of that he was sure. Father Salvatore, Brother Vincenzo, Angelo, Bartholomew, and of course Giuseppe. All dead before their time due to the evil that was the skull.

Marco swore that no more lives of his loved ones would be lost to the cursed idol. He looked at the scroll, still gripped in his hand. He was tempted to destroy it right then and there, but it was the last thing that Giuseppe had written, and he couldn't bring himself to do it. Instead, when he reached home, he would hide the scroll with his private papers so no one else might be tempted by its contents.

He opened his eyes and looked out the window to the heavens, praying that no one else should ever seek the crystal idol, lest they too suffer the fate of so many good men.

And resolved there, once and for all, to undertake one final journey.

Teufel Residence, Munich, Germany
Present day, two days after the kidnapping

Acton peered out the window at the new arrivals. Three SUVs with at least four men in each were emptying out front. His mind raced as he evaluated their situation. Outnumbered four to one. Soon to be surrounded. And no weapons. How the hell they knew they were here was a completely different question that could be worried about later. He turned to Teufel.

"Is there another way out of here?"

Teufel shook his head. "No, but the lab is a safe room."

"Then let's go!" urged Reading, herding the other three toward the basement stairs. The doorbell rang, which Acton thought was quite civilized of their besiegers. It was quickly followed by hammering on the door as they all bottlenecked at the basement entrance, Teufel taking the steps one at a time.

Acton heard something toward the back of the house and looked down the hallway to see two faces peering through a rear window then the smashing of glass. The last Acton saw was a boot crossing the window sill. He closed the door to the basement behind them as Teufel finally reached the bottom step, shuffling toward the safe room.

"They're inside!" yelled Acton as he looked for a lock, finding none. The door opened to the outside so there was no point in trying to block it or brace it; they would simply pull open the door. He looked for something to give him a better hold than a slippery metal doorknob.

Nothing.

As he gripped the knob he looked down and saw Teufel finally get into the decontamination chamber, shaking his head that the old man hadn't let Laura go first.

Chivalry dies in the face of death?

Acton frowned.

And he seems to be moving a lot slower than when we first arrived.

Again the thought of how they were found reared, but he pushed it aside, an idea suddenly occurring to him. He undid his belt buckle and pulled his belt off as he heard heavy steps coming down the hall. He looped the belt back through the buckle then hooked it over the door knob, pulling it tight. He then wrapped the other end of the belt around his wrist, leaning back and using his body weight rather than just muscle power to hold the door.

Looking down he saw Laura enter the chamber, Reading still at the foot of the steps. He turned to Acton. "Why don't you let me take that?" he asked, ever the peace officer.

"Because I'm faster and stronger than you?" suggested Acton with a wink as he felt the door jerk, the first attempt made. Acton saw Laura step out of the decontamination chamber. "Your turn!" said Acton before Reading could defend himself.

Reading frowned then after a split second of indecision jumped into the decontamination room as the door continued to rattle, but never opening more than an inch. Acton split his attention between the door and Reading's progress, his wrist in agony as the belt tightened further. Suddenly the door jerked open and a large knife appeared, slicing into the belt.

Acton spun his arm, releasing the grip his belt had on him, sending those pulling at the other side tumbling backward. He jumped down the steps then into the decontamination room just as Reading exited to the other side. As he was blasted with air he saw a man rush down the steps, gun extended, followed by several more. There was a beep as the cycle completed and he stepped into the room.

"How do we lock it?" he yelled, looking at Teufel.

"The red button," he said as the first man ran toward the decontamination entrance.

Acton looked and saw a large red button to the right. He pushed it and an alarm sounded, the clicking of several locks being heard. The man grabbed on the door entrance and pulled, but couldn't get it to open. He raised his weapon and pointed it at the glass. Acton stepped back as a shot, muffled by their enclosure, was fired.

Nothing.

The glass, or whatever it was, held, barely a mark on it.

"What is this place?" asked Reading.

"It's a panic room," answered Teufel. "Bullet proof, bomb proof—at least small bombs—with its own power supply, air filters, water and food. We can stay here for days if necessary. They will eventually tire of their failures and leave."

Several more shots rang out, the bullets slamming into the transparent walls, loud thuds echoing through the chamber. A grim looking man, a determined expression on his face, his jawline so fierce it looked like it might have more success cutting through the wall than the bullets, circled the chamber they were in, firing at each of the four walls. Acton hoped a ricochet might take him out, teaching the man Einstein's definition of insanity the hard way—doing the same thing over and over again and expecting different results.

Acton turned to Teufel, who had sat himself in a swivel chair off to the side, but several feet from the glass. He slowly spun in the chair, watching the ineffective progress of the shooter.

"Is there a way to talk to them?"

Teufel nodded, pointing to a panel by the wall. "Press the top button to activate the speaker so we can hear them but they can't hear us. Press the middle button to activate two way communications, or just press and hold the bottom button to talk like on a walkie talkie. Letting it go turns off our microphone."

Acton nodded, walking over to the panel and pressing the top button. Over hidden speakers he could hear the sounds of half a dozen men shuffling and muttering, one set of boots slowly clicking around the chamber as their owner gave up shooting.

Acton pressed the bottom button. "What do you want?" he asked, then let go just in case he and his compatriots needed to communicate in private.

A man stepped forward, clearly the leader. He smiled, a smile that must have been so practiced, it seemed genuine.

"Professor Acton. It's a pleasure to finally meet you in person. I've heard so much about you and your lovely fiancée"—he nodded toward Laura—"that I feel like I already know you."

Acton pressed the button, deciding the longer they played along, the longer Reading, who stood huddled with Laura in the rear corner, might be able to make contact with the outside world, he having caught a glimpse of a phone in Reading's hand. "How can I help you—what did you say your name was?"

"I didn't," said the man, his smile widening. "I like you Professor. And I don't want to hurt you or your friends. In fact, I can guarantee that no harm will come to you. Perhaps a sign of trust." He bowed slightly. "My name is Mitch Reynolds. My card," he said, stepping forward and pushing his watch down, exposing the inside of his left wrist.

"Triarii," observed Acton, his lips pursed. "But not the real Triarii."

Mitch smiled. "We're all *real* Triarii, just some of us have a different view on things."

"So you're the ones who kidnapped President Jackson's son?"

Mitch laughed, motioning to one of his men who ran up the steps to the main floor. "Kidnapped is such a strong word, with so many negative connotations." Two sets of feet appeared at the top of the steps, the first set descending tentatively into the basement, the face hidden by a bulkhead. When they finally came into view Acton gasped, causing the others in the room to look.

Before them stood Grant Jackson, apparent kidnap victim, looking none the worse for wear, with an awkward smile on his face as he stood facing Acton.

"As you can see, Professor Acton, Mr. Jackson is *with* us. He is not our captive, and is free to go at any time. Mr. Jackson has decided to see his father's work through, voluntarily."

"If you leave, I promise to tell the authorities that so they'll stop chasing you," said Acton, the sarcasm dripping through the speaker. He heard Laura giggle behind him.

Mitch tossed his head back, laughing, soon joined by the others, Grant as well, but if Acton didn't know better, more for show than anything else.

That guy looks far too uncomfortable to be here voluntarily.

"I love a good sense of humor, Professor Acton, but unfortunately don't have time for it." Mitch stepped closer to the glass. "You have found the location of the thirteenth skull. I want it."

Acton's eyes narrowed. "How did you find out we were here?"

Mitch waved his hand. "As much as I would like to discuss this situation further, I only have time for what we came for. You have the second half of the scroll?"

Acton removed his finger from the button and turned to look at Teufel, as had the others. He seemed uncomfortable in his chair, suddenly finding his fingernails very interesting. "Check his wrist!"

Reading stepped over and grabbed Teufel's left arm, shoving his watch out of the way. Reading grunted and turned the wrist so Acton could see.

"Triarii!"

Teufel tore his arm loose, giving Reading an annoyed look, then resumed his pleasant demeanor. "I'm sorry, Professors, but yes, I am Triarii. Always have been, in fact."

"And you're part of this breakaway group?" asked Laura.

Teufel nodded. "I truly am sorry for having deceived you. I must confess it wasn't always the case, but I was recently persuaded that the time has come to test our faith. If the skulls truly have powers, then the only way to prove so is to unite them. If nothing happens, then they are mere trinkets to be forgotten. But if something does happen, even if it is another cataclysmic event as our history tells us happened eight hundred years ago, then it will prove our faith hasn't been misguided, and will unite the Triarii once again in purpose!"

"You're all barmy!" exclaimed Reading, his phone to his ear. He suddenly spun away, talking low enough that Acton couldn't hear him from the other side of the room.

"Regardless of your opinion of us," continued Teufel, "you are under our control." He reached into his pocket and pulled out what looked like a small remote. He pressed a button and the dim red light that had surrounded the chamber suddenly went green. Acton grabbed a chair as Mitch stepped toward the decontamination chamber. He shoved it between the inner doors, preventing them from closing, which in turn prevented the outer doors from opening.

"Nice try," said Acton, making sure the chair wasn't at risk of rolling away as the doors tried again to close on it. He walked toward Teufel, his hand outstretched. "How about you hand that over."

Teufel reached in his other pocket and drew a gun. Acton raised his hands and stopped. Suddenly Reading's hand whipped out, his back still to Acton, but his side open enough for him to have a clear view of what was going on. The back of his hand made contact with Teufel's, the jarring impact causing the old man's hand to reflexively open, sending the gun clattering into the corner.

Acton pounced on it, immediately checking the safety then ejecting the magazine to see if it was indeed loaded. It was. He pointed the weapon at the floor as he faced Teufel. "Now how about you hand over that remote control?"

Teufel, his face flushed with anger and embarrassment at the frailty old age brings, handed the remote to Acton who immediately reactivated the lockdown. He turned back to Mitch, whose smile was gone. Reading stepped up beside him and pushed the button on the panel to talk.

"I just got off the phone with my friends at INTERPOL. German police have already been dispatched. I figure you have three minutes."

Mitch motioned for everyone to leave, but not before taking a step forward.

"This isn't over, Professor Acton. And next time I may not be so friendly."

Acton bowed slightly, as did Mitch, who then followed the rest of his men up the stairs. Acton turned to Reading.

"Why did you tell them? We could have just waited and they'd have been arrested."

Reading shook his head. "It could have turned into a firefight and that kid could have been killed. You could see just by looking at him that he's terrified. He has no clue what he's gotten himself into."

Acton bit his cheek, looking at the now vacant basement, remembering the look on the young Jackson's face, agreeing with Reading.

"He's going to have to get himself out of it on his own, otherwise he's not going to survive."

CIA Headquarters, Langley, Virginia
Present day, two days after the kidnapping

CIA analyst Chris Leroux jabbed at the screen, a smile on his face, spinning in his empty office cubicle on instinct, hoping to share his success with someone. As usual he was disappointed. He turned back to his keyboard, his fingers flying furiously as he packaged up the footage he had accessed by hacking the airport security feeds. Tracking the second plane to its destination outside of Munich, Germany had been easy—they had filed a flight plan and followed it. He had to admit the decoy aircraft was genius and fooled everyone, even if it had made no sense.

But now everyone was tasked with trying to find out where the passengers had gone. His boss, Director Morrison, had decided to bypass regular channels and have him hack the security system to save time, the red tape of getting it from the Germans would have probably taken at least a day.

Now Leroux had footage showing four men exiting the plane along with Grant Jackson, who was unrestrained and by outward appearances happy, or at a minimum, unafraid.

Something's not right.

He forwarded the footage to Morrison then began what he did best. Finding connections between apparently disparate things. The footage at the airport had shown them clear customs with incredible ease, especially since they had an apparent hostage with them. Grant Jackson could have at any point said something to security to ask for help, but he didn't. And he didn't even show a passport, merely being waved through with the others.

He sent a message to Morrison advising the security guard be investigated for collusion.

The cameras outside showed them being met by two men, handshakes exchanged, but not before young Mr. Jackson—easily five years older than Leroux—was put in the back of an idling SUV with blacked out windows. The new arrivals then split between two vehicles and what turned out to be a three vehicle convoy left the airport.

Leroux captured the license plates and sent off a request for traffic cameras feeds to be tapped to see if they could be traced, and for the local authorities to be on the outlook for the vehicles. As he leaned back in his chair, tapping his fingers on both armrests, he closed his eyes.

Why Munich?

If the aim were to hold on to Jackson, it made sense to keep him within the country and mobile. Placing him on a plane, even with the decoy, was very risky, then moving him to Europe with its larger population and confined spaces didn't make sense.

Unless their purpose was to deliver Jackson to a destination.

He knew from his briefing that the Triarii were based in London but were spread throughout every corner of the planet. Their wealth and numbers meant they most likely had contacts and safe houses pretty much everywhere, as was demonstrated with the Potomac farmhouse. A records search showed it belonged to the same family for generations, and they just happened to be away on vacation for a few days.

Leroux had no doubt they were Triarii, the tunnel proving it in his mind though they claimed to have known nothing about it.

But if the Triarii had taken Jackson to Europe, there had to be a purpose. The Triarii didn't need money, and the storage locker they had raided and the maid's testimony suggested they already had what they were looking for—a crystal skull. And that Jackson had gone willingly with them.

The maid's testimony had been corroborated by the footage with respect to the willingness of Jackson to remain with his captors, which meant he was probably intending to follow in his father's footsteps.

But what was the plan?

He knew from his briefing that apparently President Jackson's intent was to try and unite several skulls to unleash their supposed power. So if that were still the plan, then they must be on their way to retrieve other skulls.

And who are the skull experts?

He could think of only two, and quickly punched in the two professors so closely associated with the events in London. He smiled when he saw they had just landed in Munich the night before.

Coincidence? I think not!

Further checking showed the flight originating from Rome with INTERPOL Special Agent Hugh Reading also aboard.

Family reunion?

He launched several searches and within minutes had his answer. An emergency call had been made by Special Agent Reading that very morning local time. Leroux pulled up the police report. Neighbors had reported seeing three SUVs arrive and at least a dozen men exit with weapons. When police arrived they were all gone and only the home owner, a Mr. Teufel, remained, locked in a panic room. He claimed he had been alone when the men broke in and tried to gain access to his collection. They left when he had called the police.

At this point there appeared to be no explanation as to why the call had come from Reading except for Teufel's claim he had used the name to speed the process. It was clear to Leroux that the professors and Reading had been there when the Triarii arrived and had left before the police arrived. The question now was whether they left with the Triarii, or on their own. And if they left *with* the Triarii, was it willingly?

One of his searches popped up on his screen and he smiled as he saw a flight plan for Professor Palmer's plane filed earlier in the day. He now knew where the Professors were, and most likely where the Triarii and Grant Jackson were now heading.

Aboard Laura Palmer's Private Jet, En route to Israel

Present day, two days after the kidnapping

"Doesn't this thing cost you a fortune?" asked Reading as he leaned back in the sumptuous leather seating of the Gulf V. "Aren't they twenty or thirty million pounds?"

Laura laughed as she returned from the bathroom. "I don't own it, silly. I'm part of a leasing network. I have a share in the ownership of a fleet of planes positioned around the world. When I need one, I just call and it's arranged. *Much* cheaper."

"Still probably more than I make in a lifetime," said Reading with a sigh. "I need to start buying lottery tickets."

"It does help improve the odds of winning," said Acton as he took Laura's hand and gave it a triple-squeeze. "I still can't believe how quickly you were able to arrange the flight."

"Neither can I," replied Laura. "Last time I went to Israel I'm sure it took a few days. That was some time ago so perhaps things have improved."

Reading shook his head. "Don't count on it. I called Martin and he had his friends grease the wheels."

Acton blew a blast of air between his lips. "The Triarii are everywhere," he murmured, his mind drifting to his best friend Greg Milton and how he had been shot in the back and left for dead. Only recently had he begun to walk again, and still with effort.

"How is Martin doing?" asked Laura.

"Like he'd tell me," laughed Reading. "But I will say he sounded good. Lots of energy, spirits seemed to be up. I think us finishing this little mission of his will have him feeling fantastic."

Acton had to smile. Reading and Chaney were close, and he knew Reading thought of Chaney almost as a son, there being a significant age gap. Reading and his own son were estranged, only recently had he managed to even get the boy, now a young man, to talk to him, so Chaney, his younger partner for years, became his surrogate.

"I don't think I've ever seen you so enthused to come with us on one of our projects," observed Laura. "Perhaps we'll make an archeologist out of you yet!"

Reading's lips fluttered. "Phht! I don't think so. And this isn't archeology, this is a security job. You should have some of your SAS friends with you."

"They're too busy protecting the dig sites in Egypt and Peru," replied Laura. "I guess you'll have to do!"

"Bloody hell," muttered Reading.

Acton's phone buzzed, causing him to nearly jump in his seat. He pulled it from his pocket and looked at the message. It was a number with only two words accompanying it. *Call now!*

"It's him," said Acton, unable to hide the excitement in his voice. CIA Special Agent Dylan Kane was a former student of his. He had been in Acton's first year archeology course on a full ride football scholarship when 9/11 had happened. Within months the young man had sought Acton's counsel, wanting his opinion on Kane's thoughts of leaving college and joining the military.

Acton, himself a former reservist who had served in Gulf War I, was never one to discourage military service, and had merely acted as a sounding board. Kane had left and joined the army, excelling and quickly reaching the rank of Sergeant. As soon as he attained the rank he had applied for and won a spot in the Delta Force. Within a couple of years of that he had been recruited by the CIA. None of his latter career had been known to Acton until Kane had shown up at his class one day about a year ago, a different man, a damaged man, a secret from his past haunting him.

Acton had seen or spoken to him several times since, and was given an email address that was monitored either by him or on his behalf should he need his help.

Getting into the West Bank was something Acton thought Kane might indeed be able to help them with, so when they had left Teufel's house before the police arrived, he had sent a simple message. *Need your help.*

He dialed the number, Laura and Reading now silent.

"Hello, Doc!"

Acton smiled at the energy in the young man's voice. "Hello Dylan, how are you?"

"Not too shabby, Doc. How's the future Mrs. Acton?"

Acton glanced at Laura, winking. "She's fine and sitting here with Special Agent Hugh Reading. Can I put you on speaker?"

"Go ahead, you'll tell them everything I say regardless."

Acton laughed and pressed the button to go hands free. "Okay, you're on speaker."

"Hello Laura, Special Agent Reading. I understand you need my help. Are you guys about to cause another international incident?"

Laura laughed with Acton, Reading merely grunted in agreement. "With these two it's always something like that," he said.

"Yes, I've read their files," laughed Kane. His voice became serious. "What can I do for you?"

Acton quickly gave him a rundown of what had happened, being careful to include his thoughts on Grant Jackson's involvement and how willingly he may actually be participating. "So the bottom line is we need to get into Israel, specifically the West Bank near the city of Jericho, St. Gerasimos Monastery."

"Christ, Doc, when you ask a favor they're big!" laughed Kane. There was a pause then Kane's voice came through, serious again. "When you get there you'll be met. Follow their instructions to the letter. Understood?"

"Yes," said Acton. "Met by who?"

"I'll worry about that. And Doc?"

"Yes."

"Be careful. What you're asking for is big, and it's dangerous. These people will kill you as soon as help you. Do what they say, don't ask questions, and try not to look around too much."

Acton felt a shiver race up and down his spine. "Understood Dylan. And thanks."

"Don't thank me Doc until you make it out of this alive."

The line went dead and Acton looked at Laura who was clearly disturbed by Kane's words. He glanced at Reading whose teeth were clenched, his jaw square.

"You know who we'll be dealing with, don't you?" asked Reading.

Acton nodded. "I'm assuming Mossad?"

Reading shook his head. "No. Based on that conversation, either Fatah or worse, Hamas."

"Oh dear," murmured Laura, curling her legs up under her.

Acton nodded slowly.

We're being delivered into the hands of terrorists.

Over the Adriatic, En route to Israel

Present day, two days after the kidnapping

Grant Jackson picked at his fingernails, absentmindedly staring out the window at the waters far below. He had barely had any sleep since he had been kidnapped, the drug induced stupor he had been in the first night barely counting, and last night in Munich at a safe house was filled with tossing and turning and nightmares.

And now he was on his way to Israel, a country he had always wanted to visit, but not this way.

What the hell am I doing?

These people were criminals, wanted by every police force in the world by now, and were chasing crystal skulls around the planet thinking they had godlike powers. It was ridiculous. And his father had believed in it? The more he thought about what was going on right now, and what he had been told happened when his father was killed, the more he began to second guess his decision to see his father's work through.

Lesley Darbinger had been a friend to the family for as long as his memories went back. Darbinger was a good man, and now that he knew the brain tumor story was pure fiction, it meant that Darbinger had killed his father as a completely sane man. And if Darbinger didn't have a brain tumor, then who ordered the Delta Force to murder those students in Peru and all those people in London? If it wasn't Darbinger, then it was obviously his father. Which would make sense.

Darbinger killed Dad to stop him from killing any more people!

He felt the blood drain from his face as he suddenly felt faint. He sucked in a deep breath, trying to calm himself, continuing to stare out the window, praying no one noticed he had begun to shake.

Keep it together!

His mind was reeling with the implications. It was his own father that had given the Delta Force their orders. It was his own father that was responsible for all those deaths.

He deserved to die!

Tears filled his eyes at the thought, and he silently begged forgiveness for thinking them, but he knew he was right. Any man who would order so many innocent deaths over something as trivial as a stone carving didn't deserve to live. Lesley Darbinger had done the right thing.

And now here he was surrounded by his father's allies, those who supported him in his cause, and those who he had no doubt wouldn't hesitate to kill if anyone got in their way.

And they're everywhere!

They had just breezed through customs in Germany, the guard just giving them a nod when Mitch had flashed the tattoo on his wrist. Now they were on their way to Israel with a false passport for him that had been waiting for them in Munich.

How do you escape a group that's everywhere?

There were eight of them on the plane. When there were only four he could have walked away, but now he was in so deep he had no idea if they'd let him go. Even asking the question terrified him, the response potentially a bullet to the head.

For now his best bet was to continue playing along with them and try to find an opportunity to escape. But if he were to escape, how could he guarantee his safety from them? His shoulders dropped in defeat. He knew there was no escaping.

The only question that was relevant, was whether or not he even had to.

Over the Mediterranean, En route to Israel

Present day, two days after the kidnapping

Dawson sat in the back of the Hercules C130J as it rattled on even louder than its predecessors. *You'd think they'd invest a little in quieting things down!* He lay on one of the cots attached to the fuselage, the rest of his team, including one last minute addition from the CIA, Agent Sherrie White, doing the same, some asleep, some reading, some playing with their smartphones. For once he had finally managed to remember his Kindle and had read himself to sleep. But something had woken him.

The comm screeched in his headset again.

"Sergeant Major, you've got a call."

Dawson was immediately alert, swinging his legs off the cot, sitting upright. "Put it through," he said, adjusting the large noise cancelling headset wrapped around his head.

"Hey, old buddy! I didn't wake you, did I?"

Dawson immediately recognized the voice of Dylan Kane, a former member of his unit gone rogue—CIA Special Activities Division. If Dawson thought what *he* did was under the radar, it was nothing like what Kane was up to. Dawson had been approached to join the CIA on more than one occasion, but had refused, preferring the company of The Unit rather than the solitary existence of an operative.

"As a matter of fact you did," said Dawson with a smile.

"Good. Too much beauty sleep will make you stand out in a crowd," laughed Kane, then his voice became serious. "Can you talk?"

"I'm in the back of a Herc. Not even God can hear me."

"Good to see you're still a blasphemer," jabbed Kane. "Listen, our professor friends contacted me."

"Uh oh."

"Exactly. It looks like they're somehow mixed up with this Grant Jackson bit."

Dawson's eyes rolled. "How the hell did they manage that?"

"It would appear that Jackson was taken by an offshoot of the Triarii, the same offshoot that Jackson senior was part of. They're after crystal skulls to try and unite them or some bullshit like that. Anyway, the professors were in Munich in search of a skull when guess who shows up?"

"The nutbars with Jackson happily at their side."

"Good guess."

"Good intel from your friend."

"Ahh, my good buddy Chris is still proving to be valuable, excellent. Well, here's the latest. Acton and his fiancée along with that Special Agent from INTERPOL are heading to Israel right now."

"So are we."

"I figured you'd be on the case what with your previous involvement. Now here's a part of the puzzle I'm pretty sure you don't know about."

"What's that?"

"I've arranged for them to get into the West Bank."

Dawson's eyebrows shot up and he let out a slow whistle that he was sure sounded like static on the other end. "How the hell did you manage that?"

"Don't ask and I won't have to kill you. Let's just say these guys aren't playing for our side, and money is the only thing keeping our friends alive. They're supposed to be going to an old Greek monastery outside Jericho called St. Gerasimos. Apparently there's a skull hidden there."

"Of course there is."

Kane chuckled. "Exactly, but whatever we think of it, somebody believes and is willing to kill with respect to it. Here's the bottom line. I'm getting them in. If they survive and actually reach the monastery, they're going to need a way out. I don't trust my guys to do it since they're probably going to kill them and steal whatever they found. You're probably going to have to get them out."

"Just how the hell am I supposed to manage that?"

Dawson could almost imagine Kane grinning on the other end. "You'll think of something. You're coordinating with Mossad, aren't you?"

"Yeah, but now I have to kill you."

"Next time. Anyway, if the Triarii are after the professors, then there might be trouble so be ready for it. And remember, don't trust Jackson. He seems to be working with them now."

"Got it. And Dylan?"

"Yeah."

"Lose my number."

Kane roared in laughter then the call ended. Dawson motioned Red over.

"What's up, BD?"

"You're not going to believe the shit I just heard."

Ben Gurion Airport, Israel

Present day, two days after the kidnapping

James Acton handed over his passport to the customs officer. Reading had gone first, his INTERPOL identification speeding the process along somewhat. Laura had gone next and her smile and treasure chest had her through almost as quickly.

He, they decided to give the third degree to.

Endless questions, repeated questions, examining of the passport, reexamining of the passport, searching of his luggage, scanning of his luggage.

Do I fit the profile of a terrorist?

"You are an archeologist, Dr. Acton?"

"Yes." *For the fourth time.*

"And do you intend to seek out any of our cultural treasures while you are here?"

"If they're in a museum, yes."

"Do you intend to remove any of these treasures from our country?"

"Of course not."

"Our information says otherwise, Dr. Acton."

Acton's heart leapt but he kept it hidden from his face. He hoped.

"Then your information is wrong."

"Why are you really here, Dr. Acton?"

"As I said before, we're here on vacation. We want to visit the holy sites. A sort of pilgrimage."

"With a flight plan filed today?"

"We were surprised how quickly we got that approved as well, but my fiancée is rather wealthy and we are both well-known in our field, so that may have sped up the process."

"I've never heard of you, Dr. Acton."

"But you're not an archeologist."

The man handed over Acton's passport then scratched his wrist, moving his watch band. Acton nearly pissed his pants.

The Triarii tattoo!

"Remember, Dr. Acton, we are always watching. Should you need any assistance, call our tourist bureau."

The officer slid a card over the counter toward him. Acton took it and quickly pocketed it.

"Thank you."

"Have a good day, Doctor."

"You too."

He grabbed his bags and as casually as he could walked toward where Laura and Reading were waiting. The three said nothing as they exited the terminal.

"Hallo, what's this?" asked Reading, motioning toward a man holding a sign.

Dr. Action.

"You're a superhero, honey!" gushed Laura, elbowing him.

"Don't let it go to your bloody head," muttered Reading as they walked over to the man in a chauffeur's uniform.

"I'm Dr. Acton."

The man bowed, crumpling the paper and stuffing it in his pocket. "I am here to take you to your hotel."

"I don't remember ordering a car," said Acton, thoughts of Rome flashing through his head.

"He did say we'd be met," whispered Laura.

Acton nodded, his suspicious nature getting the better of him. He smiled at the driver who pointed to a large black limo parked nearby. "Please, leave your luggage, I will take care of it," said the man who scurried over to the rear door and opened it. Laura climbed in then Acton followed by Reading. The door was shut and they watched as the man, whose name they never got, loaded their bags in the trunk.

"What do you think?" asked Acton, glancing at Reading.

"I don't know. This cloak and dagger thing was never my area. Your friend Kane said we'd be met. I would assume if we were being met by someone else, they would have intervened."

"That's a good point," agreed Laura, looking out the window. "I don't see anybody making a scene."

Acton had to agree. If Kane had sent somebody to meet them, and they were actually here on time, then they wouldn't have let them get in the limo. *But if they weren't on time?*

The front door opened and their chauffeur/kidnapper climbed in, then looked through the rear panel with a smile. "Relax, my friends. We have about a forty minute drive ahead of us. But before you know it, you'll be at your hotel!"

The car started forward gently, the man pulling out into the light airport traffic as the rear panel closed. Within minutes they were heading toward Jerusalem, nobody saying anything, all just watching out the windows for anything out of the ordinary. Acton was dying to tell the others about the Triarii border guard and what he had said, but couldn't risk the limo being bugged.

It will have to wait for the hotel.

Acton decided to take the opportunity to nap, succeeding in minutes. A gentle elbow woke him as they pulled up to their hotel, the King David.

Their driver stopped and popped the trunk, bellhops immediately jumping at their luggage. Their door was opened and Reading climbed out followed by Acton. He looked around and saw nothing suspicious. Holding out his hand he helped Laura out then followed Reading into the hotel, their bags trailing them on a luggage cart. Check-in was swift, tips were paid—generous for the driver since he hadn't kidnapped them—and within minutes they were in their rooms, Laura and Acton sharing one, Reading in an adjoining.

Laura showered as Acton examined the amenities, then he joined her, tired of waiting. A good round of hanky panky was interrupted by knocking at their door. Acton frowned as Laura gave him a kiss then left him wagging as she stepped out of the shower and wrapped a towel around herself.

"It's Hugh!" he heard her yell, allowing him to relax slightly as he finished showering, evidence of the team sports having receded by the time he finished. He stepped out into the room and Laura returned to the bathroom. He pulled a pair of underwear on under his towel so Reading wouldn't have to be embarrassed by a locker room kibble and bits display, then tossed the towel on the back of a chair.

"So what are we supposed to do now?" asked Reading.

"He said we'd be met."

"And we were."

"Were we?"

"Bah! You professors talk in riddles. What the bloody hell do you mean?"

Acton smiled, recognizing Reading's frustration with the situation. Like him, Reading hated not being in control, and right now they clearly weren't in control. They were in a foreign country, waiting for person or persons unknown to smuggle them illegally into a very dangerous part of Israel, where the rule of law meant little.

Thank God we're not going to Gaza.

The West Bank was a paradise compared to Gaza. He sometimes wondered why everyone spoke of a "two state solution". Why not three? Israel could recognize the West Bank, make peace with that one territory, leaving the Gaza Strip to rot with its terrorist Hamas running the show. Word would get back pretty quick on how much better things were on the other side.

He dismissed the thought. *As long as the leadership on one side of the negotiations insists the other be extinguished from existence, there can be no peace.* But today they were hoping to gain access to the more peaceful enclave, retrieve an artifact hidden there for over seven hundred years, then somehow miraculously make it back out alive.

"I wonder…" he began.

"You wonder what, dear?"

Acton looked up as Laura entered the room, ready to go, her clothes "dig-site" chic—shorts, button up shirt with sleeves rolled up, lots of pockets, hat sitting on the chair, work boots on the floor.

And she's still smokin'!

Acton lost his train of thought for a moment as he appreciated how lucky a man he was, then quickly jumped up realizing he wasn't ready himself. He began to dress and talk at the same time.

"I was thinking about how we're going to get out," he began. "Let's say we can't trust these guys to get us out without killing us, or stealing the skull once we have it—"

"We can probably count on that," muttered Reading.

"Well, what if we get ourselves away from them—"

"And just how would we do that?" interrupted Reading.

"Bear with me," said Acton as he buttoned up his shirt. "Perhaps they abandon us, perhaps there's another way out, who knows. Bottom line, let's say we need to get out having survived their attempt on us, there's still a way out."

"How?" asked Laura, waving off Reading's retort.

"The border," replied Acton as he rolled up his sleeves. "Just go to one of the checkpoints, go through with our passports and deal with the consequences on the other side."

"It might work, but you'd probably have that crystal bastard taken away from you," said Reading.

"Oh! Which reminds me!" exclaimed Acton. "At the airport, the security guy was Triarii!"

Reading almost burst from his chair. "What?"

"Yeah, he showed me his tattoo when he handed me back my passport. He said something like, 'we're watching you and if you ever need help we'll be there.' He gave me a card." He grabbed his pants from earlier and rifled through the pockets. On his third go he found the small rectangle of thick paper and pulled it out, holding it up triumphantly. "This could be our way out!"

There was a knock at the door.

Acton shoved the card in the pocket of his shorts and he positioned himself between the door and Laura, Reading already peering through the peephole. He looked over at them. "It's the driver."

Acton's eyebrows jumped for a moment. "Let him in, I guess."

Reading nodded, unlocking the door with a frown. He pulled it open and stepped back, Acton noticing a clenched fist at the ready.

Their driver stepped inside.

"Are we ready?" he asked.

"For what?" asked Acton, examining the man for any obvious weapon bulges.

The man closed the door, but not before looking up and down the hallway. “I was told you require transport to a—shall we say—*difficult* destination. I am it.”

“And just how do *you* expect to get us in,” asked Reading, fists still clenched.

“Because I am Alamar, and it is my job to get people and things in and out.” He looked at Reading then at the man’s clenched fists, frowning. “I suggest you don’t ask too many questions. They can be dangerous, especially with my friends.” He pointed at the fists. “And those won’t help you.” Alamar slapped his hands together, a smile suddenly returning to his face. “Now, are we going, or what?”

Acton nodded, realizing they had no choice, and this was probably as friendly as it was going to get. “Yes.”

“Good. Then take everything you need with you, and I suggest”—he nodded at Laura’s left hand—“you leave all valuables in the safe.” Laura looked at her engagement ring, it in Acton’s opinion embarrassingly modest compared to what he felt she deserved, but on a professor’s salary, modesty was the order of the day.

But she loved it, that much was obvious. She nodded, removing it, along with her earrings and a bracelet. Acton took them then put them in the room’s safe, along with his own watch.

“What about our passports?” asked Laura.

Alamar shook his head. “They will do you no good where you are going and are worth more than gold. Definitely leave them.”

As Acton complied he had the distinct impression that all of their valuables were merely being put into one convenient place for someone to come along after they were gone and help themselves. As he put the passports into the safe, he palmed the engagement ring.

"Okay, let's go," he said, Alamar immediately opening the door and looking both ways. They followed him, Acton taking up the rear as he unrolled his sleeve, deposited the ring in the fold of the cuff, then rolled it back up.

Now as long as I don't lose my shirt.

Alamar walked past the elevators, leading them farther down the hall.

"Ah, where are we going?" asked Reading.

"Service elevator. More private."

Acton could feel his pulse quicken and the hairs on the back of his neck tingle as he traded glances with Reading, the silent exchange making it obvious they were both thinking the same thing.

Something's wrong.

But then again they were with someone who was going to illegally get them into the West Bank. He was obviously either a criminal or a terrorist—either way an undesirable—and those they were going to probably meet over the coming hours just as much so.

They arrived at the large doors of the service elevator and Alamar pressed the button. Acton watched as Alamar looked up and down the hall, clearly nervous about being seen. Acton wondered if Alamar realized the big black dome above his head was a security camera.

A chime sounded and the doors opened, the elevator empty. They all boarded and Alamar pressed the button for the parking level. The doors closed and Acton had the odd feeling that this might be his last trip in an elevator. He squeezed Laura's hand and she squeezed it back.

The chime sounded again and the doors opened. Alamar stepped outside, Reading first to follow. As Acton stepped into the parking garage a van burst from nowhere, screeching to a halt directly in from of them. The side panel slid open and four men burst out, AK-47s aimed at the trio. The doors behind them were just beginning to close. Acton shoved Laura back toward the doors and she fell inside with a yelp as Acton spread his arms trying to cover her escape. Reading already had a barrel pressed against his chest, two approaching Acton as he backed up, still trying to block the elevator.

He glanced over his shoulder and saw Laura climbing to her feet, reaching for the panel to press a floor, the doors almost closed, when Alamar calmly stepped into sight and waved his arm between the door sensors causing them to open again. Acton made eye contact with Laura, his chest tight with the knowledge he had failed to protect her.

Suddenly the wind was knocked out of him and he dropped to his knees, gripping his stomach where someone had butted him with their Kalashnikov. His hands were grabbed and he was zip tied, a black sack pulled over his head. Dragged to his feet, he was tossed into the back of the van where he smacked his head on something hard and unforgiving, knocking him out cold, the last sounds he heard those of Laura screaming and Reading cursing them all to hell.

Unknown location, Israel

Present day, two days after the kidnapping

Acton awoke, his head pounding, a searing pain making itself known through the side of his skull. Everything was black and he felt something over his face. He tried to reach up to remove it but found his hands bound, his situation suddenly rushing back with a gasp.

"Laura!"

"No talking!" yelled a voice he didn't recognize.

"I'm here," came a whisper from his left. He sighed in relief knowing she was okay.

He kept his voice as low as he could, the sounds of an engine whining ahead of them and an exhaust in desperate need of repair roaring behind them making it difficult for them to hear, and he hoped for their abductors as well. "Hugh?"

"I'm bloody well here," came the muttered return through what Acton was sure was a clenched jaw.

"I said no talking!" Acton felt a kick to his legs.

A burst of Arabic from what sounded like Alamar had his kicker sounding contrite. After a few minutes of what seemed like quite calm driving, signal lights clicking, stops seemingly obeyed, they came to a halt, the engine turning off. Acton had no way of knowing how long he had been unconscious, but it couldn't have been that long. The sound of the side door opening to his left then the feeling of hands pulling him toward the door had him hoping this portion of their ordeal was over.

The question was what was next? Were they now to be held prisoner, ransom demands made for their release? Laura was rich. Getting ten or twenty million out of her would go a long way to fund their terrorist activities.

We never should have come!

At this very moment he hated the Triarii. He hated the crystal skulls. He hated the Pope. He hated Martin Chaney. He hated every goddamned thing connecting to any of them. He wanted them all out of their lives, permanently. He just wanted to get back to his college, stand in front of his class and teach. No guns, no terrorists, no constant threats to his life.

He wanted to get married and start a new life.

A powerful grip on his arm led him somewhere, where, he had no idea, but he had the distinct impression they were inside. Suddenly the bag was yanked off his head and he began to blink rapidly, trying to adjust his eyes to the sudden flood of light. He felt a jerk at his wrists as the zip tie was cut and he instinctively rubbed them as he looked around. Laura was to his left and he immediately put his arm protectively over her shoulders, pulling her toward him. Reading was to the right, glowering at the group of men standing in front of them, including Alamar.

Alamar held out his hands. "I must apologize for this, but we couldn't risk you knowing where we were going."

"And just putting us in the van and asking us to wear the hoods wasn't an option?" asked Reading, his voice dripping with sarcasm.

Alamar shrugged then smiled. "Usually they don't go willingly." He smacked his hands together as the other men laughed. He pointed to a table. "Now, sit. We will eat and have something to drink, then when it is morning, we will go."

"You still haven't told us how we're getting there," said Acton, holding a chair for Laura as she sat down.

"You will see soon enough," said Alamar as he shouted in Arabic for food to be brought. Several women appeared in traditional Arab garb with platters of food that to Acton at this moment smelled fantastic. His stomach rumbled and Reading gave him a "how can you be hungry at a time like this?" look. Acton shrugged with his eyes, and dug in.

"Eat up," he said. "You're going to need your strength for tomorrow, that I can guarantee."

Laura was already reaching for the hummus. "He's right," she said. "Who knows if we'll get to eat at all tomorrow."

Reading shook his head, poster boy for the "don't break bread with thine enemy" campaign, finally overwhelmed by the delicious aromas and his own hunger.

They were left alone, the "guards" in the next room. One of the women would occasionally check on them as they ate in relative silence, afraid that any conversation would be overheard. After they were finished they were shown into a room with several cots and questionably clean linens.

"You sleep! You sleep!" urged an elderly woman who then closed the door.

"Sounds good to me," said Acton, lying on one of the cots, Reading again the reluctant follower.

"If I ever get out of this I'm putting Martin back in a coma," he muttered.

Acton chuckled, rolling to his side and falling asleep within minutes, trying not to worry about what hell the crystal skulls would bring them when they woke up.

Unknown location, Israel

Present day, three days after the kidnapping

"James!"

Acton grunted then rolled over, opening his eyes to find Laura leaning over him, her hand on his shoulder shaking him gently. He blinked a few times, rubbing the sleep out of them, feeling far better rested than he thought he should.

"What time is it?" he asked as he slowly swung out of the cot.

"Almost four in the bloody morning," replied Reading as he stretched his arms behind his back. "I *just* fell asleep I'm sure ten minutes ago."

Laura gave him an accusatory look. "I can assure you from that god-awful sound erupting from your throat you were asleep for hours."

"What god-awful sound?"

"You snore."

"No I don't."

"Yes you do." Laura held up her phone and tapped it. Immediately a sound emerged from the speaker that had Reading flush, his cheeks burning red and Acton roaring with laughter.

"That's not me," muttered Reading, standing up and doing some more stretches. "You just downloaded that from the Internet. There's no way Martin would have let me get away with that in Egypt. We were sharing a bloody tent!"

Laura laughed, killing the recording. "You got me! I downloaded it. Although there were a few good snorts out of you."

"You're getting his bloody sense of humor," said Reading, bending over to touch his toes but failing miserably, instead tapping his knees as if that were his intention. "Bah! Getting old sucks!"

Acton nodded in sympathy, his own bones and muscles needing more tender loving care lately than he remembered. He stood, did a quick check of himself in the mirror, nobody having brought any toiletries and none apparently available. Reading did the same, and Laura, looking impeccable, Acton assumed had already partaken before waking them up.

As if on cue Alamar stepped into the room.

"Ready?"

Acton nodded and took Laura's hand. They followed Alamar through several rooms then down a set of stairs into what appeared to be a basement where several bearded men with green and white balaclavas pulled down over their faces stood, only the glare of angry eyes showing. Acton had the distinct impression they weren't happy to have them as visitors.

A cabinet was moved aside by two of the guards and an entrance was revealed. Alamar went first, motioning for them to follow. Acton bent over and stepped inside a rather larger room than he was expecting, bags of food and crates of weapons piled everywhere. Laura and Reading quickly followed and Alamar pointed to a hole in the floor. Acton stepped toward it and saw a set of steep stairs dropping at least thirty feet.

"This tunnel leads to the West Bank, as you call it. Be careful going down the stairs, they are *very* steep. Once you get to the bottom, walk as quickly as you can to the other end. There you will find another set of steps. Once at the top, if the entrance is closed, knock three times, then once, then three times again. This is important," said Alamar, pausing. "Three, then one, then three. Like this." He knocked the pattern out on the wall. "They will then knock twice. If you do not hear that knock, wait five minutes and try again. If you hear three knocks in response, there is a problem and you must return here, as fast as you can. Repeat the knock at this end."

"What kind of problem could there be?" asked Acton.

"If Fatah has raided the house, they will kill anyone coming through. If you do not do the proper knock and wait for the proper acknowledgement, *we* will kill anyone who comes through. Understood?"

Acton understood perfectly, as did the others by their concerned looks. Fatah was the quasi-terrorist organization that now ran the West Bank. Hamas was the out-and-out terrorist group that controlled Gaza. During "elections", Fatah won in the West Bank, but Hamas won in Gaza, promptly killing all the Fatah party members in their territory. No further elections have been held.

So much for Middle Eastern democracy expanding beyond Israel.

"What should we expect at the other end?" asked Acton.

"You will be provided with transport to the monastery as requested. You will be blindfolded again for a short period so you can't lead anyone back to the tunnel. Acceptable?"

"Absolutely," replied Acton. "I assume we won't have any *misunderstandings* like last time?"

Alamar smiled. "I like you, Professor Acton. I think in another life you could have been a diplomat." He paused suddenly, eyeballing Acton. "None of you are Jews, are you?"

Acton shook his head. "No, otherwise I'm certain we wouldn't have been delivered into your hands by our friend."

Alamar's lips pursed as his head bobbed, examining the three of them for a moment.

"No, I don't think you are. I can recognize Jews. They look much like swine!" He laughed and the guards roared with him. Acton made it a point to not have even a hint of frivolity show on his face.

Swine are those who have no intention of ever living in peace.

"Shall we go?" he asked, motioning toward the hole.

Alamar, still laughing at his own joke nodded. "Please."

Acton eyed the hole, debating how to get to the first step without breaking his neck, there no handholds or anything to hold on to at the top. He opted for sitting down on the floor and dangling his legs over the edge then placing his feet on the first step. From there he pushed himself up, using his hands on the floor to steady himself, then step-by-step began the long climb down. He paused to make sure Laura was able to begin the trip safely, then resumed his descent.

It felt like half an hour but was more likely five minutes before he came to the bottom of the steps. He had no doubt those who used the tunnel on a regular basis would make the descent in less than a minute, but Acton wasn't willing to risk his neck, or those of his companions, by setting too eager a pace.

He glanced down the tunnel and found it to be about seven feet tall, four feet wide and stretching for as far as the eye could see, lights every fifty feet showing the way. He turned, his arms out, ready to catch Laura should she fall, but she reached the bottom without incident, as did a none-too-pleased Reading.

"Don't forget! Three then one then three!" yelled Alamar down the stairwell. "Oh, and if the lights go out, just keep walking until you reach the stairs. They go out all the time!"

Acton looked up, frowning at this latest revelation, then saw something moved over the hole, covering it and blocking the light from above.

"Let's get this done with," he said, setting a brisk pace forward. There was no point in running; being exhausted at the other end when they had no idea what to expect was senseless. And the last thing he wanted was to be running at a sprint and have the lights go out.

They walked for a good five minutes, the tunnel far longer than Acton would have imagined, the amount of work necessary to dig such a hole jaw dropping. *Where did they put all the dirt?* He was reminded of one of his favorite movies, The Great Escape. Loosely based on a true story, the inmates at a Prisoner of War camp in Germany began digging three tunnels resulting in massive amounts of dirt that had to be cleverly hidden or disposed of.

And those tunnels were barely big enough to crawl through.

This was a feat of engineering.

And it was a Hamas tunnel. Not aimed at helping those on the other side, but of arming a rebellion to try and either overthrow the elected Fatah government, or begin a civil war to destabilize it.

No construction supplies were moving through these tunnels.

The lights flickered and Acton looked up at the incandescent bulbs then down the tunnel.

"I think I see the end," he said over his shoulder. He looked again. *Or maybe not.* There was a darkness in the distance that either was the end, or else the lights weren't working farther on.

As they approached his heart began to sink. *It's the lights.* "Sorry, I was wrong. Lights are out ahead."

"Blast!" Reading's outburst echoed up and down the tunnel. "Sorry," he mumbled.

"Let's all join hands for the rest of the way," said Acton as they approached the end of the functioning lighting. He reached back and felt Laura taking his hand. They continued into the darkness, slower now that he could see nothing, his left hand behind him, his right out front, waving back and forth as if it were some sort of sensor.

His foot hit something sending him tumbling forward, his outstretched hand breaking his fall as it encountered something hard almost directly in front of him. Instinctively he had let go of Laura's hand, reaching forward with both. He felt Laura bump into him then Reading into her.

"I think we might be there," whispered Acton, not wanting to startle anyone who might be above. He felt in front of him and confirmed they were definitely steps. "Okay, I can feel the steps. You two wait here, I'll go up."

"I should go," said Reading.

"Forget it. I need you to get Laura back to the other end if there's a problem. Don't wait for me, take care of her. Understood?"

He could only imagine the expression on Reading's face, it pitch black where they were, the lights in the far distance not even casting a shadow.

"Understood. At least let me get ahead of you, Laura. If anything happens, you run, don't wait for me," said Reading.

"Okay, but don't you two play hero."

"Who, me?" asked both Reading and Acton in unison.

"You two have been spending too much time together!"

Acton flashed a smile at where he thought Reading stood, imagining one in return. "Okay, here goes nothing." He felt with his foot for the first step and gained it, then began slowly climbing toward the top, it too pitch black. There wasn't a sliver of light above them, and as he climbed, he could actually see a hint of light below, reinforcing how dark this new area actually was.

His head hit the top first. He instinctively ducked, massaging the top of his head, then reached up, knocking three times, pausing, knocking once, pausing, then knocking three times, mimicking Alamar as closely as he could.

He waited for a reply, but none came. Cocking an ear, he could hear nothing at all. No footsteps, no talking, nothing.

"Anything?" came a harsh whisper from below. It was Reading.

"No," he replied with barely a whisper. Alamar had said to wait five minutes before trying again, but to him that sounded an eternity, especially as he balanced on the stairs, the balls of his feet barely fitting on them, his heels hanging off the ends, no rails to hold on to. At the moment he was balanced with both hands out at his sides, pushing against the walls.

He reached up to knock again when he heard two short raps then a scraping sound. Sweet, brilliant, blinding light shone through as the opening was revealed. A hand reached in and he took it, the powerful grip almost hoisting him from the hole. Acton smiled at the man, thanking him with a nod. He glanced around and saw several men in a windowless room, most likely another basement, all armed, all with Hamas balaclavas covering their faces.

Acton made a judgment call, kneeling by the hole, the staircase now well-lit from above. He could see Reading's face looking up.

"It's okay, come on up."

Laura switched places and began the climb, Reading several steps behind her should she fall. Within a couple of minutes they were both in the room, dusting themselves off and enjoying the light.

"What now?" asked Acton of the room. One of the men stepped forward, handing them three black sacks. Acton frowned. "That's what I figured."

At least this time there's no hitting.

Megiddo Airport, Israel

Present day, three days after the kidnapping

If Grant Jackson had any hope of gaining his freedom through the guards at the airport he was sadly mistaken. As he followed Mitch and the others down the small stairs of yet another private aircraft, this one different from the one they had left the United States in, he looked around to find it dark out and their plane having been taxied to the far end of the airport.

At the foot of the steps stood two men in uniforms of some type. Both shook Mitch's hands before leading them to four large sedans parked nearby, all with drivers waiting behind the wheels.

"I trust these will meet your needs," said what appeared to be the senior of the two Israeli's who had greeted them.

"I'm sure they will. Any word yet on where our friends have gone?"

"Yes, as a matter of fact," replied the first. "As suspected they used one of the illegal tunnels to enter the West Bank."

Mitch whistled. "I'm stunned they knew how."

"So was I so I did some digging and found out that *they* didn't arrange it. It was arranged for them by somebody else."

"Who?" asked Mitch.

The man shook his head. "My contacts wouldn't tell me. I got the distinct impression they were more afraid of whoever arranged their passage than they were of me."

"Understood. And did they cross?"

"Yes," nodded the man. "They were seen leaving not even an hour ago."

"And their destination?"

"A monastery near Jericho. St. Gerasimos."

Mitch frowned, looking at his watch. "How quickly can you get us there?"

The man shook his head. "Not before they get there, but soon."

Mitch motioned for everyone to get in the vehicles. "Let's go. Fast as possible."

The man nodded and Grant climbed into the back of one of the cars, Mitch joining him along with two others. Doors slammed all around and the driver tossed several black sacks into the back seat.

"Put these on!" he ordered.

Mitch handed one of the bags to Grant, shrugging his shoulders. "When in Rome."

Grant frowned but placed the bag over his head, and as the darkness enveloped him, his hopelessness grew, yet another opportunity to escape gone. The Triarii seemed to be everywhere.

But are they Triarii, or the offshoot?

He wondered how a breakaway group could have so many contacts, so many people helping them around the world. And then a thought occurred to him.

What if the Triarii helping them don't realize they're part of the breakaway group?

From what he could gather in talking with Mitch over the past day, they were a small but growing group who didn't want to destroy the Triarii, but merely take it in a different direction, and if they were proven wrong in their beliefs, they were perfectly willing to come back into the fold. And from what he could also gather, the Triarii were tightlipped, the members fed little information they didn't need to know, which in Grant's mind meant that outside of the leadership circle, few if any Triarii knew about this breakaway group.

Which might mean they were helping them not because they supported their beliefs, but merely because their orders were to help any Triarii that requested it.

It gave Grant a sliver of hope to cling to. His theory might not even be right, but for now it was all he had, otherwise he had to believe that he was in the hands of an organization so big, it stretched the world, and was at war with an even bigger organization.

He leaned his head against the window, his memories of three nights ago and a simpler life flooding back. A pit formed in his stomach as he remembered Louisa begging him not to go, and he, the fool, ignoring her pleas, instead smiling and waving at her.

Idiot.

Tel Nof Airbase, Israel

Present day, three days after the kidnapping

Burt Dawson watched as his men prepped their civie clothes, walking through Jerusalem in their spec ops gear probably not a good idea. CIA Agent Sherrie White was already in civilian attire and Dawson had to admit was a fantastic looking woman who was apparently spoken for. He gave his head a mental shake as he pictured the CIA geek that apparently had won her heart.

Lucky bastard.

He had met Leroux during the New Orleans crisis. He seemed like a good kid. Brilliant, of that there was no doubt. Good looking too in an awkward kind of way.

There's no accounting for taste.

His mind drifted to Maggie. At least ten years White's senior, but another fantastic looking woman. He just wondered if she were right for him, and whether or not getting into a relationship was the right thing.

Why the hell not? Half the guys are married, the other half have girlfriends. Why not you?

Their Hercules came to a halt and he took a look out one of the small windows. It was dark outside, little artificial light in the area. Several vehicles were pulling to a stop nearby, clearly their escort.

"Ready?" he asked their CIA liaison who gave a quick nod.

The rear ramp lowered and Dawson exited first, chivalry having no place in the military. Agent White followed as the others began to collect their gear, the orders to keep it light.

"Mr. White, I presume," said a smiling young man wearing civilian clothes, his hand extended. "Call me David."

Dawson nodded, shaking the man's hand, who glanced at Agent White but didn't introduce himself to her. *The less bullshit with aliases the better.* He led the two of them toward one of the vehicles as the Herc's engines continued to power down.

"Any word on our friends?" asked Dawson when they were far enough away to have a conversation without having to shout.

"Unfortunately, yes. Your friends were kidnapped from their hotel at gunpoint. We're trying to trace them now, but don't expect much success."

Dawson didn't like the sound of that. Clearly Kane had used Hamas or Fatah to get them into the West Bank, probably through an illegal tunnel.

What the hell were you thinking?

Dawson knew Kane would do nothing to intentionally harm Professor Acton, they apparently having history, so if Kane trusted these people enough to put somebody important to him in their hands, he had to assume they would be taken care of.

"How bad was it?"

"The footage I saw in the parking garage looked a little rough, but nothing too bad. Unfortunately this Professor Acton put up a bit of resistance. I read his file. He's got quite the history over the past few years."

"Yeah, he's a goddamned magnet for trouble, that guy."

David laughed. "I know the type. Some say I'm one as well. Others say I enjoy the hunt too much."

Dawson cracked half a smile. "I think we've all been accused of that once or twice in this business."

David nodded. "So we're assuming your friends have made it into the West Bank by this point. You will want to follow them, of course?

"Yes. Will it be a problem?"

The man shook his head, his lips jutting out. "No, not at all. We're inserting teams all the time. Do you know where they were going?"

"Some Greek monastery. St. Gerasimos."

David's head bobbed. "Yes, I know of this place. The Arabs call it Deir Hajla." He paused, his eyes narrowing. "Why the hell would they want to go there?"

Dawson shook his head, deciding to leave the crystal skulls and Triarii out of the conversation. "They're archeologists. We're pretty sure they're being coerced into this," said Dawson. "And we're pretty sure it involves those who kidnapped President Jackson's son. We expect them to either be here already, or to be here shortly."

David frowned. "We had a plane arrive a couple of hours ago from Munich. An anonymous tip told us it didn't properly clear customs. We're interrogating those involved now."

"Any luck?"

"No, but we have our methods."

Dawson knew what that meant and didn't need any more details to know it went way beyond what people were worried about at Guantanamo. He looked behind him to see his team ready, Red giving him the nod.

"How quickly can you insert us?" asked Sherrie.

"Within the hour."

Dawson nodded, pleased with the speed. *We just might catch up to them.* "How?"

"I'll deliver you myself," said David with a smile, turning and pointing to a white cube van with UN markings.

"Ahh, a diplomatic vehicle," said Dawson.

"How will you get us through their checkpoint?" asked Sherrie. "Won't they want to search it?"

"Good question," said David as they walked toward the vehicle, "*if* we were using a border crossing. We will use one of our—shall we say 'express?—methods of entry."

Dawson and Sherrie exchanged glances.

"Can't wait," said Sherrie as she climbed into the back of the already opened van. The eight man Delta team, including Dawson, joined her, David closing then locking the back. Dawson frowned, not liking that part. He turned to his men.

"Anyone have C4?"

Several nods and the patting of a pocket or two was the response.

"Good. Let's keep in mind we have keys just in case our friend decides not to let us out."

There were several chuckles as the van started to roll.

Toward what he wasn't sure. Were they about to simply escort the professors and their INTERPOL friend out of the West Bank? Were they going to have to fight those who had brought them in—most likely terrorists? Would Jackson's kidnappers be there? Would Jackson himself be there? And whose side would he be on? And would the Triarii be there, manipulating things in the background as they always did?

I hate cults. Give me a good terror cell any day.

South East of Jericho, West Bank, Israel

Present day, three days after the kidnapping

"You can take your hoods off," said a voice that sounded much like Alamar. Acton yanked his off immediately, breathing a sigh of relief as he was finally able to take a full breath without sucking in the cloth or feeling the humidity from his lungs fill the bag. He looked about, giving Laura a squeeze on the leg and a nod to Reading who looked equally relieved. His eyes rested on Alamar.

"When did you get here?"

Alamar turned in his seat. "I came through a few minutes after you, just in case there was a problem."

"I see," said Acton. "Why stick your own neck out when you can stick someone elses?"

Alamar threw his head back and laughed. "Exactly!"

"Where are we?" asked Acton, noticing they weren't on a road but instead some type of trail.

"We're almost there. We're taking back roads to avoid the checkpoints."

"I thought this was Palestinian territory?" asked Laura, leaning forward and looking ahead.

"Hah! That's what you are meant to believe! The reality is less than twenty percent of the land is controlled by Palestinians. Another twenty percent the Israeli's *graciously* let us administer while their soldiers watch over us. The rest, the vast majority, is under complete Israeli control, including the area where you want to go."

Laura looked at Acton then back at Alamar, her expression one of concern. "What will happen if we're stopped?"

Alamar slapped the AK-47 sitting in his lap. "We kill them, or they kill us."

Acton didn't like the sound of that and hoped for everyone's sake the rest of their journey was uneventful. He suddenly tweaked on what was said. "We're almost there already?"

Alamar nodded. "This isn't Kansas, Professor. The West Bank is maybe forty kilometers wide. If we could take the highway we would have been there long ago."

A burst of Arabic from the driver and some pointing.

"It looks like we fight!" yelled Alamar as a military jeep crested a ridge in front of them, four men jumping out, automatic weapons at the ready. The driver hammered on the brakes and they skidded to a halt on the dirt road. Alamar and the driver jumped out along with two other men who were in the back with Acton, Laura and Reading. Gunfire erupted from all around them and Acton could see one of the Israeli soldiers already on the ground, wounded. He was grabbed by a comrade and pulled to the other side of their jeep, the other two providing cover fire as they retreated.

Acton looked out the back and saw no one. He climbed over the third row of seats and stepped out. The two men from the back were on either side of the vehicle, near the opened front doors, firing at the Israeli patrol. The windshield took several hits, the bullets racing through and tearing up the cabin. Acton looked at Laura and Reading.

"Let's get the hell out of here," he said in a harsh whisper. Laura jumped over the seats, Reading following and the three of them were soon running away from the vehicle, keeping it between them and the Israelis. They cleared a ridge and dropped to the ground. Acton scrambled back up and looked, the gun battle continuing, one of the terrorists now on the ground, the sides evenly matched at three apiece.

Acton pulled out his phone and activated the GPS. He turned to the others. "Let's follow this ridge and go around them. According to this"—he shook his phone—"we're only two kilometers west of the monastery."

"Let's do it," said Reading. "The Israeli's will be sending in reinforcements any minute now."

"You don't have to ask me twice," said Laura, turning and running at a crouch along the bottom of the ridge. Acton grinned at Reading then followed, the gunfire quickly fading. They turned east, toward the monastery, and within about ten minutes Acton came to a halt.

"The shooting stopped."

Laura and Reading paused and listened as well.

"I wonder who won?" asked Laura, resuming their walk. "I hope it was the Israeli's."

Reading grunted. "Just remember, those bastards were our way out. Now we're stuck in Palestinian territory, having illegally entered. Even if we get this blasted skull, we have no way out."

"You heard Alamar. This is Israeli controlled. We just need to turn ourselves in, claim we were kidnapped, and get things straightened out at the embassy," said Acton.

"Riiight, with a bloody crystal skull slung over your shoulder." Reading shook his head. "They'll confiscate it—defeating the entire purpose of this trip—and toss us in jail for antiquities theft. You two will probably just get more street cred or whatever the hell it is you Americans call it, and I'll lose my job."

"That's the spirit!" laughed Acton as they crested a ridge. He pointed. "That must be it."

Below, a well maintained road crossed from north to south, and beyond that was a cluster of buildings, many looking quite old.

"It must be," agreed Laura as they crossed toward the road. A quick scan up and down showed it empty.

"We still need a plan to get out of here," reminded Reading as they walked up the small drive toward a large parking area before the walled compound.

"One thing at a time," replied Acton. "Maybe we call the tourist bureau for help getting out."

"Tourist bureau?" asked Reading.

Acton realized he hadn't given that detail of his conversation with the airport customs officer who was Triarii. He decided not to get into it now as the entrance of the monastery neared. "Look on the bright side," he said, turning to Reading. "Maybe the skull isn't even here, and we can just get arrested for trespassing instead of trespassing and theft!" He grinned.

Reading frowned. "Bloody Yanks and their sense of humor." He turned to Laura. "And you better watch yourself. You're becoming just like him!"

Laura laughed and wrapped an arm around Acton's waist. "I wouldn't have it any other way!"

Reading threw his head in the air in frustration as they passed through the gates. The monastery appeared to be a tourist attraction now, but apparently not a very popular one since the parking area was empty save a truck that appeared to belong to the monks.

"We're not open yet," called a voice. Acton turned to see a middle-aged woman approaching along the south wall. "You're welcome to wait, of course, but we don't open for a few more hours." The woman came to a halt, her jaw dropping. "Are you Professor Acton?"

Acton flushed slightly, and nodded. "Yes I am. Do we know each other?"

The woman's hand flew to her chest. "*You* know *me*? Heaven's no. But I of course know about you. And you must be Professor Palmer! I feel like I'm meeting celebrities!"

Acton wasn't sure what to say, but decided to play on the woman's apparent celebrity worship. "We were hoping to see the burial sites. Specifically those from around the late thirteenth century?"

"Of course! Of course! The Abbot will be thrilled to meet you. He's an archeology buff as am I. We've both followed your career with great interest. I have all of the National Geographic articles on you, newspaper articles—oh, just everything!" She suddenly turned to Reading. "Are you anybody?"

Reading shook his head. "Apparently not."

The woman eyed him for a few more seconds, then waved for them to follow her inside. Acton grinned at Reading and whispered.

"You're somebody to me, Hugh."

Reading slugged him in the shoulder.

Unknown Location, Israel

Present day, three days after the kidnapping

Dawson instinctively ran his finger over his Glock as someone unlocked the rear door of their delivery vehicle. The door was thrown open and a smiling "David" stood there, Dawson positive that wasn't their Mossad contact's name any more than Mr. White was his.

"Delivered, as promised. And in less than thirty minutes, I might add," he said with a wag of the finger and a grin. "Israel expects a big tip for helping you retrieve President Jackson's son."

Dawson climbed out and looked about before turning to David. "Well, the White House is currently a different political stripe than Jackson was, so you might have to wait awhile for that favor."

David roared in laughter, clearly more comfortable where they now were. From what he could tell they were still at a military installation, this not an airport, however at least half a dozen black, heavily armed helicopters were within sight along with mock-up training areas. If he had to guess, they were now at a Mossad base.

Agent White joined them, helped down by Niner. She looked about and turned to David.

"Where are we?"

"I could tell you, but then I'd have to kill you, and I haven't had lunch yet."

"I'm sorry to hear that's all that's holding you back," said Sherrie.

David tossed his head back, laughing. "You are the first female CIA agent I have met. In Israel we have let our women participate in all areas of the military for a long time—after all, there weren't many of us to defend against a sea of Arabs who wanted to kill us just because of our religion. Telling our women to stay at home and tie a yellow ribbon on the old oak tree wasn't an option." He extended his hand, apparently now thinking she was worthy of hearing his alias. "David."

"Agent Black."

"Of course it is!"

She grinned then stopped as a man approached.

"Your chopper is ready," said the man to David who nodded then turned to Dawson. "It's time. We'll insert you near the monastery and out of sight of any patrols or locals. Two vehicles have been pre-positioned for you. The monastery is north of your position on the right—you can't miss it."

Dawson looked over the UH-60 Black Hawk helicopter that was starting to power up. "Extraction?"

David handed him a radio. "It's already tuned to the frequency. You are Sheep Dog, we are Goliath. Extraction code is Lightning and should you need assistance as in some firepower, the code is Thunder. Got it?"

Dawson raised his eyebrows. "Sheep Dog?"

David shrugged his shoulders. "My choice. I kind of like it."

"Sure you do," replied Dawson as he climbed aboard the now roaring Black Hawk. David stayed outside. "Not coming with us?"

David shook his head. "No need. I'll see you when you get back. Good luck, Mr. White."

Dawson gave him a casual salute then held out a hand, pulling Sherrie into the chopper. As the rest boarded, he wondered how far off mission they really were. Their job was to retrieve Grant Jackson, not save Professor Acton from another one of his "situations". Then again he usually didn't intentionally get himself into trouble, trouble just seemed to follow him. But from all outward appearances he and the good doctor Palmer, along with their friend Reading, had willingly entered the West Bank. Mossad thought they were kidnapped, but he knew that was just a ploy set up by Kane. This very helicopter they were on was Israeli cooperation in retrieving a citizen of an ally, and if they knew what was really going on, they'd probably toss them all out of the country.

But Dawson had a hunch that everything was somehow connected. There was no way that Acton would be in Munich then Israel, with the Triarii only hours behind them, if that. It appeared that Jackson's kidnappers were following Acton for some reason, and he could think of only one, a crystal skull, which meant once again his men's lives were at risk over a chunk of rock.

It pissed him off, especially after what had happened in Peru and London. Manipulated by a madman, and now, once again, they were being controlled. Not by one man, but by events beyond their control.

But if we can get there first, we might be able to put an end to it.

The Black Hawk rose off the ground, its nose dipping forward as it picked up speed.

"ETA five minutes," said the pilot over the comm.

"Equipment check!" ordered Dawson, his men immediately pulling out their body armor and weapons from their bags. They were travelling light so if they ended up in a heavy firefight, he just might need that Thunder code. And if they were only five minutes away, it just might arrive fast enough to save their skins.

Fatah. Hamas. Israeli patrols. Good Triarii. Bad Triarii.

Dawson shook his head.

Hopefully the monks are friendly.

Unknown Location, West Bank, Israel

Present day, three days after the kidnapping

Grant Jackson crept forward in the dark, longing for the dangling bulbs far behind them. He could hear Mitch's footsteps ahead of him, as well as the rest of their group behind him, the occasional grumble erupting when someone would step on someone else's heel. When he had given his speech a few nights ago he would never have expected three days later to be in a terrorist tunnel entering the West Bank with a cult of what he was afraid were nuts after a piece of carved crystal, apparently willingly.

He could guarantee to everyone including his God that there was no place he rather wouldn't be than here. If he could drill a hole through the planet and push up somewhere near home, he'd do it. If he could pinch himself out of this nightmare, he'd do it.

God I wish I could turn back time and not get on that helicopter.

He should have stayed with Louisa, should have made sure she was safe, and ended his involvement with these people when he had the chance. His obsession with that moment in time was becoming all-consuming and he could think of little else. Brief bouts of hating his father for being involved with these people provided little relief from the moment in time he seemed now trapped in.

"We're here," said Mitch in front of him and Grant stopped. "Give me a minute."

Grant heard Mitch begin to climb the stupidly steep stairs—why not just make it a ladder?—and a few minutes later the coded knock at the top. There was an answering knock and a light appeared above as the opening was revealed. Grant began to climb the steps and when he reached the top he felt two strong arms on him, yanking him the rest of the way. He looked about, blinking in the bright light and was shocked to find at least half a dozen weapons pointed at him, ushering him to the far wall where Mitch stood with his arms held up. Grant stood beside him, turning to face the room, his own arms high.

"What's going on?" he whispered.

"Don't know, but they're pissed about something."

The rest of the surprised group were hauled out one by one, each stripped of their weapons, nobody bothering to warn the others. If they were pissed at this end of the tunnel, they were sure to be pissed at the other end, so retreat wasn't possible. In fact retreat would probably get them all killed.

As the final member of their team was pulled out, the hole was quickly covered and one of the terrorists, his face covered with a balaclava, stepped forward. "Who is in charge here?"

Mitch stepped forward slightly. "Clearly *you,* sir, are in charge *here.* I am in charge of my men only."

The man paused as he probably replayed the words in his head, trying to determine if he had just been insulted. There was a grunt that seemed to suggest he was satisfied with Mitch's reply.

"There has been a problem. You will come with us."

Mitch nodded. "Of course we will, but first, we must have our weapons back."

The man looked at the pile of weaponry far nicer than anything they were sporting. He nodded, barking something in Arabic. Mitch and his crew rearmed as Grant continued to stand against the wall, hands up.

Mitch walked over and handed Grant a Glock 22. "Do you know how to use this?"

Grant nodded. "My Dad taught me."

"Good. Try not to shoot any of us," said Mitch with a grin, handing him two extra magazines. "You're one of us now."

Grant's chest tightened to the point where he was certain a panic attack or a heart attack was setting in. He secretly prayed for a heart attack to strike him down dead, right then and there, so this nightmare would be over.

But instead he felt Mitch's hand on his back, urging him forward. As they stepped from the room, they were each handed a black sack to put over their heads once again.

Lovely.

"Get in the truck then cover your heads," ordered the man in charge. "We will leave immediately."

Grant looked about curiously. Four trucks were roaring to life, the Triarii being loaded into two, the other two filling up with armed militants. Something was definitely going on, and Grant was certain he wanted no part of it. These men looked like they were going to war. He turned to Mitch.

"What do you think is going on?" he whispered.

Mitch shook his head, preparing his head cover. "I don't know, but I don't like it. First opportunity we get we're out of here."

"And just how do you propose that?"

Mitch patted his gun. "Only one way I can think of." He grinned then pulled the sack over his head. Grant covered his head, once again leaning his head on the glass, an overwhelming sense of self-pity rolling over him.

I'm going to die.

Monastery of St. Gerasimos, West Bank, Israel
Present day, three days after the kidnapping

"When was the last time anybody was in here?" asked Acton as they walked deeper and deeper into the manmade cave. The caves were remarkably well preserved though there had been some collapses over the past fifteen hundred years. This particular cave had survived, and was part of a large network painstakingly carved out of the side of a cliff about a mile from the actual monastery.

Known as a lavra, these caves were begun by St. Gerasimos himself around the year 450 AD. He lived in these caves as a hermit with others, eventually expanding the hermitage by building a monastery for the faithful. The story of him helping an ailing mountain lion, pulling a thorn from its paw then taming the wild creature, is a legend well known by Christians.

Acton found himself examining everything, Reading continually having to urge him on as he would stop to point out something to Laura who was as equally enthralled.

God I love archeology!

The Abbot was more than accommodating, giving them an ongoing travel guide explanation of everything as they passed. The woman who had greeted them at the monastery, Rita, wasn't kidding when she had said the Abbot was a big fan. He had insisted on both Acton and Laura autographing his copies of National Geographic and had as a courtesy begrudgingly offered up a pen to Reading who had politely refused, amused by the entire thing until it started to drag past sixty seconds.

Now they were heading for the ancient burial chambers of the monks from the crusade period, hidden deep inside the rock to protect them from

Saracens seeking revenge. When the Kingdom of Jerusalem had fallen, many Christians had fled the Holy Land, but others formed clusters, moving into towns and cities such as Bethlehem and Jerusalem with the thought that there was safety in numbers. After things calmed down with the defeat of the crusaders, most Christians lived in peace with their Muslim neighbors, returning to their previous homes, or choosing to remain in their newly created communities.

In the monastery's case, it was still occupied to this day by monks devoted to their founder, and to their God, apparently sharing their surroundings with thousands of tourists as they went about their daily business.

But what they were about to be shown today had been seen by no tourists in the history of the monastery unless they had gone well off the guided tour. At the end of a long twisting passage they stepped into a larger chamber, this appearing to not be manmade, but carved out by water millennia ago.

Dozens of holes carved into the walls contained the carefully wrapped bodies of what appeared to be scores of monks.

"Amazing," whispered Laura as she stepped into the center of the cavern, slowly spinning to take it all in. Even Reading's jaw had dropped as flashlights played around the room. The flick of a lighter from a nearby wall suddenly had the Abbot bathed in light as a torch was lit. He took the torch then walked around the cavern, lighting a series of others. Soon the flashlights were of no use, Acton switching his off.

He turned to the Abbot. "We're specifically looking for the tomb of somebody named Giuseppe—"

The Abbot gasped, his hand darting to his mouth before Acton could finish his sentence, tears welling in the elderly man's eyes.

"It is you!" he whispered, his hand reaching out to touch Acton's arm as if in reverence.

"What? What's wrong?" asked Acton. "Are you okay?"

Laura stepped over, putting a hand on the old man's shoulder as he began to shake. Reading spotted an old wooden chair nearby and brought it over. They all helped the old man to sit, Laura retrieving a bottle of water from her bag. The Abbot waved his hand, refusing it.

"Forgive an old man who is apparently shocked quite easily," he said, his voice weak but regaining some of its strength. He looked up at Acton. "Tell me, have you been to the Holy See recently?"

Acton nodded. "Two days ago."

"Do…do you have…" The Abbot stopped, almost as if he were afraid to ask the question. He looked up at Acton, his eyes filled with almost childlike wonder. "Do you have the scroll?"

Acton stood up straight, shocked at the question, his jaw dropping as he looked at Laura then Reading, both equally as stunned as he was. Acton nodded to Laura who removed the two halves from her bag—they having liberated the other half from Teufel—holding them together so the Abbot could see.

She was rewarded with a burst of tears and heaving shoulders as the old man sobbed, a smile on his face as he stared at the two pieces of ancient parchment preserved between Plexiglas.

"I can't—" He had to stop, choking on his words. He took a deep breath, holding it for a moment, then wiped his face dry with the sleeves of his robes. "I'm so sorry, forgive my emotions, but this is a great day. A glorious day." He sniffed several times, then stood up, looking sheepishly about. "It has been foretold for almost a millennia that you would arrive."

"Me?"

"A man from a faraway land on a mission for the Holy See, will return to Jericho and reclaim that which was never meant to be ours."

Acton had to admit it sort of fit their situation, but it was so generic it could have been a dude from Rome picking up his phone from the monastery's lost and found.

He decided to play along. "Can we see him?"

The old man nodded. "Of course, but he's not here. Follow me."

They exited the cavern, retracing their steps for about thirty paces, then turned down a previously passed corridor. Moments later they were in a manmade chamber. The Abbot lit several torches leaving Acton stunned as he stared at a wall of letters that had him feeling like he was in an Indiana Jones movie.

"What's this?" he asked, his mouth agape. Before them stood a hand chiseled wall, about ten feet across, eight feet high. To the left were what appeared to be the entire Latin alphabet carved into the wall, to the right the same thing. Each letter was squared out, and if Acton wasn't mistaken, could be pushed in, almost like an ancient stone keyboard—with keys the size of your fists.

"The possessor of the two parts of the scroll, written by Brother Giuseppe himself, must enter the *decoded* first word from the left part of the scroll here"—he motioned to the letters on the left—"and the decoded *last* word from the right part of the scroll here." He pointed to the set of letters on the right.

"Who built this?" asked Acton, approaching the left set, running his hand over the carved letters.

"It was built shortly after Giuseppe's death. His original wishes were to be buried as one of us, but we realized that the secret he guarded was too great to have left out in the open. This chamber was built to protect the secret when it became apparent we might be forced from our home during the crusades."

"And just what happens if someone enters the wrong code?" asked Reading, ever the pessimist. Acton though had to admit it was an extremely relevant question.

The Abbot pointed up at the ceiling. "The chamber will be filled with sand."

"Has anyone tried to enter a code?"

The Abbot shook his head. "No. You will be the first."

Acton turned to Laura and Reading. "You two wait outside, just in case."

"I'm not leaving you alone!" exclaimed Laura.

"Please, hon, if something goes wrong, I want you outside so you can figure out how to help me." He turned to Reading. "You too. I have every intention of surviving this, and in the unlikely event something goes wrong, it's you two who are going to pull my ass out of here."

Laura frowned but nodded. "Okay. But if you get yourself killed, I'm stuffing your bloody body in one of those holes back there and forgetting about you."

Acton grinned. "That's the spirit!" His face suddenly became serious as he pulled a pad from his pocket along with a pencil. "How about we triple check the translation of the first and last words?" Laura nodded, immediately huddling with her fiancée as Reading examined the room, the doorway and played his flashlight over the ceiling. Acton glanced at him as he muttered, apparently not pleased with what he saw.

"Are you sure?" asked Laura. "There's no second chances here."

Acton nodded. "Both decoded words are actually words. They are both Latin, and they are spelled correctly." He took a deep breath. "Yes, I'm sure."

Laura nodded. "So am I." She leaned in and gave him a kiss. "I love you."

Acton smiled, closing his eyes and holding his forehead against hers. "I love you too," he whispered. "But I'm going to be fine." He straightened, handing her the originals of the scroll then pointing at the door. "Everyone out."

Reading immediately headed for the door, holding his hand out for a reluctant Laura who finally broke away from Acton and stepped through the door. Reading followed, but not before looking at him. "Good luck, mate."

Acton nodded his thanks, then turned to the Abbot. "You better leave too. There's no telling what might happen."

The Abbot smiled. "There is no danger here. You possess both halves of the scroll. I have no doubt you are the one prophesized to return. There is no way anyone could prevent me from remaining here and witnessing over seven hundred years of history come to an end."

Acton frowned. "I'm not sure I like how that sounds."

'Come to an end.' Let's hope not, Abbot.

Acton stepped over to the set of carved letters on the left. He looked at the pad, the two words written out in block letters, clearly labeled 'Left' and 'Right'.

To say he was jumpy would be an understatement. He reached for the first letter, his hand shaking.

"Have faith, my son. God will protect you," said the old man gently.

"I'm entering the first letter now!" he called.

"Okay," came Laura's reply. "Good luck!"

"From your lips to God's ears," replied Acton, quietly, as he pushed on the first letter. It receded about two inches. He turned to the Abbot. "Is that a good sign?"

The old man shrugged. "I am but an observer."

"Do you know the words that must be entered?"

The old man shook his head. "I have no idea. I have never seen the scroll. The two words were left with the Abbot at the time to be used to authenticate any scroll that might be used to try and gain access to Giuseppe's body, but they instead chose to create this"—he motioned at the wall—"as a more permanent solution should the words be lost in time. As a result, we don't know the words, as we don't need to know. The device will determine whether or not you are worthy of entering."

Acton frowned.

"What's happening?" asked Laura.

He glanced back to see her head poking through the door. He waved her off. "I've entered the first letter. It receded into the wall about two inches. I'm entering the second letter now." He pushed on the next letter, it too receding, the first letter pushing back out to its original position. "Second letter went in about two inches, the first letter came back out!"

"Is that good or bad?" asked Reading.

"Haven't a clue. Nothing's caved in on us yet, and the Abbot hasn't started running, so I'm guessing good," replied Acton with a smile at the Abbot who bowed slightly in response.

"Here goes. I'm entering the rest of the first word."

He carefully pressed each of the remaining three letters, each receding, each of the previous returning to their former positions, except the last letter, which when pressed receded, but resulted in a clicking sound to their right.

Acton's head shot back as he stared up at the ceiling, waiting for it to collapse.

Nothing.

"First word is in. I heard a clicking sound to my right. I'm guessing that means it has activated the second set of letters," relayed Acton as he stepped over to the second set. "I'm entering the second word now."

"*Last* word!" yelled Reading.

"He knows!" hissed Laura. "Don't confuse him!"

"Sorry," mumbled Reading resulting in Acton grinning as he pictured his chastised friend.

He began entering the letters until he reached the last one. He sucked in a deep breath and looked at the Abbot, his expression inscrutable. *Does he know we're about to die?* Acton looked over his shoulder at the entrance. He could see Laura crouched down just outside, looking at him.

"Here goes nothing," he muttered. "I'm entering the last letter now!"

He pushed it and suddenly there was a loud rumble, the sounds of a mechanism clicking behind the wall then stone scraping on stone. Acton began to step back toward the entrance, the Abbot remaining in place, as Acton eyed the ceiling overhead.

Suddenly everything stopped.

"What's happening?" asked Laura.

Acton looked about. "I don't know. I don't think anything changed!" He looked again, carefully, playing his flashlight over every square inch of the ceiling and the walls, and it wasn't until he began to look down that he saw it. An opening in the floor between the two sets of letters. He had spent so much time looking up, he had missed it.

"There's an opening here!" he exclaimed, rushing over to it and dropping to his knees. He heard Laura rush into the room behind him, Reading cursing as he followed. Acton turned to the Abbot. "What does this lead to?"

The old man shrugged. "That is for the prophesized one to find out."

The hole had been created by a stone in the floor, perhaps four feet wide by five feet deep, dropping about three feet. Acton poked his head inside, shining his flashlight down what looked like a passageway about ten feet long.

"I think this leads to another chamber," he said. He pulled off his satchel and handed it to Laura. "I'm going in."

"So am I," replied Laura, handing the satchel to Reading, then her own.

"Of course, hon, but wait until I make sure it's safe."

"Fine," she said, her disappointment clear in her voice. He could understand her feelings, being the first to see something so old was almost irresistible—nobody wanted to be Buzz Aldrin when it came to these things. He dropped inside the hole and crouched down, half crawling, half sliding through the tunnel, his flashlight jumping about until he finally poked his head through the other side and gasped. It was a similarly sized chamber as the one he had just left, and in the middle was a large stone structure that he assumed was the sarcophagus holding the remains of Giuseppe.

Fascinating that a Venetian slave could become so revered among a group of monks that they would go to such lengths to preserve him!

Acton climbed to his feet, quickly examining his surroundings, then shouted back to Laura. "Okay, I think it's safe!"

"Okay, I'm coming." A minute later Laura poked her head out from the tunnel and Acton helped her up from the hole. Directly behind her was the Abbot.

"Hugh, are you coming?" yelled Acton.

"Are you bloody barmy? There's no way I'm climbing in there."

"Okay, hold the fort, we shouldn't be too long."

"Riight."

Acton winked at Laura who knew perfectly well they would quite often get lost in their work for hours, thinking it was only minutes. Acton returned to the center of the room, a large stone "box", perhaps six feet by three feet on the top, about three feet deep, sat on a slightly raised platform. It was simple in design, nothing fancy carved on it, only a few markings chiseled at the head.

"Here lies Giuseppe Polo of Venice. Slave, friend and brother to Marco Polo. Died April 17th, 1281," translated Laura. She couldn't hide her excitement any better than Acton could. His heart was slamming in his chest. The loyal slave of Marco Polo, lost in the Holy Land for over seven hundred years, guarding a secret apparently entrusted to him by his long dead master. Acton could only imagine how a crystal skull so sought after by the Triarii could end up in the hands of Marco Polo.

"Shall we?" asked Laura, grabbing the corners at the far end.

Acton nodded, placing his hands at the other two. "Clockwise on three. One…two…three!" He pulled with all his might, Laura doing the same on the other end, and the large stone cover began to turn, slowly gaining momentum. Within seconds the cover was now perpendicular to the sarcophagus, revealing a very unexpected surprise.

"Where's the body?" asked Laura.

Acton looked inside at the nearly empty vessel. All that it seemed to contain was a chiseled tablet where the head of Giuseppe should have been. Acton reached inside and removed the tablet, carefully placing it on the turned top.

"How about an update?" yelled Reading, clearly getting impatient.

"The body is gone!" replied Laura. "But there's a stone tablet inside."

Muttered curses could be heard, the odd word drifting down the tunnel suggesting Reading was of the opinion they had come all this way for nothing.

"I can't make this out," commented Laura. Acton looked at the letters on the tablet and it too made no sense.

"Another code?" he suggested to which the Abbot shook his head.

"Not a code, but a type of shorthand if you will, only understood by those of us in the order. Let me translate." He cleared his throat and began to read as Acton whipped out his pad and pencil. "*As Abbot I take responsibility for my actions. Disturbing the remains of our beloved Giuseppe fills my heart with despair, however with the continued harassment by the Saracens, I have felt it necessary to move his body, and his charge. I hope one day he will be returned to slumber in peace. Forgive me.*"

Acton leaned his elbows on the empty sarcophagus, grabbing his hair. "We're too late."

"About seven hundred years too late," agreed an exasperated Laura. "What now?"

Acton pointed at the tablet. "Take a rubbing for the records, I guess, but unless anyone knows where this Abbot would have taken the remains, I think our journey is over."

The old man cleared his throat.

"I just may know where he went."

Approaching the Monastery of St. Gerasimos, West Bank, Israel
Present day, three days after the kidnapping

"What's the hurry?" asked Mitch as their vehicle bounced over a very poor excuse for a road. Grant had given up his forlorn looks out the window, face pressed against the glass, instead now gripping the "Oh Jesus!" handle and praying they'd make it there in one piece.

"Our men who left with your friends haven't been heard from! They might be in trouble!" shouted one of the Hamas terrorists from the passenger seat. "They might have run into a Jew"—the man paused to spit on the floor—"patrol."

"Isn't the West Bank controlled by Fatah?" asked Mitch.

"Fatah!" Another loogie. "They couldn't control anything. That's why we eliminated them in Gaza. Soon we will have enough men and arms here to do the same. Only then with a united, strong Palestinian leadership will we be able to negotiate with Israel, and once we've lulled them into a false sense of security, we will strike with our Arab brothers and push them into the sea!"

The dogma was impressive. The man was clearly insane, which most terrorists were, but to actually hear it spoken in person had Grant almost shaking his head. *How can you go through life filled with such hate?* It made no sense to him; he had to assume ignorance of history on their part. The UN had promised a Palestinian *and* a Jewish state and tried to implement that after World War II. The Jews had cooperated, the Palestinians hadn't. Israel had never started a war—unless they knew they were about to be attacked—but they definitely finished them. Did Hamas hate Israel because they kept winning the wars Arabs foisted upon them? Or was it just because they were Jews and the Koran told them so? Or was it just because they were Jews?

Grant knew the Koran had a lot of hateful things in it. His father had made him read a translation of it years ago—"know your enemy"—and he had been shocked that much of the anti-Islam propaganda was true. What he had learned was the surahs, or chapters, were written in the order they were supposedly delivered to Mohammad, and if there was a contradiction between an earlier surah, and a later one, the later one superseded the earlier. This was where much of the confusion lay for Westerners being lectured by Muslims who defended their religion by quoting earlier surahs that sounded peaceful, but were actually overridden by later surahs that were much more intolerant.

He knew the Bible had many references that if interpreted strictly were unsavory now, but most Christians had adapted, realizing the Bible was a product of its time, and quite often what seemed literal was actually metaphorical. Christians had had their Crusades, their Inquisitions but also their Reformation and Enlightenment. Until monsters like their escort moved beyond the hate, the world had little hope of ever being at peace.

Their driver yelled something, pointing ahead, ending the political stump speech. The vehicle skidded to a halt as they came alongside two men, exhausted and disheveled. Rapid Arabic began to be fired back and forth, and nobody looked happy, angrier and angrier glances being aimed at the passengers.

Mitch turned back to look at the others, pulling his weapon out and readying it, making certain to hide it from the two Hamas men in front.

"What's going on?" asked Chip.

"The two guys outside are saying they were betrayed by the professors. They were intercepted by an Israeli patrol. When the gunfight was over their vehicle was useless and the professors were gone. They decided to walk back before another patrol arrived. The guy talking outside says we can't be trusted."

Mitch spun around, placing his gun against the back of the driver's head. Chip jumped forward, pointing his own gun out the window at the other two men as Mitch turned to Grant. "Cover the passenger!" he yelled and Grant fumbled with his gun, finally retrieving it from his belt and pointing it at the stunned man.

Arms shot up in the air as Mitch opened the door, stepping outside. Almost immediately the two vehicles filled with Hamas emptied, their weapons aimed in the direction of the first vehicle. Mitch positioned himself behind the talker outside, holding the gun to his head, motioning for the other man to drop his weapons. He did, then Mitch said something in Arabic and the man ran toward the rear two vehicles. More orders barked and the driver and passenger dumped their weapons out their windows and stepped outside, joining the others in the rear.

Grant, freed of having to cover anyone, turned around in his seat and saw the second vehicle was in a similar situation, the Triarii men all with their weapons out, pointed at their escort in the front seat. More shouting in Arabic from Mitch, then rapid head bobbing from his prisoner and more shouting from him—which sounded more like pleading—had the two rear vehicles loading up then departing, leaving only the one Hamas member behind.

Mitch shoved the man between Grant and Chip. "Shoot him if he moves." Grant hoped the order was for Chip to follow. Mitch climbed in the driver's seat and soon the two vehicles were moving forward, at a more reasonable pace, but still quicker than Grant's liking. He glanced back and there was no sign of the other two terrorist laden vehicles.

"What did you tell them?" he asked.

"That I'd kill their friend if we saw them again."

"He must be important to them," replied Chip. "I was half expecting them to shoot the shit out of all of us including him."

"You think you've gotten away from my men but you haven't. You're merely delaying the inevitable," sneered the man.

"Oh, you speak English?" Mitch glanced over his shoulder at the man. "If I see even one Hamas flag, in fact if I even see any green on someone, you're a dead man."

"If Allah wills it, then so be it."

"Bettin' on those seventy-two virgins, are we?" asked Chip, poking the man's ribs with his gun.

"You are so ignorant of our beliefs it is pitiable."

"Why should I give a shit about your ways? *I* don't want to kill *you*, but *you* want to kill *me*. *I* have nothing against Muslims, but *you* want to kill Christians and Jews and Hindus and Buddhists and just about everyone else. *You* want to create the grand Caliphate and rule the world under the flag of Islam. *You* want to blow up our buildings and our civilians." Chip shook his head. "You're not my enemy, but somehow I am yours. Why is that? Is it that you hate everything so much peace just never occurs to you as an option? Look at the West. We have democracy, freedom, equality. Why wouldn't you want that?"

"Because it goes against the Koran and Sharia. These things are blasphemous according to God himself!"

"You're an effin' idiot," spat Chip, turning away from the man and looking at Mitch. "How long do we have to put up with this asshole?"

"Until we're free and clear of the West Bank."

"You and your professor friends will be dead before the day is out," said their captive. "All of you."

Mitch looked in the rearview mirror at the man. "I don't think you'll be killing the good doctors today," he said as he slowed, smoke rising ahead of them in the distance. “In fact,” he continued as he turned the vehicle to the right, apparently intending to go around the possible danger, “I think your killing days are over.”

“Amen,” grinned Chip, poking the man in the ribs again. “We should hand him over to the Israelis.”

The man spat on Chip whose face turned a burning red. He wiped the insult off his face with his sleeve then leaned forward, suddenly jerking his left elbow back and into the man’s nose three times. Grant swore he heard the crack.

Blood poured from the man’s nose as he cried out in pain. Mitch slammed on the brakes, bringing their vehicle to a stop, the second one coming up beside them.

“Get him out. Make sure he doesn’t have a phone on him.”

Chip smiled, stepping out of the vehicle and pulling the man along with him. A quick pat down was followed by a kick in the ass.

“Get the hell out of here!” yelled Chip as the man stumbled away. Chip climbed back in the vehicle and they were on their way again, this time a little faster than before.

“We need to get to that monastery and get the hell out of here before that guy’s friends come back.”

Grant looked behind them, wondering just how long it would be before the terrorists came after them. Dust on the far horizon behind them had him thinking it wouldn’t be too long.

Ten miles south of the Monastery of St. Gerasimos, West Bank, Israel
Present day, three days after the kidnapping

Dawson jumped from the helicopter, the rest of his men following as the bird touched down for only seconds, it immediately rising as the last boot cleared. He squinted behind his shades, shielding his face as best he could as he scanned the area. They were in the middle of nowhere by all outward appearances, two tan colored SUVs sitting nearby as promised with no roads or civilization in sight.

Perfect.

He climbed in the passenger seat of the nearest SUV, Red taking the second team. Niner took the wheel, Spock and Atlas, along with Agent Sherrie White occupying the rear.

"Aw, shit BD, does he have to drive?" whined the massive Atlas from the rear seat. "You know how he is!"

"Hey, no backseat bitching or driving," shouted Niner as he started the vehicle. "If you wanted to drive you should have been quicker."

"I would have been if you hadn't got in my way."

Niner looked at Atlas through the rearview mirror. "Are you kidding me? You're built like a tank! How the hell do *I* get in *your* way?"

Dawson pointed to the left, a map on his phone showing the way, and Niner put it in gear, pulling out like a grandmother. "Is that more to your liking?" he asked.

"Much better," replied Atlas. "I have a sensitive bottom, you know."

Dawson chuckled as Sherrie bit her finger, snorting. "Is it always like this?" she asked.

Spock shook his head. "No, it's usually worse."

"He's right," agreed Niner. "You should hear some of the stuff that comes out of their mouths. I must admit sometimes I blush. Other times they're so insensitive, I get all verklempt"—he bit his finger, faking a cry—"and just can't go on." He suddenly spun in his seat, reaching for Dawson. "Hold me!"

"Watch the goddamned road!" laughed Dawson as he shoved Niner back in his seat, the rest of the team roaring with laughter.

Niner looked back at Sherrie.

"See? So insensitive. Sometimes a man just wants a hug."

"When we get out of here I'll give you a hug so hard it'll break your back," said Atlas.

"With your arms? That's like getting hugged by two tree trunks. I'll pass, thanks."

"I'll give you a hug, Niner," said Sherrie, delivering her line with a syrupy tone.

"Sold!" yelled Niner, then with a sly voice, "Sympathy card. Works every time."

Atlas turned to Sherrie. "You know, sometimes my feelings get hurt too."

Dawson decided to save Sherrie. "ETA five minutes."

Everyone became all business as they checked their equipment, Dawson turning slightly to make eye contact with Sherrie, giving her a slight wink. She grinned and pulled her Glock, inspecting it, giving Dawson the distinct impression he was dealing with "one of the boys".

Now let's just hope Acton and crew are still there.

He frowned as he wondered how he would justify this leg of the operation. Acton wasn't their target, and though they had intel that Grant Jackson might be in the area, they couldn't be sure.

Wouldn't it be nice if they were all there, waiting for us?

Monastery of St. Gerasimos Lavra, West Bank, Israel

Present day, three days after the kidnapping

"So you really think they may have taken him to Bethlehem?" asked Acton as he followed the Abbot down the passageway toward the outside. Several tourists were passing them by, smiling nods in greeting from most as they continued on their spiritual journey. It made him wonder, since the tour seemed unguided, whether or not anyone else had found the entrance to the secret chamber they were just in. He doubted it, since everyone seemed to be sticking to the front of the caves, light pouring in from the outside and through slits cut in the roof previously used as natural chimneys. Where they had emerged from was dark and foreboding, probably enough to stop anyone from venturing too far.

He glanced over his shoulder as a woman asked, "What do you think is down here?"

"Nothing you want to see," replied what appeared to be her husband. "Read the sign."

Acton saw the no admittance sign standing beside the passage they had just come out of, not noticing it in his excitement the first time.

"But *they* were there," replied the whine.

"And they're with a monk," came the exasperated reply.

"But how can we go there? I want you to ask someone, Leroy. When we get back down there you ask them."

"Yes, dear," groaned the man, his voice subtly suggesting to the world around him that this was his daily life and if God took him now he would be a content man.

Acton glanced at Laura and she smiled, leaning toward him. "That will never be us!"

He laughed as they emerged from the cave entrance, the sunlight almost blinding him. Shielding his eyes, he nearly bumped into the Abbot.

"Oh my!" exclaimed the elderly man as Acton stepped around him to see what was wrong. His chest tightened at what was waiting to greet them.

Eight men, all armed, along with a young man Acton instantly recognized.

Grant Jackson.

Armed and unharmed.

Acton raised his hands, as did Laura and a smoldering Reading.

"Please, Dr. Acton, lower your hands. We don't want to make a scene now, do we?" Acton lowered his arms as he put himself between Laura and the armed men. "Now, Dr. Acton, I believe you have something that belongs to us."

"I have no idea what you're talking about." Acton knew it was playing dumb, but at the moment he was playing for time. What he hoped to gain he had no idea, it just seemed the natural thing to do. Delaying them would just delay the inevitable, since nobody except Hamas terrorists knew they were here, and counting on their help was ludicrous.

"Tsk, tsk," said the man, waving a finger, then running it over the handgun tucked in the front of his belt. "We're all friends here," he said, showing them his Triarii tattoo. "We're Triarii, and you have something we want."

"You're not Triarii, you're the Deniers."

"True Believers, actually. But still Triarii." The man's face lost all pleasantries. "I must insist, Dr. Acton."

Acton shrugged his shoulders. "Search us, we don't have it."

"Then why are you here?"

"It was supposed to be here, but it wasn't."

"Then where is it?" asked the increasingly frustrated man.

"I have no idea. We were just about to contact London to tell them we failed."

The man frowned.

"Dr. Acton? Why do I get the impression that you're lying to me?" The man drew his weapon, flicking it to his right. "How about we go discuss this somewhere less public, shall we?"

Acton noticed Grant Jackson place a hand on his own weapon, but when he made eye contact with him, the eyes immediately darted away, confidence completely lacking in the young man's expression.

Are you my enemy, Mr. Jackson?

Approaching the Monastery of St. Gerasimos, West Bank, Israel
Present day, three days after the kidnapping

"This is it!" announced Dawson as they turned off the road and onto a narrower one, the monastery now in front of them. It seemed to be a cluster of old and very old, several structures that appeared to have been built in the past fifty years scattered around the main complex, then the monastery itself surrounded by massive, thick walls. Signs of damage over the millennia were evident, much of it appearing to have been built or rebuilt over the centuries. Dawson would love to know the history of the place, but right now, what he saw in the large parking lot had him frowning.

To their right, ahead about fifty feet, were the two professors, their INTERPOL friend and an old monk, being herded by a group of nine men.

Things are never easy.

He activated his comm. "Four friendlies at our three o'clock surrounded by hostiles. Remember one of those might be Grant Jackson. Team two, take position past the second bus, we'll take the first. Let's use the element of surprise here, hopefully no gunfire will be needed. Copy?"

Red's voice came over the comm. "Copy, team two taking the second bus, over," as their vehicle pulled past them at a speed that shouldn't draw anyone's attention. Niner continued forward and Dawson pointed to a tour bus that had two identical vehicles, much rougher looking than most of the vehicles, parked near it. "Fifty bucks says those are theirs." Red's team pulled in behind the tour bus and out of sight. Dawson pointed to another bus their targets had just walked by. "Put us on this side of that bus."

Niner turned, parking beside the bus as the doors all opened, everyone jumping out, weapons at the ready. Dawson activated his comm, stuffing the Israeli radio in his belt. "Bravo Two, Bravo One. Status, over?"

Red's voice came back immediately. "Team two in position, over."

Dawson looked past the bus and saw the group approaching their vehicles. *We have to take them before they gain that cover!* He motioned for Atlas and Spock to go to the other end of the bus and once in position, he held in his comm button. "Execute in three—two—one—Execute!"

He burst from around the back of the bus, Niner and Sherrie flanking him, weapons extended in front of them as he saw Red and his team explode from either end of their bus.

"US Army!" shouted Dawson as he rushed forward. "If you move, you die!"

Several of the men reached for their weapons but with nine armed operatives rushing them, they immediately stopped, hands shooting up into the air, some eagerly like Grant Jackson's, others much more leisurely. Stepping away from the group were the two professors and Special Agent Reading, who had his hand on the back of the old monk.

Acton approached him as Dawson's team quickly disarmed the men, lining them up against the side of the bus. "Man, am I glad to see you!" exclaimed the professor, his hand extended.

Dawson shook the man's hand with a smile. "A little birdie told me you might need help."

Acton shook his head, still smiling. "I only asked for a ride, not an armed escort."

Dawson nodded toward the group of men by the bus. "Looks like you needed one."

"Agreed," said Acton as Laura Palmer approached and shook Dawson's hand.

"Thank you so much, Sergeant Major. You have a knack for showing up just in time."

Dawson nodded. "Just like the movies."

Suddenly gunfire erupted from behind them, the windows of the bus shattering. Dawson shoved Laura to the ground as he whipped around, using his right leg to sweep Acton off his feet. As Dawson hit the ground, his weapon extending in front of him, he counted at least half a dozen vehicles racing toward them, men hanging out of the windows and doors, a mix of weapons firing wildly as their vehicles bounced on the uneven road.

"Take cover!" yelled Dawson as tourists screamed, running toward the walls of the monastery. Dawson immediately emptied a mag into the engine of the lead vehicle, bringing it to a steaming halt, the next vehicle ramming the back of it causing the entire convoy to jerk to a stop. "Get inside!" he yelled, pointing at the Triarii weapons. "And take their weapons!"

Dawson and Acton grabbed Laura, Reading already with a weapon as the four of them raced toward the entrance that stood about sixty feet away. Dawson reloaded and looked over his shoulder, firing several rounds, two of them true. To his left he spotted two elderly tourists trying to escape the gunfire, their legs just too slow to save them. He broke off from the professors and raced toward the old couple, the elderly man, his arm around his wife, trying to shield her as best he could.

As Dawson approached, the dirt began to explode in front of him in small bursts as an automatic weapon missed him but raced toward the couple. The old man turned and Dawson recognized the look of someone who knew he was going to die. Two bullets tore into his side, sending him to the ground, his wife screaming in horror as she tried to bend over and help her fallen partner.

Dawson scooped her up and carried her protesting form toward the entrance of the compound, and glancing over his shoulder he saw that

Acton and Reading had picked up the body of the old man and were close behind, once again renewing his respect for these men.

As he cleared the entrance he broke to the left, putting down the old woman then taking up position at the gate as his men poured through along with the Triarii prisoners. Several tourists were trapped in the parking area, some huddling behind vehicles, others running toward the entrance, still others either writhing on the ground in pain, or unmoving, their nightmare over.

The attacking vehicles had emptied themselves of their occupants, the militants spreading out, pouring fire on the monastery. "Is everyone okay?" he yelled, looking about and doing a quick headcount.

"We're all good," yelled Red.

"Conserve your ammo! Make every shot count!" ordered Dawson, now regretting the decision to travel light.

"How can we help?" came a voice to Dawson's right. He spun and saw three men, Stars and Stripes worn proudly on their person through patches, ball caps and pins, all looking to be about seventy. Dawson recognized the look immediately.

These guys are vets.

Dawson pointed to Atlas. "Arm them." He pointed at the Triarii group. "Guard them." He pointed to the old man who had been wounded outside. "Any of you a medic?"

One man stepped forward. "Sergeant Webber, retired! I was a corpsman in 'Nam."

"Good. Niner!"

Niner tossed a med kit to the man who immediately went to work, the other two taking up position and covering the nine prisoners, lining them up against the very wall now being peppered by a near constant barrage of weapons fire.

He heard something behind him and turned to see another group of older men approaching and he felt his heart swell with pride in his country, and his chosen profession. Atlas tossed them weapons and Dawson pointed to Red. "Take them and two of ours and cover our six!"

He turned back to the entrance and took a look. Several more bodies lay on the ground thanks to the precision shooting of his men, but they were facing at least two dozen hostiles.

He pulled the Israeli radio from his belt.

"Goliath, this is Sheep Dog. Code word Thunder, I say again, Code word Thunder, acknowledge."

There was a pause and Dawson was about to retransmit when the radio squawked.

"Sheep Dog, Goliath. Code word is Thunder, repeat, Code word is Thunder, out."

Now we just need to hold out.

Monastery of St. Gerasimos, West Bank, Israel
Present day, three days after the kidnapping

Grant Jackson stood with his back pressed against the wall, his hands, once raised over his head, now covered his ears as he tried to crouch, terrified of what was happening on the other side of the wall, and even more so of the grim looking vets now pointing weapons at him and the Triarii.

This is a nightmare!

As his breathing continued to increase its pace, once deep breaths turning into shallow gasps, he began to lose focus of what was happening around him. It was clear they were going to die, and deservedly so. If he had just left them at the storage unit he'd be at home right now and these American troops wouldn't have been here looking for him, most likely here to save his life, with no idea he was here voluntarily.

And the terrorists that had brought them here, that were now attacking him, no doubt knew exactly who he was from the beginning, and wanted him as a hostage to parade around and humiliate America on the world stage, then either demand the release of prisoners—men who would absolutely go on to kill other innocents—or money, again undoubtedly to fund further attacks on civilians.

Either way, if he weren't here, the soldiers wouldn't be here and the terrorists wouldn't be here. The dead innocent tourists would be alive, and today would be another peaceful day at the St. Gerasimos Monastery.

It's my fault.

The world suddenly came into focus.

"It's my fault!" he screamed, bolting to the right before any of the vets guarding him could take action. He ran in front of the entrance and stopped, spreading his arms and legs, trying to make himself the biggest target he possibly could. "Kill me! End this now!"

The two soldiers on either side of the gate spun to see what was happening when Grant felt himself tackled, his right side screaming out in pain as someone hit him square in the ribs, sending him sailing to the other side, away from the gate opening. He hit the ground and turned to see who had saved him.

It was the professor they had been talking about, Acton. Acton had successfully saved his life but now found himself on his knees in the middle of the entrance. He pushed himself to his feet, beginning to scramble for cover, when he suddenly spun, a burst of blood misting the air as he collapsed on his back.

Unmoving.

A woman's anguished scream cut through the mayhem, bringing a human moment to something so inhuman.

"James!" screamed Laura as she jumped to her feet, racing for his unmoving body. She felt hands grab her from behind, yanking her back to the cover of the ancient walls. She struggled against the grip, jerking back and forth and kicking her legs as she continued to scream, tears pouring down her face.

"Don't get yourself killed too!" cried Reading, trying to drag her to safety. Her entire view of what was going on was now tunnel vision, everything black except the body of her beloved James lying completely still in the open entrance to the outside, the bullets still pouring in, the stone he now lay on bursting apart as fresh bullets ricocheted.

"Covering fire!" yelled Niner as he and Spock rushed from their positions, grabbing the body of her poor James and began dragging him toward safety, the large trail of blood on the stone sickening.

He's dead! My James is dead!

She collapsed to the ground, Reading's arms making the fall gentle. He dropped to his knees beside her and she threw her arms around him, sobbing uncontrollably, even more than the day her brother had died in the cave collapse. The thought that she would hurt more for James than her brother had her feeling even more guilty.

I should have never let him agree to this.

A momentary flash of hatred for Martin was pushed aside by even more guilt as she focused her hatred on the Triarii. She looked up again as the two brave soldiers risked their lives for her James, when suddenly Niner spun several times, collapsing on the ground only feet away, he too unmoving.

Spock dragged the body of her fiancé toward Niner then grabbed his comrade by the collar, pulling them both to safety, his straining face red from the effort as nearly every vein was screaming for relief.

Another dead because of them!

All of this was the Trairii's fault, and she swore at that moment she would have her revenge if she lived to see another day.

Dawson picked off another of the terrorists then glanced over his shoulder to see Niner suddenly gasp and rise up halfway, grabbing at his chest, double-checking that he was still alive. Dawson said a silent prayer to the inventor of body armor and resumed looking for another target of opportunity. He could still hear the sobs of Professor Palmer to his right and his heart went out to her, and when time permitted he would grieve her loss with her, but now wasn't the time.

Over the gunfire he heard thumping in the distance and knew the Israeli's were arriving. He poked his head out and quickly scanned the area.

He could find no civilians anymore, all either dead or having successfully fled the scene.

The Israeli radio squelched and he held it to his ear.

"Sheep Dog, Goliath. Code is Thunder. Where do you want us, over?"

"Goliath, Sheep Dog, parking lot north side of complex. Your targets are six technicals, lead vehicle smoking, then anything with a gun, over."

"Roger that, Sheep Dog. Keep your heads down, out."

Dawson looked up and gave a wave as two AH-64 Apache gunships raced overhead, missiles streaking from their weapons pods, lead belching from their chain guns. He watched as the six vehicles the terrorists had arrived in were blown to pieces, the shrapnel from the shredded metal tearing apart the Hamas militants who were using them as cover.

This turn of events had the remaining dozen or so hostiles scrambling away from the other vehicles and into the open as they sought alternate cover.

"Take them out!" yelled Dawson as his team rushed forward, taking up positions across the gate, eliminating the enemy as they concentrated their fire on the choppers. A final burst from one of the gunships was followed by silence, nothing at all in the parking area moving.

Or even twitching.

Israeli efficiency. Hooyah!

Footsteps sprinting behind him had Dawson spinning but he stopped, Professor Palmer rushing to Acton's side, grabbing him and holding his lifeless body in her arms. He activated his comm as two of the choppers landed in a clearing nearby.

"Bravo Two, Bravo One, report, over!"

Red's voice came in loud and clear. "Bravo One, Bravo Two. All clear on this side, over."

"Roger that, report back to the front gate and thank our vets, out."

A platoon of Israeli soldiers rushed from a Black Hawk that had just set down, quickly securing the area as Dawson waved at them. A gasp behind him and a cry of joy from Palmer had him turn to see the bravest civie he knew suddenly moving.

"Medic!" yelled Dawson to the arriving Israeli's, one of them breaking off from the group and rushing toward the entrance. Dawson directed him to Acton and the man immediately went to work as Reading dragged Palmer away from her fiancé so the medic and Niner could do their job.

One of the Israeli's ran up to him and Dawson smiled as he recognized David.

"I didn't think you were coming," said Dawson.

"I heard there was a little excitement, so decided to take a peek." The Mossad agent looked around at the carnage. Dozens of terrorist bodies littered the parking area, too many tourists lay dead, the façade of the old monastery had been torn apart, and inside remained eight Triarii prisoners, one suicidal ex-President's son, sobbing in a corner, a handful of senior vets guarding them, and a former corpsman still working on an elderly tourist.

And Professor James Acton, ten paces away, fighting for his life.

Grant Jackson sat huddled in a corner of the wall, hugging his knees for several minutes before he realized the gunfire had stopped. He slowly lifted his head, looking around. Mitch and the Triarii were on the other side of the entrance, still lining the wall, several old tourists guarding them. To his right, twenty feet away lay the man who had saved his life. A man he had never met before, and whose name he had never spoken.

Professor James Acton.

Uniformed soldiers were now here, the previous group of Americans wearing casual clothes under their body armor and weaponry. He assumed the new arrivals were Israeli, two of them now working with one of the

Americans on the wounded professor. As he watched, the professor was placed on a stretcher, a woman who clearly cared about him and another man who looked almost as worried followed the medics as they carried him out of the monastery and out of sight.

Grant pushed himself to his feet and slowly walked toward the Triarii men lined against the wall. He nodded to the men guarding them, they obviously having been informed as to who he was. Stepping over to Mitch, he had a hard time keeping eye contact.

"I'm sorry about this," he said, not really sure why.

"Don't worry about it, kid, we've been in worse situations."

Grant's eyebrows jumped, wondering how much worse it could get. Dozens were dead, innocent blood spilled, all over a stupid piece of rock. "Listen, I need to say something."

"Anything."

"I-I made a mistake."

"What do you mean?"

Grant sucked in a deep breath. "I shouldn't have come. I should have stayed with Louisa. This is all my fault. If it weren't for me these soldiers wouldn't have come looking for me, these people wouldn't be dead." His voice cracked. "Today would have been a peaceful day," he whispered, his bottom lip trembling.

Mitch stepped forward and put a hand on his shoulder. "Let me tell you why you're wrong about everything you just said." Grant looked up at him then back at his feet. "These soldiers that are here now, the Americans, they're the same ones that killed those students and attacked the Triarii headquarters. Whether you were here or not, they would have been, because a skull was involved."

Grant's chest tightened as his jaw dropped slightly. He looked at Grant then around at the soldiers nearby. "You mean—"

"They're not here for you, they're here for the skull."

"But it isn't here."

"Nobody knew that until a few minutes ago. Mark my words, they were here to steal it, not save you. The fact you were here is just a coincidence. A fantastic one for them since now they have an excuse for being here, but a coincidence nonetheless."

Grant's mind was reeling with this new piece of information, but as the turmoil settled, he asked himself the important question—does it matter? Why these soldiers were here made no difference to the ultimate reason he had come to talk to Mitch. The real reason the soldiers were here was just further evidence that he needed out of this life, out of this world.

He clenched his teeth and straightened himself, looking Mitch in the eye.

"I want out of the Triarii."

Mitch laughed. "Is that what this is about?"

Grant nodded.

"Son, you were never *in* the Triarii. You can't just join up after a conversation in a farmhouse. There's indoctrination, training, oaths. It takes years."

"So I can leave and nobody will come after me?"

"Of course," laughed Mitch. "Like I said, we're friends of your father. I could never do anything to harm you."

Grant sighed and he could feel the color coming back to his cheeks as his entire body, nearly on the verge of fainting, relaxed. "You don't know how happy I am to hear that."

Mitch patted Grant's shoulder, still smiling. He reached into an upper pocket and removed a business card. On one side it had the Triarii symbol, the other side a phone number and a series of numbers.

"If you ever need anything, just call me," he said, handing the card to Grant.

Grant nodded, placing the card in his wallet. "Thank you for telling me about my father."

"Don't judge him on *your* beliefs," said Grant. "Remember what *he* believed, and use those beliefs to judge his actions. I hope in the end you will find them justified."

Grant nodded, not too sure he could ever agree with his father's actions, but deciding now wasn't the time to voice those concerns. He shook Mitch's hand, nodding to the others, Chip tossing him a wave, then walked over to the group of American soldiers, wondering what their mission actually was.

Dawson turned to Grant Jackson as he approached. "Mr. Jackson, are you okay?"

The young man nodded, looking back at his captors. "What will happen to them?"

"They'll be extradited to the United States and face charges."

Grant chewed on his cheek then looked at the ground. "There's something you should know."

"And what's that?"

"They kidnapped me, but I chose to stay with them."

"I know."

"You do?"

"I was at the storage place. I saw you get on the helicopter."

"So what happens now?"

Dawson smiled and motioned for the men to head to the helicopters for evac. "When you're kidnapped, sometimes you do crazy things. Stockholm Syndrome usually takes longer, but you already had a connection with these people, and they were probably able to manipulate you without you even realizing, because they knew your father."

"So you know about him?"

"Of course," said Dawson, choosing his words carefully. "Your father is the one who gave us orders that we followed, trusting in our handlers. Unfortunately things weren't as they seemed."

"You mean the students in Peru and the Triarii Headquarters."

"They told you about that?" asked Dawson, slightly surprised.

"Yes." Grant sucked in a deep breath and slowly let it out. "I'm sorry about that."

Dawson nodded. "So are we."

"Can I ask you a question?"

"Shoot."

"Why are you here? Honestly?"

Dawson smiled and stopped, pointing a finger at the helicopter with the Professors as it was about to lift off, the tiny old Abbot running toward the Black Hawk, waving his hand in the air.

"We're here for them. They were caught up in your father's affairs, and I nearly killed them because I was lied to. Now I spend my life living it as best I can, doing my job to the best of my ability, and whenever possible, making amends for my actions that week. And the best way I know how is to play guardian angel to those two professors whenever I can."

Grant nodded and extended his hand.

"You're a good man, sir. And I think perhaps it might be time for the Jackson family to begin to make up for the actions of one of their own."

Dawson smiled, shaking the man's hand.

"That sounds like a good choice to me."

Laura held James' hand tightly, the tears that streaked her face settling, the medics having assured her that he was going to live. He was out, something having been injected for the pain, but the bleeding had been stopped, or at least slowed significantly, and they were only ten minutes away from a trauma hospital that would take care of everything.

She heard a shout from outside. Turning, she saw the elderly Abbot shuffling as fast as he could toward the helicopter, waving a small piece of paper in his hand. He reached the helicopter, out of breath, and grabbed Laura's hand.

"For when he wakes up," he said, stuffing the paper into the palm of her hand.

"What's this?"

"The location of what you seek!"

The old man stepped back and the Black Hawk climbed into the air, the monastery quickly falling out of sight. She looked at the paper and found an address in Bethlehem.

She looked down at her beloved James as she pushed the paper into her pocket, at the moment not giving a damn about crystal skulls or the Triarii. All she cared about was James, and how close she had come to losing him. She ran her fingers through his hair, her eyes glassing over again as she squeezed his hand three times.

Hadassah Medical Center, Jerusalem, Israel
Present day, six days after the kidnapping

Professor James Acton lay in a hospital bed, the head of it in a sitting position, watching the television reports on the aftermath of their little escapade into the West Bank. Laura sat in a chair beside him, her head resting on the bed and his leg, her hand absentmindedly stroking his shin. Their good friend and protector Hugh Reading lay on the empty bed beside him thoroughly enjoying the lunch that Acton couldn't force himself to eat, hospital food quality apparently universal.

His wound had been bad compared to anything he had previously suffered, but not as traumatic as what was first thought. Nothing vital had been hit, and he had merely gone into shock when he was hit, his body shutting down to protect itself. Once the trauma unit had removed the bullet, shoved a few pints of blood into him and stitched him up, he felt fine. Now all he had to do was let the wound heal and rebuild his stamina, the ordeal having taken quite a bit of his strength away. Each day was better—a lot better—and he was hoping to be back to his regular routine within a few more days—less restrictions imposed on him by a still healing shoulder.

He could only imagine what his students were going to say when they saw him teaching again.

Reading suddenly pointed at the screen. "Hah!"

Laura's head popped up and Acton began to laugh. On the screen was a barricade built by the Palestinians outside of Jericho, black smoke billowing from oil drums alongside a stack of crushed and semi-crushed cars piled across the road, with a nearly immaculate Jaguar XK8 on top, its engine burned out, but otherwise in perfect condition.

Acton turned to Reading. "Do you think that's Dick Van Dyke's?" he asked, roaring in laughter as he remembered Dyke's brand new Jaguar catching fire on him on the highway, nearly killing the old actor.

"Dick Van who?" replied Reading.

"Dyke. You know, Marry Poppins, Diagnosis Murder?"

"Never heard of him," replied Reading, turning his attention to the Jell-O.

"You need to get out more," said Acton, gently rotating his shoulder.

"How does it feel," asked Laura, now sitting upright in her chair and facing him, her hand still on his leg as if she had made a vow to never be out of physical contact again.

"Good, actually. I can't wait to get out of here tomorrow. I'm sick of hospitals."

"Me too," came Reading's muffled reply, his mouth full of Jell-O. "I assume we're going to Bethlehem."

"Damned skippy!"

Laura frowned and Acton patted her hand.

"Hey, it's the only way we're going to get closure on this entire Triarii business."

She nodded, letting out a sigh.

"I just hope there's no more bullets."

Manger Street, Bethlehem, Israel

Present day, seven days after the kidnapping

Reading pulled the rental car to the curb, all of them looking out the driver side windows at the incredibly old stone structure across from them. Acton's trained eye knew that by outward appearances to the amateur eye it could be easily mistaken as being from biblical times, perhaps even a former inn that turned away Mary and Joseph, but he knew better. This old building had been built and rebuilt over the centuries, probably over a millennia, the wall in front that hid what was no doubt a courtyard beyond, clearly having undergone significant repairs and rebuilds many times.

"Is this it?" asked Reading, turning off the engine.

"I think so," said Laura, double-checking the piece of paper given her by the monk. "The address is correct."

"Doesn't look like much," observed Reading, removing the keys and climbing out of the car.

"What were you expecting?" asked Acton as Reading helped him from the car, his shoulder still sore, his body still a little weak from his ordeal.

Reading shrugged. "I dunno. Something fancier anyway."

"It's a nunnery. They're not known for being spectacular," said Laura as she held her hand out to block an approaching car as the three of them crossed the road a little more slowly than Acton would have liked. He could feel the beads of sweat forming on his forehead as he overexerted himself, but he refused to give in. They were so close to ending this nightmare that had hung over them for the past few years, there was no way he was going to let some bullet wound hold him back.

Laura waved her thanks to the driver who had stopped as they climbed the curb and stepped up to the humble wood door to the courtyard, a cross proudly displayed over it, nailed to the stone wall.

Reading knocked, three quick raps, then one, then three.

Acton looked at him. "Oh, very funny."

Reading grinned then his look turned to concern as he motioned toward Acton's sweating forehead. "Are you sure you're up for this?"

"Try to stop me," he said, pulling a bottle of water from the satchel Laura was wearing. He drained half it before the gate finally swung open a few inches and a sliver of a nun's face appeared.

Acton stepped forward. "Hello, my name is—"

"Professor Acton!" exclaimed the nun, pulling the gate all the way open and ushering them in. "Come in! Come in! The abbot told us to expect you should you survive, and thank the good Lord you did!" She closed the gate behind her, locking it, then excitedly led them across the small courtyard toward the main building. "I'm Sister Josephine. I understand you wanted a private tour!"

The woman was clearly excited, and Acton wasn't sure why. Perhaps the Abbot's almost fanboy appreciation had rubbed off on her, or she was just excited to have visitors, there being no indication from the outside that any type of tour was offered to the public.

As they crossed the courtyard, Sister Josephine spoke non-stop. "On your left are the living quarters, on the right are offices, workshops, storage and other things. In front of us is our humble church. We just finished prayers so your timing is perfect." She ushered them through a large set of wooden doors, lovingly maintained over time, the wood still a healthy sheen though pitted and scarred from years of service.

They stepped inside and found a small church with an altar at the head of it, a humble crucifix looking down on the congregation, with wood benches able to hold perhaps fifty worshippers. Carved into the walls were alcoves where different treasures were displayed—crucifixes, chalices, carvings of Mary with baby Jesus. Nothing of much monetary value beyond their historically intrinsic value.

"As you can see our church is simple but functional. We are a poor order, supported by visitors to the monastery. We pray, we help throughout the city where we can volunteering with the orphans, free clinics—anything we can to help the Lord's children."

She guided them to a side room, the tour whirlwind compared to others, almost reminding Acton of the White House tour.

"We're walking, we're walking!"

"Here we have gifts given by visitors over the years, some as much as a thousand years old."

Acton's expert eyes examined every piece, perhaps sixty or seventy in all, many crests from cities around Europe, music boxes, various crucifixes of varying value, an ornate mask, carvings of religious scenes and old bibles that Acton thought were of enough value to warrant much better preservation techniques than having them lying on a table, exposed to air, pollutants and worse, humidity.

Maybe I'll suggest to Laura we make a donation to preserve these items properly.

Acton could feel himself weakening and leaned on Laura a little more heavily. She noticed immediately.

"Do you have a crypt of any sorts?" she asked. "It was our understanding a body was moved here about seven hundred years ago."

Sister Josephine stopped in her tracks, turning to face her visitors. "No, no we don't. But…" She tapped her fingers on her chin, her eyes looking up as if trying to recall something. A finger pointed up, the memory apparently retrieved as an "Ah!" burst from her mouth. "Yes, I remember now. There is a story told among the nuns, obviously handed down from generation to generation, that during the crusades a body *was* moved here from the monastery to protect it from the Saracens."

"Is it still here?" asked Laura.

"No, I don't think so. At least if it is, nobody here knows where it would be, and as you can see"—she spread her arms out—"there's not a lot of places to hide a body."

"Perhaps underground?"

"Again, I don't think so. But then again I don't believe the stories myself. Neither do most of the sisters. I mean, why would the brothers only move one body? And why would a visitor not even from the Holy Land come and retrieve that body?"

"Excuse me?" interupted Acton. "A visitor?"

"Oh, didn't I mention him?"

"No."

"Oh, I'm sorry. I guess I'm just so caught up in the excitement of having visitors. I must apologize, I'm not much of a tour guide. In fact I think you're the first visitors we've had in years that weren't children. I always thought that if I hadn't given myself to the Lord I might have become a tour guide." She smiled wistfully, looking up at the sky. "Or an airline stewardess!"

"The visitor?" prompted Acton.

"Oh yes, my Lord, please forgive me! Yes, the visitor. The story, or myth if you will—as I said, I don't really believe it—is that this one body was moved here, and years later a man arrived and claimed the body as belonging to his family. He left with the remains, and that was the last he was heard of." She waved her hand in the air, as if dismissing everything she had just said. "Like I said, just a story, probably made up from bits and pieces of true stories. Bored nuns making their own entertainment, if you ask me."

It was at that moment that Acton realized their hopes of finding the body of Giuseppe at the nunnery was futile. Their search here was over, and Acton had a pretty good idea of where it just might need to take them next.

"Thank you very much for the tour, it was enlightening," said Acton. "I'm afraid I'm getting pretty weak, so we'll have to call it a day, I'm afraid."

Sister Josephine beamed at the praise, but also showed her concern for his health, pressing her palms together in prayer. "You are welcome any time, Professor Acton, should you be feeling better."

She began to lead them to the front gate, Laura and Reading helping him on either side. Sweat drenched his entire body and his shoulder was beginning to throb. He shook Sister Josephine's hand at the gate, thanking her again, then was nearly carried to the car by Reading. They helped him in the backseat and he collapsed, his arms sagging at his sides, his head lolled against the back of the seat.

"Are you okay?" asked Laura, climbing in the other side and immediately beginning to wipe his face dry with a handkerchief from her purse.

"Yeah, I just need to catch my breath," he said, taking a sip of water from a bottle Laura held to his lips. "Getting shot sucks."

"No shite," commented Reading who had the car running, looking back at his friend. "Do you want to go back to the hospital?"

Acton shook his head. "No, I'm already starting to feel better. I think I just need to get some rest, then I'll be okay." He turned to Laura. "And then I think I know exactly where we need to go."

She smiled at him, nodding. "Venice."

Reading's eyebrows shot up. "Venice? What has you thinking that?"

"The mask," echoed Acton and Laura, Acton holding out his hand, deferring to her.

Laura turned to Reading. "Do you remember in the small room where they had things that visitors had left?"

Reading nodded. "And you got Venice from that? I didn't see any bloody Gondolas."

Acton laughed then winced.

"Do you remember the mask?"

Reading's eyes shot up as he tried to recall. "Yes, actually. The very ornate thing that covers the eyes only, with a stick to hold it up with?"

"Good memory. It's a Venetian mask, usually worn at the Carnival of Venice which precedes Lent."

"I think I've seen them in movies," said Reading.

"Probably, it's quite famous. It caught on throughout Europe—the masks I mean—but Venice started it, and that mask was of a design popular at the end of the thirteenth century, exactly at the time of Marco Polo's return to Venice from China."

"You mean—?"

Acton cut him off. "That the visitor to the nunnery was Marco Polo himself, here to claim the body of his slave."

"Lot of trouble for a slave."

Laura shook her head. "No, remember that the translation called him his brother, and it was signed Giuseppe Polo. Only a freeman would do that."

Reading's eyebrows narrowed. "Sorry?"

"Giuseppe must have been offered his freedom before he died by the Polo family. This was extremely rare, and usually only granted to slaves who had proven their loyalty. And in a few cases, they were granted not only their freedom, but citizenship. And in even fewer cases, they were invited to join the family they once served as equals. I think that Marco Polo thought of this man as his brother. They most likely grew up together, played together, learned together, and in every sense of the word became brothers, to the point where Giuseppe being a servant simply became intolerable, thus the granting of his freedom."

"So what would he do with the body?" asked Reading.

"What would *you* do with the body of your brother?"

"Bury it at home."

"And if he had no wife or other family, where?"

Reading nodded. "I'd probably have him buried where *I* planned to be buried."

"Exactly," said Acton, his strength rapidly returning. "Tomorrow we fly to Venice."

Reading shook his head, turning around and putting the car in gear. "Yet another bloody city," he muttered. "At least this time there shouldn't be any guns."

The car started to roll forward and Acton turned his attention to the street.

And could have sworn he saw a man staring directly at him as he talked on his phone.

Church of San Lorenzo, Venice, Italy

Present day, nine days after the kidnapping

"I can't take you any farther," said Administrator Mitro, pointing to a closed doorway. "I really shouldn't be letting you in at all, but when His Holiness calls and asks for a personal favor?" Mitro threw up his hands. "What can one do?"

"Indeed," smiled Acton, feeling dramatically better than yesterday after nearly twenty-four hours of sleep and pampering. "We've been asked a favor by His Holiness on more than one occasion."

"It's impossible to say no," added Laura, giving Reading a glance to make sure he kept his mouth shut. Reading, standing behind the Administrator of the ancient Church of San Lorenzo, made a zipping motion over his mouth.

Acton extended his hand. "Thank you, Administrator. We will take it from here and disturb you no longer."

"You promise not to disturb anything you might find? When the church was rebuilt in the seventeenth century, much was lost," said the man, shaking his head. "To think they simply built over the old church without a thought to what was under it! Unbelievable idiocy." The man took a deep breath, then looked at his guests apologetically. "I'm sorry for the outburst, but you as archeologists must understand how I feel. The history lost! Idiocy!"

Acton smiled, almost laughing. "Believe me, we understand. So much has been lost to us through ignorance. Perhaps our little outing will bring back some of that past."

Mitro frowned. "Beyond this door no one has gone in my lifetime, perhaps many more. It is dangerous, falling apart. You take your lives in your own hands." He quickly made the sign of the cross. "May God protect you on your journey." With that he turned, marching quickly down the hall as if he wanted to be out of earshot lest any calamity unfold.

"Sounds encouraging," observed Reading. He reached for the door handle, the key used to unlock it still in the keyhole. "Shall we?"

"Do the honors," said Acton, flicking on his flashlight. Laura and Reading did the same, Reading pulling open the door. A dank, thick layer of air poured out, raising the humidity in the corridor noticeably. Acton stepped aside, almost as if a physical being had rolled past.

"Oh, what a wonderful smell we've discovered," muttered Reading as he stepped over the threshold.

"Okay, Han," grinned Acton, looking at Laura.

"Han?" she asked.

Acton was genuinely crestfallen. "Okay, when we get home, we're watching the original three Star Wars movies again."

Laura rolled her eyes. "You and your Star Wars! I might enjoy it a bit more if you didn't insist all three had to be watched in one sitting!"

Acton pursed his lips then stuck out his hand, flicking his fingers. "Okay, give me the ring back. I can't marry any woman who doesn't worship upon the altar of George Lucas."

"Are you two done?" asked Reading, already a good twenty feet ahead.

Acton gave Laura a kiss and a gentle smack on the bum and they stepped through the door. The dust and cobwebs were thick, the only footprints those of Reading.

"There's some stairs here. They look safe."

"Looks can be deceiving," said Acton. "You first."

"Sod off!"

Acton laughed, knowing full well Reading would insist on going first due to Acton's injury and Laura being of the "gentler" sex. Reading placed a tentative foot on the first step and gave it a push down.

"Seems okay."

"May I suggest a safety rope, hero?"

Reading's foot jumped off the step and back to the floor, turning to Acton a bit sheepishly. "Can't hurt, I guess."

Acton pulled a long rope from Reading's pack and tied it to a nearby stone column then wrapped it around Reading's waist. "Give it a try."

Reading pulled on it as hard as he could then nodded, satisfied. "If I can pull down a bloody column then I need to lose a few." He returned to the top of the steps. "Let's try this again." He stepped down with one foot, jumping a bit, then committed himself to the soundness of the stairs with another.

Suddenly the stairs started to shift. Reading spun around, his eyes bulging in shock as he grabbed onto the rope with both hands, his flashlight clattering to the floor below. He made eye contact with Acton who instinctively reached for the rope as the entire staircase collapsed, Reading falling out of sight with a yelp.

"Are you okay, Hugh?" cried Laura, peering over the edge and into the void below.

"What do you bloody well think?" came his voice, sounding none the worse for wear. "I can see the flashlight on the floor. I'm maybe five feet from the bottom. Give us a second." Several grunts were followed by a yelp at what Acton guessed was a healthy dose of rope burn. "Bloody hell!"

"You okay?" asked Acton, noticing the rope go slack.

"Yeah, care to join me?"

"Absolutely!" replied Acton with a smile at Laura. *As if there was any doubt.* He pulled the rope up then tied it around his waist. "I'll go next," he said.

"There's no arguing with you," she said. "Just be careful, don't forget you got shot only a week ago."

"You know me, no pain no gain."

"I've never heard you say that."

Acton frowned as he stepped off the edge, dangling on the rope. "True," he grunted as he one armed himself down, using his feet to control his descent. He reached the bottom without much trouble, Reading supporting him the final few feet. "Okay, it's safe for you to come down now!" he called as he untied the rope.

Acton shone his flashlight up as did Reading. Laura leaned backward into the void created by the collapsed stairs, then kicked off with her feet, quickly going hand over hand until she reached the bottom.

"Like a pro!" gushed Acton as he gave her a quick hug.

"Rappelling training last time we were in Peru. You should have tried it."

"Next time, I promise."

"Okay, kids, where to?" asked Reading, guiding his flashlight beam around the entire area. Acton and Laura joined in the stationary search, their lights playing out in various directions. The entire area seemed to be a junkyard of construction supplies from centuries ago. Broken rock, discarded wood, tools and equipment all cast about for as far as the beams could reach.

"Oh how I would love to catalog this place," whispered Acton as he examined some of the closer equipment. "Imagine what we could learn about construction techniques of the mid-seventeenth century!"

"I know!" agreed Laura. "This is such a treasure-trove of knowledge, it's such a shame it's been left here like this. What a waste!"

Acton pointed ahead to where the stairs had been leading. "I'm guessing that's the outer wall. It appears solid with no obvious blocked entrances. Hugh, you and Laura go left along the wall, I'll go right, just to confirm."

"Okay," said Reading, leading the way, Laura following him as they twisted their way around various obstacles. Acton struck out to the right, his flashlight playing along the floor then the wall, alternating until he reached the corner, no evidence of any hidden chambers on the other side.

"I'm at the corner, how about you?" he called, his voice echoing through the large forgotten sub-basement, there being two levels over head that were still used.

"I can see it now!" called Laura. "Still no signs of any openings or walled up ones."

"Okay, let's begin a sweep forward and see if there's anything along the next walls."

"Okay!"

They continued their survey for almost forty five minutes, finding several rooms leading off the first room, all filled with more junk, but none with any hints that they did or once did contain any sarcophagi. History recorded that Marco Polo was buried in this very church in 1324, but when it was rebuilt in the sixteen hundreds due to fire, they literally knocked down what was left and rebuilt over top of it, "losing" Venice's most famous resident's body in the process.

Acton was getting discouraged until his flashlight played out over the far wall of one of these unpromising side rooms. He froze, flicking his wrist back. There was a clear difference in the stone in one area, there obviously having been an entrance to another room at some time.

"I've got something!" he yelled, rushing over to the wall. He ran his fingers along it and could tell the stone was newer than the old walls, the stones not as tight together, there more mortar used with these joints than the other, the older stone relying more on the tightness of the fit than these newer stones clearly more hastily erected.

"What is it?" asked Laura as she stepped into the room, Reading close behind.

"Something's been bricked in here," said Acton, stepping back so the others could look.

"Definitely," said Laura as she ran her hands over the stone. She picked at some of the mortar, it crumbling in her fingers. She pressed against the bricked up area, the sound of stones shifting slightly echoing through the room. "This is pretty loose. We could probably knock it out."

"Just a bloody minute," said Reading, stepping forward. "Am I the only one who's sane here? This could be a load bearing wall for all we know! You could bring the entire church down on top of us."

Acton shook his head, pointing up at a massive wood beam. "Not to worry. That beam is covering this entire span. We should be able to safely take out these stones without compromising anything."

"And if you're wrong?"

"It's been a pleasure knowing you."

"Bah! Almost every time I see the likes of you I'm shot at, punched, kicked, kidnapped or some other blasted thing. 'Pleasure knowing you' me arse!"

Acton grinned, picking up a large mallet discarded nearby. He held it up for Reading. "Care to do the honors or shall I have my fiancée do it for you?"

"Give me the bloody thing," muttered Reading as he snatched the weighty tool from Acton. He positioned himself for the first blow then turned. "What are you, daft? Get the hell out of the bloody room! If I survive this, then you can come in, but not before."

"Yes, Dad," whined Acton as he and Laura headed for the entrance.

"Sod off! 'Dad'. I'm not old enough to be your fu—" The first blow hit the wall, cutting off his tirade with a grunt. Another swing and from what Acton's flashlight revealed the center of the stones seemed to be sagging inward. Another blow and Reading leapt back as the newer section collapsed in, almost in a single piece. He looked up, pulling his own flashlight out and examined the ceiling. Apparently satisfied, a few more blows were delivered to clear some bottom stones, then he tossed the mallet aside, leaning against the wall next to his handiwork, gasping.

Acton and Laura quickly reentered the room, Acton smacking Reading on the arm with a grin, then stepping through his handiwork. His heart leapt into his throat as his flashlight revealed exactly what they had been looking for. A large sarcophagus, carved in stone, stood in the center of the room. Frescos lined the surrounding walls, paintings of several different men evident, but one that was unmistakable from historical paintings.

Marco Polo.

Depictions of his travels had been painstakingly recreated on the walls of his final resting place, his sarcophagus a gorgeous example of early-Renaissance craftsmanship.

"Is this it?" asked Reading as he joined them, still a little short of breath.

"Yes," said Laura, already brushing away the dust on the sarcophagus. "This is definitely him."

Acton slowly walked over to the final resting place of one of the world's great explorers. His heart was slamming in his chest in excitement, the throbbing in his shoulder forgotten. He looked at Laura with a smile, reaching out and grabbing her hand as they both circled the large rectangular stonework.

"If that's him, where's the bloody slave?"

Acton stopped, his eyes narrowing, a frown emerging. *Leave it to Hugh to state the obvious. And ruin the moment.* They weren't looking for Marco Polo's body, they were looking for his slave's. Acton looked around and it was clear that there was only one body here, the entire room meant to honor one man, Marco Polo.

"Could we have been wrong?" asked Laura. "I don't see anywhere else that a body could be kept."

"Maybe there's another room? Another chamber?" suggested Acton.

"We didn't see anything else, and this is clearly Marco Polo's crypt, but it doesn't appear to be a family crypt. His parents aren't here, his wife, children. Just him."

Acton shook his head. "That doesn't make any sense. In those days they might honor him more prominently, but they would definitely make provisions to have his family buried with him eventually."

"Um, Professors," said Reading, interrupting the flow of scholarly thought.

"What?" asked Acton, turning toward Reading.

"You're standing on him."

"Huh?" Acton looked to where Reading's flashlight was shining and jumped back. Laura pounced faster than he could, his shoulder and weakened state still slowing him down. By the time he had joined her on his knees, she had already swept away the dust from the engraving in the floor.

And as Acton translated the inscription, his heart nearly stopped.

"*Giuseppe Polo. A freeman and a beloved brother.*"

"We found it!" whispered Laura. They both shuffled back, brushes out, sweeping away the dust. Acton found an edge, then followed it, sweeping out the crack in the floor, and within minutes they were all standing back, staring at the rectangle covering to what from all outward appearances was the tomb of Giuseppe Polo.

Reading left the room, returning a few minutes later with a couple of pieces of metal that Acton realized could be used as crude pry bars. Reading jammed an edge into the crevice then looked at Acton.

"So, am I giving it the old heave ho?"

Acton nodded and Reading pushed down on the bar, grunting as he did so. The scrape of stone on stone erupted and Acton dropped to the floor, wedging the second bar in. Laura pushed down on it as hard as she could, then Reading quickly jerked his, repositioning it deeper, allowing Laura to get hers inside. Acton grabbed Laura's bar, sitting back on it with his right buttock, using his weight rather than muscle power to push the lid of the recessed sarcophagus above the lip. Reading pulled his lever out, switching to the left side, near the end already pried loose, and opposite Marco Polo's sarcophagus, then shoved the bar under it, pushing down. Laura went opposite him and shoved with her hands on the stone. It shifted slightly as Reading repositioned farther down without letting the bar out. Pushing again, Laura shoved, bracing herself with her feet against Marco's final resting place, and the slab shifted several inches.

"That should be enough," she said as Acton rose, the stone settling on his pry bar but with one edge over the lip, the rest would just be muscle power. Reading removed his bar then joined the three of them at the opposite corner of the one that now sat above the lip. All three pushed, the stone shifting aside in jerks. Several more minutes of prying and pulling and shoving had the stone cover free, twisted perpendicular to the recessed outline.

They all sat on the floor, exhausted, Laura tossing out bottles of water that were quickly drained, then returned, nobody wanting to add to the mess that had been created beyond these walls.

"Shall we?" asked Acton. He was greeted with tired nods. He crawled over to the edge and smiled, almost tempted to reach out and touch the man who had affected their lives so much over the past week. "Giuseppe Polo, freeman and beloved brother," he whispered as he examined the remains of the one man who knew the secret of the thirteenth crystal skull.

"Look!" exclaimed Laura, reaching under the lid of the sarcophagus and retrieving a basketball sized object, wrapped in various leathers and cloths, most falling apart. "This has to be it!"

Acton could feel his heart pounding in his ears as he exchanged excited glances with his friends. "Open it!" he hissed.

Laura placed it on the floor and carefully removed the wrappings, and within moments it was clear what it was. As she removed the final layer she lifted the object up, all three of them shining their flashlights on it, it causing Acton to shudder as the hairs on his neck stood on end, goose bumps covering his body.

There was no doubt this was a crystal skull just like the one he had found in Peru.

And a sudden sense of foreboding swept over him.

"Let's get out of here, now," he whispered, an unreasonable fear already taking over.

"Agreed," said Reading as he jumped to his feet and single-handedly pushed the cover back over Giuseppe Polo's remains. "The sooner that thing is back in London, the sooner I'll sleep at night."

Reading led the way back to the rope. Acton put the skull in Laura's pack, lacing it tight.

"I'll go first," said Reading. "When I get to the top, I'll pull you both up." He grabbed the rope then pulled himself up, gym class style, with what Acton thought was an impressive amount of cursing even for Reading.

Once at the top their friend rolled over the edge and heavy breathing could be heard for several minutes.

Acton decided ribbing was in order, and was about to open his mouth when the end of the rope dropped at his feet.

Later.

They tied the rope around his waist, tucking it under his legs so it would act almost like a seat. Acton grabbed onto the rope with his good arm then winked at Laura.

"Here goes nothing."

He felt Reading pull and he jerked up several feet, then another couple of feet, allowing Laura to get under him and push against the seat of his pants as hard as she could. This allowed Reading to rapidly pull him up several more feet, the remaining ten a struggle, Acton unable to help, instead feeling his rope seat begin to tighten uncomfortably. It seemed like forever, and felt even worse, but eventually he could reach the floor and at least contribute a little bit of muscle power to the effort. As his head cleared he could see the beet red face of Reading as he continued to pull with all his might. With one final yank, Acton managed to get his chest onto the floor, then swing his leg up, rolling to safety, Reading collapsing beside him, his chest heaving and sagging rapidly.

Acton slowly untied the rope, and when the knot gave, he felt a flood of relief as his circulation returned. He tossed the rope into the void and before either of them could catch their breath to help, Laura was at their side, brushing the dust off her clothes

"Should I call an ambulance for you two?"

"Sod"—deep breath—"off!"

Acton laughed and pushed himself to his feet, offering to help Reading who batted his hand way, getting up himself. Acton's knees were shaking but the smile on his face was unwavering. *We found the tomb of Marco Polo!* At the moment he couldn't give a damn about the crystal skull. All he cared about was the incredible historical find just below them. They would have to keep it secret at first, but with permission hopefully to come from the Vatican, they should be able to do a proper study of the tomb, then perhaps even have it restored so the public could honor the man who introduced the Far East to the masses of Europe.

They exited the main doors of the church, clearing the steps and heading toward the closed gates when they suddenly opened, a man stepping inside from the street, followed by another, and within moments there were at least a dozen people blocking their exit.

"Get behind me," said Reading as he stepped forward, Acton already moving in front of Laura as he looked around for another escape route.

"Let's fall back to the church," he whispered.

"Professor James Acton, Professor Laura Palmer, Special Agent Hugh Reading." The voice came from one of the men blocking their way, he having stepped forward. "I assume congratulations are in order?"

Acton stepped forward. "Who are you?"

The man stepped closer, extending his left arm and exposing his wrist and the Triarii tattoo.

"I believe you have something that belongs to us."

Acton turned to look at Laura, his eyes resting momentarily on her backpack containing the skull. He turned back to their interrogator. "How do we know you're the real Triarii?"

The man smiled, then stood aside, motioning toward the door. As Acton looked, he saw a wheelchair emerge from the darkness, the lights of the courtyard lighting an all too familiar face.

"Martin!" cried Reading, already charging forward, the Triarii stepping aside. "What the bloody hell are you doing here you daft bastard! You should be in the hospital!"

Acton grabbed Laura by the hand as they walked over to their friend, Martin Chaney, smiles on both their faces. Handshakes, hugs and insults were exchanged, then Acton looked about him, the looks all expectant.

He untied Laura's backpack and removed the carefully wrapped skull. He handed it to Chaney. "Please take this as far away from us as possible."

Chaney smiled, cradling the skull in his hands as if it were precious, and Acton suddenly realized that to these people surrounding them, some with tears pouring down their faces, others with more control having merely glassed over eyes, this was a truly religious moment, something probably none of them had ever expected to experience—the discovery of another crystal skull.

"We will take this back to London immediately," said Chaney, handing it to the man who had first spoken, the others filing out of the courtyard, weapons drawn. "And Professors, Hugh?"

"Yes, mate?" asked Reading, his hand still on his friend's shoulder.

"The Triarii thanks you, and owes you a debt of gratitude. Should you ever need our assistance, it will be there for you. Forever."

Chaney motioned for the person pushing his chair to proceed, and moments later they were alone in the courtyard, possessing nothing they hadn't already had when they entered, except increased wisdom, and the knowledge their ordeal was finally over.

"Now we have just one more stop to make," said Acton, eliciting a groan from Reading.

Papal Office, Apostolic Palace, The Vatican
Present day, ten days after the kidnapping

"So everything has been returned to its rightful place?"

Acton nodded at the Pope. "Everything that was removed has been returned, the skull has been delivered into the hands of the Triarii, and with your permission, we will begin examination of the burial site of Marco Polo."

"It seems the least I can do. I will sign the decree tonight. Tomorrow I will be announcing my resignation as my work here is done."

"I really wish you would reconsider, your Holiness," said Mario Giasson, Vatican's head of security. He shifted in his seat. "Forgive me for saying so, however resignation from your position is almost unheard of."

The old man raised a shaking finger. "But *not* unheard of." He shook his head. "No, I must resign. It is the right thing to do, and in time, hopefully God will forgive me for what I have done."

Giasson made the sign of the cross, clearly uncomfortable with this turn of events.

"What will you do?" asked Laura, sitting between Acton and Reading.

"I'm not sure what my title will be. I'm sure the lawyers will figure that out. I hope to remain here, a simple priest, should my successor permit it. If not, perhaps I'll return to a monastery in Germany." He shrugged. "God will provide."

Acton, staring at Laura, suddenly focused on every detail as she smiled sympathetically at their host. *What will you do?* His thoughts thrust to when he too would be that age. *What will you be doing when you're eighty? What will you have done?* His chest tightened, his heart slammed against his ribcage, his ears pounded with the flow of blood as he realized at that very moment exactly what he needed to do *now* in order to secure the future he so desperately wanted.

"Will you marry me?" he blurted out.

Laura's head spun toward him in shock, then her eyebrows narrowed in confusion. "Of course, dear. I already said yes!" she smiled, flashing the ring he had needlessly protected in his cuff, their hotel possessions untouched. She glanced at Reading and Giasson with a grin. "Just how badly were you shot?"

Acton shook his head, turning his chair to face her, taking both her hands in his. "No, I mean right now! Let's get married right now!"

"What!" exclaimed Laura, her eyes instantly glistening over.

Acton turned to the Pope. "Sir, I mean your Holiness, will you marry us?" Acton paused a second. "*Can* you marry us?"

The old man beamed, his smile as great as any Acton had seen from the man in their years of contact. "Yes I *can*, and yes, I absolutely will!"

Acton turned back to Laura. "What do you think?"

A tear rolled down her cheek as she smiled, ear to ear, a smile he knew was of complete joy, matching his own. "I think it's a fantastically impulsive idea!" she replied, then her smile grew even broader. "I say, let's!"

Acton rose, still holding her hands as Laura joined him, tears pouring down his own cheeks. Acton glanced over at Reading who couldn't stop grinning, even he wiping his eyes dry.

"Do you have the rings?" asked the Pontiff.

Acton's heart stopped. "Oh my God, no, I don't!"

Giasson jumped forward, pulling his wedding band off his finger and handing it to Acton. "Here, use this."

Reading reached for his own hand then stopped. "Blast! I'm not married anymore!"

"I'll go get one from someone!" said Giasson as he rushed out the doors. The elderly pontiff rounded his desk, Bible in hand, and stood in front of the two lovers. Giasson rushed back into the room, holding up a second ring triumphantly, handing it to Laura, leaving Acton to wonder what poor soul in the hallway had given up their ring, and whether or not an explanation was even given. The pontiff began to recite the vows, but Acton didn't hear a word, his entire world engulfed by the smile of the woman he loved.

Suddenly the pontiff paused, his eyebrows narrowing as if something were occurring to him.

"Ah, are you two Catholic?"

Acton threw his head back and nearly cursed as he groaned to the heavens. He looked at Laura who was beginning to laugh, then at the pontiff. "How about a snap conversion?"

The old man chuckled, shaking his head as his Bible snapped shut. "I think God has other plans for you tonight."

Acton exchanged glances with Laura then Reading, not sure he liked the sound of that.

What more could He possibly do to us?

THE END

ACKNOWLEDGEMENTS

For those who have followed the James Acton series, the Triarii and their crystal skulls are familiar territory. Loose ends had been intentionally left through the previous seven novels, with the idea of this novel left to tie everything up. It is always a challenge to write an Acton novel so that it can be a standalone story that everyone can enjoy, not just those who in this case have read the previous seven installments. In order to do so, repetition is quite often necessary, and with this novel tied so intimately with The Protocol, more was necessary than normal.

I hope I got the balance right!

For those who haven't read The Protocol but enjoyed the lore of the Triarii, check it out. It was my debut novel and led to this entire best selling series. For those who had already read it, I hope this was an enjoyable experience revisiting the past.

I'd like to thank my researcher—my Dad—who knocked himself out again, and once again was left spinning from time to time when I changed my mind about where the story was heading. Fun fact: the monastery was supposed to be in Syria, but when he found St. Gerasimos in the West Bank, I thought that would be even more fun to write.

Acton #9 is on the way, ideas already percolating in the old brain. I can't wait to see how it turns out!

And one final thing as a reminder to those who have not already done so, please visit my website at www.jrobertkennedy.com then sign up for the Insiders Club. You'll get emails about new book releases, new collections, sales, etc. Only an email or two a month tops, I promise!

And as always, to my wife, daughter, parents and friends, thank you once again for your support. And to you the readers, thank you! You've all made this possible.

ABOUT THE AUTHOR

J. Robert Kennedy is the author of over one dozen international best sellers, including the smash hit James Acton Thrillers series, the first installment of which, The Protocol, has been on the best sellers list since its release, including a three month run at number one. In addition to the other novels from this series, Brass Monkey, Broken Dove, The Templar's Relic (also a number one best seller), Flags of Sin, The Arab Fall (also #1), The Circle of Eight (also #1) and The Venice Code, he has written the international best sellers Rogue Operator, Containment Failure, Cold Warriors, Depraved Difference, Tick Tock, The Redeemer and The Turned. Robert spends his time in Ontario, Canada with his family.

Visit Robert's website at www.jrobertkennedy.com for the latest news and contact information.

The Protocol

A James Acton Thriller, Book #1

For two thousand years the Triarii have protected us, influencing history from the crusades to the discovery of America. Descendent from the Roman Empire, they pervade every level of society, and are now in a race with our own government to retrieve an ancient artifact thought to have been lost forever.

Caught in the middle is archaeology professor James Acton, relentlessly hunted by the elite Delta Force, under orders to stop at nothing to possess what he has found, and the Triarii, equally determined to prevent the discovery from falling into the wrong hands.

With his students and friends dying around him, Acton flees to find the one person who might be able to help him, but little does he know he may actually be racing directly into the hands of an organization he knows nothing about...

Brass Monkey

A James Acton Thriller, Book #2

A nuclear missile, lost during the Cold War, is now in play--the most public spy swap in history, with a gorgeous agent the center of international attention, triggers the end-game of a corrupt Soviet Colonel's twenty five year plan. Pursued across the globe by the Russian authorities, including a brutal Spetsnaz unit, those involved will stop at nothing to deliver their weapon, and ensure their pay day, regardless of the terrifying consequences.

When Laura Palmer confronts a UNICEF group for trespassing on her Egyptian archaeological dig site, she unwittingly stumbles upon the ultimate weapons deal, and becomes entangled in an international conspiracy that sends her lover, archeology Professor James Acton, racing to Egypt with the most unlikely of allies, not only to rescue her, but to prevent the start of a holy war that could result in Islam and Christianity wiping each other out.

From the bestselling author of Depraved Difference and The Protocol comes Brass Monkey, a thriller international in scope, certain to offend some, and stimulate debate in others. Brass Monkey pulls no punches in confronting the conflict between two of the world's most powerful, and divergent, religions, and the terrifying possibilities the future may hold if left unchecked.

Broken Dove

A James Acton Thriller, Book #3

With the Triarii in control of the Roman Catholic Church, an organization founded by Saint Peter himself takes action, murdering one of the new Pope's operatives. Detective Chaney, called in by the Pope to investigate, disappears, and, to the horror of the Papal staff sent to inform His Holiness, they find him missing too, the only clue a secret chest, presented to each new pope on the eve of their election, since the beginning of the Church.

Interpol Agent Reading, determined to find his friend, calls Professors James Acton and Laura Palmer to Rome to examine the chest and its forbidden contents, but before they can arrive, they are intercepted by an organization older than the Church, demanding the professors retrieve an item stolen in ancient Judea in exchange for the lives of their friends.

All of your favorite characters from The Protocol return to solve the most infamous kidnapping in history, against the backdrop of a two thousand year old battle pitting ancient foes with diametrically opposed agendas.

From the internationally bestselling author of Depraved Difference and The Protocol comes Broken Dove, the third entry in the smash hit James Acton Thrillers series, where J. Robert Kennedy reveals a secret concealed by the Church for almost 1200 years, and a fascinating interpretation of what the real reason behind the denials might be.

The Templar's Relic

A James Acton Thriller, Book #4

The Church Helped Destroy the Templars. Will a twist of fate let them get their revenge 700 years later?

The Vault must be sealed, but a construction accident leads to a miraculous discovery--an ancient tomb containing four Templar Knights, long forgotten, on the grounds of the Vatican. Not knowing who they can trust, the Vatican requests Professors James Acton and Laura Palmer examine the find, but what they discover, a precious Islamic relic, lost during the Crusades, triggers a set of events that shake the entire world, pitting the two greatest religions against each other.

Join Professors James Acton and Laura Palmer, INTERPOL Agent Hugh Reading, Scotland Yard DI Martin Chaney, and the Delta Force Bravo Team as they race against time to defuse a worldwide crisis that could quickly devolve into all-out war.

At risk is nothing less than the Vatican itself, and the rock upon which it was built.

From J. Robert Kennedy, the author of six international bestsellers including Depraved Difference and The Protocol, comes The Templar's Relic, the fourth entry in the smash hit James Acton Thrillers series, where once again Kennedy takes history and twists it to his own ends, resulting in a heart pounding thrill ride filled with action, suspense, humor and heartbreak.

Flags of Sin

A James Acton Thriller, Book #5

Archaeology Professor James Acton simply wants to get away from everything, and relax. A trip to China seems just the answer, and he and his fiancée, Professor Laura Palmer, are soon on a flight to Beijing.

But while boarding, they bump into an old friend, Delta Force Command Sergeant Major Burt Dawson, who surreptitiously delivers a message that they must meet the next day, for Dawson knows something they don't.

China is about to erupt into chaos.

Foreign tourists and diplomats are being targeted by unknown forces, and if they don't get out of China in time, they could be caught up in events no one had seen coming.

J. Robert Kennedy, the author of eight international best sellers, including the smash hit James Acton Thrillers, takes history once again and turns it on its head, sending his reluctant heroes James Acton and Laura Palmer into harm's way, to not only save themselves, but to try and save a country from a century old conspiracy it knew nothing about.

The Arab Fall

A James Acton Thriller, Book #6

The greatest archeological discovery since King Tut's tomb is about to be destroyed!

The Arab Spring has happened and Egypt has yet to calm down, but with the dig site on the edge of the Nubian Desert, a thousand miles from the excitement, Professor Laura Palmer and her fiancé Professor James Acton return with a group of students, and two friends: Interpol Special Agent Hugh Reading, and Scotland Yard DI Martin Chaney.

But an accidental find by Chaney may lead to the greatest archaeological discovery since the tomb of King Tutankhamen, perhaps even greater. And when news of it spreads, it reaches the ears of a group hell-bent on the destruction of all idols and icons, their mere existence considered blasphemous to Islam.

As chaos hits the major cities of the world in a coordinated attack, unbeknownst to the professors, students and friends, they are about to be faced with one of the most difficult decisions of their lives. Stay and protect the greatest archaeological find of our times, or save themselves and their students from harm, leaving the find to be destroyed by fanatics determined to wipe it from the history books.

From J. Robert Kennedy, the author of eleven international bestsellers including Rogue Operator and The Protocol, comes The Arab Fall, the sixth entry in the smash hit James Acton Thrillers series, where Kennedy once again takes events from history and today's headlines, and twists them into a heart pounding adventure filled with humor and heartbreak, as one of their own is left severely wounded, fighting for their life.

The Circle of Eight

A James Acton Thriller, Book #7

Abandoned by their government, Delta Team Bravo fights to not only save themselves and their families, but humanity as well.

The Bravo Team is targeted by a madman after one of their own intervenes in a rape. Little do they know this internationally well-respected banker is also a senior member of an organization long thought extinct, whose stated goals for a reshaped world are not only terrifying, but with today's globalization, totally achievable.

As the Bravo Team fights for its very survival, they are suspended, left adrift without their support network. To save themselves and their families, markers are called in, former members volunteer their services, favors are asked for past services, and the expertise of two professors, James Acton and his fiancée Laura Palmer, is requested.

It is a race around the globe to save what remains of the Bravo Team, abandoned by their government, alone in their mission, with only their friends to rely upon, as an organization over six centuries old works in the background to destroy them and all who help them, as it moves forward with plans that could see the world population decimated in an attempt to recreate Eden.

The Circle of Eight is the seventh installment in the internationally best selling James Acton Thrillers series. In The Circle of Eight J. Robert Kennedy, author of over a dozen international best sellers, is at his best, weaving a tale spanning centuries and delivering a taut thriller that will keep you on the edge of your seat from page one until the breathtaking conclusion.

The Venice Code

A James Acton Thriller, Book #8

A SEVEN HUNDRED YEAR OLD MYSTERY IS ABOUT TO BE SOLVED. BUT HOW MANY MUST DIE FIRST?

A former President's son is kidnapped in a brazen attack on the streets of Potomac by the very ancient organization that murdered his father, convinced he knows the location of an item stolen from them by the late president.

A close friend awakes from a coma with a message for archeology Professor James Acton from the same organization, sending him along with his fiancée Professor Laura Palmer on a quest to find an object only rumored to exist, while trying desperately to keep one step ahead of a foe hell-bent on possessing it.

And seven hundred years ago, the Mongol Empire threatens to fracture into civil war as the northern capital devolves into idol worship, the Khan sending in a trusted family to save the empire--two brothers and a son, Marco Polo, whose actions have ramifications that resonate to this day.

From J. Robert Kennedy, the author of fourteen international best sellers comes The Venice Code, the latest installment of the hit James Acton Thrillers series. Join James Acton and his friends, including Delta Team Bravo and CIA Special Agent Dylan Kane in their greatest adventure yet, an adventure seven hundred years in the making.

Rogue Operator

A Special Agent Dylan Kane Thriller, Book #1

TO SAVE THE COUNTRY HE LOVES, SPECIAL AGENT DYLAN KANE MIGHT HAVE TO BETRAY IT.

Three top secret research scientists are presumed dead in a boating accident, but the kidnapping of their families the same day raises questions the FBI and local police can't answer, leaving them waiting for a ransom demand that will never come.

Central Intelligence Agency Analyst Chris Leroux stumbles upon the story, and finds a phone conversation that was never supposed to happen. When he reports it to his boss, the National Clandestine Services Chief, he is uncharacteristically reprimanded for conducting an unauthorized investigation and told to leave it to the FBI.

But he can't let it go.

For he knows something the FBI doesn't.

One of the scientists is alive.

Chris makes a call to his childhood friend, CIA Special Agent Dylan Kane, leading to a race across the globe to stop a conspiracy reaching the highest levels of political and corporate America, that if not stopped, could lead to war with an enemy armed with a weapon far worse than anything in the American arsenal, with the potential to not only destroy the world, but consume it.

J. Robert Kennedy, the author of nine international best sellers, including the smash hit James Acton Thrillers, introduces Rogue Operator, the first installment of his newest series, The Special Agent Dylan Kane Thrillers, promising to bring all of the action and intrigue of the James Acton Thrillers with a hero who lives below the radar, waiting for his country to call when it most desperately needs him.

Containment Failure

A Special Agent Dylan Kane Thriller, Book #2

THE BLACK DEATH KILLED ALMOST HALF OF EUROPE'S POPULATION. THIS TIME BILLIONS ARE AT RISK.

New Orleans has been quarantined, an unknown virus sweeping the city, killing one hundred percent of those infected. The Centers for Disease Control, desperate to find a cure, is approached by BioDyne Pharma who reveal a former employee has turned a cutting edge medical treatment capable of targeting specific genetic sequences into a weapon, and released it.

CIA Special Agent Dylan Kane has been given one guideline from his boss: consider yourself unleashed, leaving Kane and New Orleans Police Detective Isabelle Laprise battling to stay alive as an insidious disease and terrified mobs spread through the city while they desperately seek those behind the greatest crime ever perpetrated.

The stakes have never been higher as Kane battles to save not only his friends and the country he loves, but all of mankind.

In Containment Failure, eleven times internationally bestselling author J. Robert Kennedy delivers a terrifying tale of what could happen when science goes mad, with enough sorrow, heartbreak, laughs and passion to keep readers on the edge of their seats until the chilling conclusion.

Cold Warriors

A Special Agent Dylan Kane Thriller, Book #3

THE COUNTRY'S BEST HOPE IN DEFEATING A FORGOTTEN SOVIET WEAPON LIES WITH DYLAN KANE AND THE COLD WARRIORS WHO ORIGINALLY DISCOVERED IT.

While in Chechnya CIA Special Agent Dylan Kane stumbles upon a meeting between a known Chechen drug lord and a retired General once responsible for the entire Soviet nuclear arsenal. Money is exchanged for a data stick and the resulting transmission begins a race across the globe to discover just what was sold, the only clue a reference to a top secret Soviet weapon called Crimson Rush.

Unknown to Kane, this isn't the first time America has faced this threat and he soon receives a mysterious message, relayed through his friend and CIA analyst Chris Leroux, arranging a meeting with perhaps the one man alive today who can help answer the questions the nation's entire intelligence apparatus is asking--the Cold Warrior who had discovered the threat the first time.

Over thirty years ago.

In Cold Warriors, the third installment of the hit Special Agent Dylan Kane Thrillers series, J. Robert Kennedy, the author of thirteen international bestsellers including The Protocol and Rogue Operator, weaves a tale spanning two generations and three continents with all the heart pounding, edge of your seat action his readers have come to expect. Take a journey back in time as the unsung heroes of a war forgotten try to protect our way of life against our greatest enemy, and see how their war never really ended, the horrors of decades ago still a very real threat today.

The Turned

Zander Varga, Vampire Detective, Book #1

Zander has relived his wife's death at the hands of vampires every day for almost three hundred years, his perfect memory a curse of becoming one of The Turned—infecting him their final heinous act after her murder.

Nineteen year-old Sydney Winter knows Zander's secret, a secret preserved by the women in her family for four generations. But with her mother in a coma, she's thrust into the front lines, ahead of her time, to fight side-by-side with Zander.

And she wouldn't change a thing. She loves the excitement, she loves the danger. And she loves Zander. But it's a love that will have to go unrequited, because Zander has only one thing on his mind. And it's been the same thing for over two hundred years. Revenge.

But today, revenge will have to wait, because Zander Varga, Private Detective, has a new case. A woman's husband is missing. The police aren't interested. But Zander is. Something doesn't smell right, and he's determined to find out why.

From J. Robert Kennedy, the internationally bestselling author of The Protocol and Depraved Difference, comes his sixth novel, The Turned, a terrifying story that in true Kennedy fashion takes a completely new twist on the origin of vampires, tying it directly to a well-known moment in history. Told from the perspective of Zander Varga and his assistant, Sydney Winter, The Turned is loaded with action, humor, terror and a centuries long love that must eventually be let go.

Depraved Difference

A Detective Shakespeare Mystery, Book #1

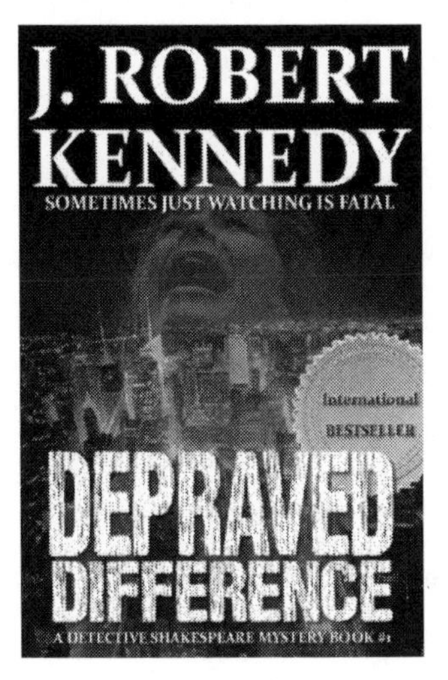

WOULD YOU HELP, WOULD YOU RUN, OR WOULD YOU JUST WATCH?

When a young woman is brutally assaulted by two men on the subway, her cries for help fall on the deaf ears of onlookers too terrified to get involved, her misery ended with the crushing stomp of a steel-toed boot. A cellphone video of her vicious murder, callously released on the Internet, its popularity a testament to today's depraved society, serves as a trigger, pulled a year later, for a killer.

Emailed a video documenting the final moments of a woman's life, entertainment reporter Aynslee Kai, rather than ask why the killer chose her to tell the story, decides to capitalize on the opportunity to further her career. Assigned to the case is Hayden Eldridge, a detective left to learn the ropes by a disgraced partner, and as videos continue to follow victims, he discovers they were all witnesses to the vicious subway murder a year earlier, proving sometimes just watching is fatal.

From the author of The Protocol and Brass Monkey, Depraved Difference is a fast-paced murder suspense novel with enough laughs, heartbreak, terror and twists to keep you on the edge of your seat, then knock you flat on the floor with an ending so shocking, you'll read it again just to pick up the clues.

Tick Tock

A Detective Shakespeare Mystery, Book #2

Crime Scene tech Frank Brata digs deep and finds the courage to ask his colleague, Sarah, out for coffee after work. Their good time turns into a nightmare when Frank wakes up the next morning covered in blood, with no recollection of what happened, and Sarah's body floating in the tub. Determined not to go to prison for a crime he's horrified he may have committed, he scrubs the crime scene clean, and, tormented by text messages from the real killer, begins a race against the clock to solve the murder before his own co-workers, his own friends, solve it first, and find him guilty.

Billionaire Richard Tate is the toast of the town, loved by everyone but his wife. His plans for a romantic weekend with his mistress ends in disaster, waking the next morning to find her murdered, floating in the tub. After fleeing in a panic, he returns to find the hotel room spotless, and no sign of the body. An envelope found at the scene contains not the expected blackmail note, but something far more sinister.

Two murders, with the same MO, targeting both the average working man, and the richest of society, sets a rejuvenated Detective Shakespeare, and his new reluctant partner, Amber Trace, after a murderer whose motivations are a mystery, and who appears to be aided by the very people they would least expect—their own.

Tick Tock, Book #2 in the internationally bestselling Detective Shakespeare Mysteries series, picks up right where Depraved Difference left off, and asks a simple question: What would you do? What would you do if you couldn't prove your innocence, but knew you weren't capable of murder? Would you hide the very evidence that might clear you, or would you turn yourself in and trust the system to work?

From the internationally bestselling author of The Protocol and Brass Monkey comes the highly anticipated sequel to the smash hit Depraved Difference, Tick Tock. Filled with heart pounding terror and suspense, along with a healthy dose of humor, Tick Tock's twists will keep you guessing right up to the terrifying end.

The Redeemer

A Detective Shakespeare Mystery, Book #3

SOMETIMES LIFE GIVES MURDER A SECOND CHANCE

It was the case that destroyed Detective Justin Shakespeare's career, beginning a downward spiral of self-loathing and self-destruction lasting half a decade. And today things are only going to get worse. The Widow Rapist is free on a technicality, and it is up to Detective Shakespeare and his partner Amber Trace to find the evidence, five years cold, to put him back in prison before he strikes again.

But Shakespeare and Trace aren't alone in their desire for justice. The Seven are the survivors, avowed to not let the memories of their loved ones be forgotten. And with the release of the Widow Rapist, they are determined to take justice into their own hands, restoring balance to a flawed system.

At stake is a second chance, a chance at redemption, a chance to salvage a career destroyed, a reputation tarnished, and a life diminished.

A chance brought to Detective Shakespeare whether he wants it or not.

A chance brought to him by The Redeemer.

From J. Robert Kennedy, the author of seven international bestsellers including Depraved Difference and The Protocol, comes the third entry in the acclaimed Detective Shakespeare Mysteries series, The Redeemer, a dark tale exploring the psyches of the serial killer, the victim, and the police, as they all try to achieve the same goals.

Balance. And redemption.

Made in the USA
Las Vegas, NV
11 September 2021